Contents

The Snows of Yorkshire

Angela Waller

Pen Press

First published in Great Britain by Pen Press
an Imprint of Indepenpress Publishing Ltd
25 Eastern Place
Brighton
BN2 1GJ

ISBN 978-1-906710-27-9

Printed and bound in the UK

A catalogue record of this book is available from
the British Library

Cover design by Jacqueline Abromeit

Angela Waller was born in Cheshire and worked as a secretary in London before becoming an Air Hostess for six years in the 1950s and 1960s. After returning to secretarial work, she lived and worked in Libya, U.S.A., and Canada. She met her American husband in Libya and they moved to England in 1992.

Angela has written articles for magazines including "Hello!" and "Sussex Life" and has appeared on TV's "Newsnight", "Ready To Wear" and was a champion on "Countdown". She now lives in West Sussex and is a frequent guest speaker at clubs and societies.

To Harry, with love and gratitude
for his constant encouragement and support.

Part I
1415

Chapter 1

It was starting to rain, and dark clouds scurried across the sky. Kate peered down the drive, straining to see any movement. She had been sitting by this window for hours every day, watching the long drive to the house, ever since the messenger had come to her a few weeks ago. The message he carried from her husband, Richard, was brief and said only, 'We have won an outstanding victory. I am well and have not been injured. I am coming home as soon as I can arrange passage on a ship to England.'

How long would it take for him to travel home from France? No doubt there were many tasks to be finished after the battle; he would be taking care of the men from the estate that he had taken with him, especially any who had been injured or become ill. And then, even after he had found a ship that could carry them all, the journey itself depended on the winds in the English Channel. Sometimes, ships couldn't sail for days or even weeks. But, longing for his return, she sat day after day in one of the upper rooms so that she could see all the way to the gatehouse, which lay on the edge of the estate.

It was not a large estate – about 1,000 acres – and the Manor House was a modest size. Built by Richard's ancestors over 100 years ago in the style of that time, the Manor House had a central Great Hall which was open to the rafters and on either side of the Hall were two floors of smaller chambers. Alongside the courtyard of the Manor House was a single storey of lodgings for some of the families who worked on the estate and others lived in cottages that had been built in small groups around the estate.

Just beyond the gatehouse were the parish church and the house for the priest, and near to that were the blacksmith's forge and cottage, and an alehouse that also served as an inn that could accommodate travellers, and stable and feed their horses overnight. The forge, the alehouse and the church were grouped around a small green area that was always left uncultivated. It was a piece of land for common use as a meeting place for all the estate workers and it was also used for the annual village fair. The road that ran from London to York passed close by this green. The whole estate had been handed down through four generations of the Snowwe family and Richard, who was the fifth generation to live there, had inherited the house and estate when he was only 22 years old. Both his parents had died of a bloody fever that had swept across England, killing thousands. Richard had been trained from an early age in the management and business affairs of the estate and also in agriculture and animal husbandry, in readiness for the time when he would inherit and administer the estate.

There was a gentle touch on Kate's shoulder.

'Madam, will you eat? Just a little?' Beth, the housekeeper, stood beside her, her face full of concern. Beth supervised the domestic staff and took charge of the day-to-day running of the house and she was married to Thomas, their steward, who was in charge of all estate matters.

During these past months Beth had become more than Kate's servant. Although the manner between them was still that of mistress and maid, and Beth showed proper deference, she had become a companion to her during the lonely days after Richard had left with the band of men he had raised to join the King's armies in the wars in France. And Beth had been a comfort when their son, also named Richard, but they called him Dickon, had died. Kate's joy at the thought of her husband's return was dampened only by the thought that she would have to break the news to him that their only child, their son, had died while he had been away. Although Kate knew that many children died in infancy, that knowledge didn't lessen the sorrow, or assuage the grief that she felt.

'Please eat,' Beth said again.

Kate turned to her. 'Yes, I will eat ... but I will take my food here so that I can keep watch until it is too dark to see any movement.'

Beth called to one of the servants to bring food, and then she moved a chair and placed it so that Kate could sit and eat at the table but still keep watch on the long drive.

Kate stood and stretched; she ached with stiffness from sitting so long. While she waited for her food to be brought up from the kitchens, she paced up and down, still peering into the darkness. Soon two of the maids brought in steaming bowls of a thick mutton stew, along with platters of freshly baked bread. The cook had used some of the first of the crop of winter vegetables and the stew smelled good.

She was surprised how hungry she was and how much she ate. Beth lit more candles and after she'd finished eating, Kate asked her to group several candles close together so that she would have enough light to work on her embroidery. She had started this piece when she was first married and intended to make several long pieces that would serve as hangings on each side of their bed. Richard, thought Kate, was an unusual man. He had watched her working on the embroidery and while most men would dismiss it as simply 'women's work' he had complimented on her fine stitching and said, 'When we have a daughter, you must teach her to sew and embroider. I would like our daughter to become a good needlewoman.'

Kate woke with a start. She must have dozed off and her embroidery had fallen to the ground at her feet. As she bent to pick it up, she realised that what had woken her was the sound of horses' hooves, and the shouts of some of the servants.

She knew straight away … she knew, she could feel … Richard was home! She sprang to her feet and hurried to the stairs.

As Kate opened her eyes and came awake, a feeling of contentment swept over her. Richard was home. At last, the long wait was over. They had not talked much the night before. After Richard had eaten, he had turned to her, reached out a hand and said, 'It's been so long Kate … let's go to bed.' She had not had the heart to spoil the moment and tell him about their son's death, and so they had tumbled into bed, made love and fallen asleep still with their arms around each other. Before she slept she could hear the sounds of merrymaking continuing as all the house and estate workers celebrated with the returning soldiers.

Richard stirred beside her, turned and looking deeply into her eyes said, 'Oh Kate … how good it is to be here with you again. Sometimes I felt that I might never see you and Dickon again.' He pulled her close and started to caress her.

Wrapping her arms around him and pulling him close she said, 'Richard … Dickon … I must tell you …'

He interrupted her. 'He must have grown so much while I've been away. I wonder if he will have forgotten me. I can't wait to see him, let's wake him now.'

She pulled back and half sat up, but keeping her hands on his shoulders she said, 'Richard, I have the most awful news to tell you … Dickon …' She gulped, took a deep breath and swallowed. 'Our Dickon, our beautiful boy, was taken from us with the fevers that came in late September. One day, he played as usual and he was perfectly well when I put him into his bed, but he awoke in the night and cried out. When I touched him, his face and body were burning. His nurse and I bathed him but the fever seemed to worsen and just before dawn, he whimpered, stretched out his arms and legs, and … and … he was gone.' She gulped again but this time she couldn't hold back the tears. As Richard's arms went round her she fell into deep sobs, wrenching, gulping sobs, as the agony and grief of a mother whose only child has been taken from her poured out.

Richard cradled her in his arms but said nothing. He knew that there were no words that he could say that would ease her grief, and besides he did not trust himself to speak. The shock and the misery of hearing that their only child, their beloved son, was dead brought tears very close. After some minutes, he said, 'You must show me where he is buried. We will go together to his grave and offer prayers for him.'

At the church that lay just beyond the gatehouse, they stood together beside the grave of their small son. For a long time they were both silent. Then Richard said, 'We will have a stone marker made for his grave, and we will also have a brass memorial made to go on a wall inside the church. And I will plant an oak tree in his memory. It will grow and stand for many years, perhaps hundreds of years, as a living memorial to our baby boy. In memory of something so tiny, a mighty tree will grow and we will plant it so that we can see it from the house.'

Very softly Kate said, 'I like that idea very much. I sat for so many hours looking out of the windows, watching and waiting for your return, and in future I will look out of those same windows and I will see something that is in memory of our son.'

'Also,' said Richard, 'there is one thing more for me to do. I must talk to the priest and make plans for a celebration in the church to give thanks for the safe return of all the men from this area. Every man that went with me has returned safely. Not one was killed and the only injuries were flesh wounds that are now healing. Oh, and young Ben's foot was damaged when a horse trampled on it, but that wasn't a wound inflicted by the enemy. There is so much cause for thanksgiving, and afterwards we will have a feast. An ox will be roasted, and a sheep, and all the people of our estate and their families will join with us to celebrate. This place is indeed a fortunate place to have had all our men come safely home.'

Chapter 2

The day before the thanksgiving service was to be held in the church, the courtyard of the house was filled with noise and people and the smell of wood smoke. Two great fires had been made and the ox was already turning on a spit over on one of them. The estate brewery master had had three large barrels of ale brought up to the courtyard and placed on stands ready to be tapped. Although the sun shone and it was a bright winter day, it was late in the year and Christmas was approaching. It was too chilly for everyone to eat and drink out of doors, so Richard had instructed the estate carpenter to construct long tables in the great central hall of the house. With two of his apprentices, the carpenter had worked for more than two days, laying long flat planks of wood on to trestle supports so that everyone could sit at these long plank tables to eat together.

One of the men working on the fires suddenly cried, 'A rider is approaching,' and everyone turned to look down the drive. As he drew nearer, it could be seen from the quality of his horse and his clothing that the visitor was a gentleman. He rode into the courtyard and young Ben ran forward to take hold of the horse's bridle.

'I have messages for your master,' said the rider.

Thomas, the steward, came forward and said, 'I will conduct you to the master of the house, if you will tell me on what business you wish to speak with him.'

'The King's business,' came the reply and a hush fell in the courtyard.

'The King's business … King's business …' the words

were repeated among all the people working there. 'Did you hear what he said? The King's business … 'Tis a messenger from the King himself.'

Richard appeared in the great doorway. 'What's happening here? Who is our visitor?'

The rider dismounted and came towards Richard. 'I must speak with you privately, Sir. I carry messages from the King.'

'You have had a long ride and you must be tired and hungry. Thomas, have ale and food brought to us in my chambers and have a bedchamber prepared for our guest.'

As the two men went into the house, the rider said, 'Allow me to introduce myself. I am Sir Roger De Terrell, in the King's service at Court.'

After the two men were settled in comfortable chairs and the food and ale had been served, Sir Roger said, 'The documents I have brought with me contain a personal message for you from His Majesty. The King has been pleased to recognise the assistance you gave to him by raising a small army from among the workers on your estates. Most of the armies to support the King were raised in the south and the middle of England. Yours was the only army raised in the north. To show his gratitude and also to commend you on your gallantry in battle, His Majesty is pleased to confer on you a title granting you Lordship of this area. His Majesty also makes a gift to you of land that is in the next county of Derbyshire, a day's ride away from your estate here in Yorkshire. You will, of course, enjoy the benefits of those lands, which include the rents from a number of tenant farmers, and the income from the active lead mines. These documents confirm both your title and your ownership of the lands in Derbyshire.'

'But I only did what I felt was right in supporting our King,' said Richard. 'I never expected honours or recompense for what I did.'

'Nonetheless,' Sir Roger said, 'you will find that the "recompense" as you put it, is quite considerable. The lands that have been granted to you are at Matworth in Derbyshire and have been in the royal possession for decades, ever since the last owner died without heir and without making a will to determine disposition of his goods and lands. You will find that the lead mines will provide an excellent, regular income.'

The Great Hall in the old house was filled with people. All the men who had gone with Richard to fight at Agincourt and their families had come to the great celebration feast, as had everyone who lived and worked on the estate. They all ate and drank together, along with the priest who had conducted the service of thanksgiving earlier in the day. Meat had been carved from the ox and from the sheep, and large platters of food were carried in and placed on the long tables. The three barrels of ale had now been tapped and the drink flowed freely. There would be plenty for everyone to drink, even if the merrymaking went on all night.

Richard got to his feet and called for silence. Gradually a hush fell in the Great Hall.

'As many of you know, we have a visitor, a distinguished guest, who has come from London with messages from His Majesty, the King. Our visitor, Sir Roger de Terrell, wishes to tell you himself the reasons for his coming here.'

Sir Roger got to his feet. 'I will not keep you long from your feasting and merrymaking. I am happy to tell you that I brought with me a proclamation from His Majesty, the King, conferring upon Richard Snowwe a title so that henceforth he will be known as Sir Richard Snowwe, and will hold also the title of Lord of this manor. This honour is given by His Majesty in recognition of Sir Richard's service to the Crown in raising a goodly army of men to fight in France. In addition, in commendation of his bravery in battle, the King has been graciously pleased to grant to Sir Richard additional lands with the rights and privileges pertaining to them. And now,' he raised his drinking vessel, 'good people, join me in drinking to the health and long life of the newly entitled Lord of this manor, Sir Richard Snowwe.'

Everyone joined in the toast, calling out 'God bless you, Sir Richard …' and 'Long life to you and her Ladyship …', and cheering, and banging their fists on the tables and stamping on the floor, making a great noise.

Richard rose from his place and raised his hand to ask for silence.

'I, too, will not keep you long from these celebrations, but I want you all to join me in drinking a loyal toast to His Majesty, the King.' Everyone stood, drinking mugs and vessels raised, and drank to the King's good health and long reign. 'And,' Richard continued as everyone sat down again, 'I want to thank you, each one of you men who accompanied me to France in the service of our King. My thanks also go to God for bringing us all safely home. God did indeed grant us good fortune, and in recognition of that good fortune, I intend to change the name of this house and estate to Fortune. No longer simply The Manor House. From today onwards, the name is Fortune House and it is at the heart of the Fortune estate.' Richard raised his own drinking vessel and said, 'I thank God for watching over us, and I thank God for such good people.'

As he sat down again a voice from the crowd shouted, 'And we thank God for such a good Lord!' The cheers rang out again, echoing up to the rafters of the old Hall. Once more tankards were banged on the table, and everyone stamped their feet.

Chapter 3

Christmas followed soon after the celebrations for the safe homecoming of the men, and in January the estate settled into its usual business. It was a mild winter with snow falling for only a few days. Plough Monday came and the season's ploughing of many acres began, ready for the sowing of seeds in the spring. Young Ben's foot had healed better than had been expected, and he was able to walk behind the plough and horses and cover as much ground in a day as did the other men. It had become such a habit to refer to him as 'Young Ben' that Kate often said that she thought he would still be called 'Young Ben' even when he was an old man.

Through all the years that he was growing up and learning about managing the estate, Richard had worked closely with Thomas and the two men had developed a close bond. After Richard had inherited the house and the land when his father died, he and Thomas had worked together to improve and build up the stock of cattle, sheep and pigs. Both men took great pride in all their work, and they had gained a reputation for producing animals of excellent quality. Each year they sold some of their beasts for good prices at local markets and they had bred sheep that produced a heavy fleece of very fine wool for which there was a growing market. All over England farmers and landowners were becoming prosperous as the demand for English wool grew throughout Europe. Most of the wool was sold to traders who, in turn, sold it to cloth makers all over England. A smaller amount of the wool was sold to local spinners and weavers, and Yorkshire cloth was already gaining a reputation for its fine qualities, with growing numbers of spinners, weavers and dyers moving to the area.

While the younger men from the estate had been away with Richard in France, all the work of the land had been done by the older men and, often, their wives and children had worked alongside them. Their help had been needed especially at harvest time because all the crops had been good this year. Every able-bodied person had worked all the hours of daylight, from just after dawn until the light faded in the late evening. With all the crops safely harvested, Thomas told Richard how abundant the harvest had been. Sufficient hay was stored in the barns to feed all the beasts through the winter, and the plentiful crops of vegetables and fruits meant that there was food for the winter for everyone living on the estate. The excess crops had all been sold for good prices, so Richard was well pleased with Thomas's management in his absence. Everyone living and working on the estate felt great loyalty to Richard Snowwe and his family and many of them were the fourth or fifth generations of the same families who had worked there since the first Snowwes settled on the land over 100 years ago. At the time that the Snowwes built the large house for themselves, they had also built lodgings alongside the courtyard for their household staff. At first the farm workers had lived and slept in parts of the barns but gradually cottages had been built for them. People who worked on the estate had good housing and plenty of food, and the Snowwes always took good care of their workers, especially if they were ill or injured, and when they grew old and were unable to work.

Richard decided that once the spring sowing was underway, and the weather was improving, it would be a good time to visit his newly acquired lands in Derbyshire. Since his return he had spent many days talking with Thomas, and walking over all the land, inspecting the cattle and the sheep. He was well satisfied with Thomas's handling of estate affairs while he'd been gone, and he knew that everything could be left in Thomas's capable hands while he went to visit Derbyshire. By the beginning of April the roads were dry and passable, and it would be a good time to make the journey. The day before he left, Richard told Kate that he would probably be away two or maybe three weeks.

'I need to visit and inspect the lands in Derbyshire that are now mine, and meet all the people who live and work there. Particularly I want to meet the man who is in charge of everything there, including all the mines and mine workers,' he told Kate. 'As you know, Sir Roger told me that the income from the lead mines is considerable, so I must be sure that I have a good man in charge, who can oversee everything connected with the mines. Also, I shall meet all the people, both the miners and those who work on the land, because I want to know the workers and their families there, just as we know all the people who work and live on this estate,' he went on. 'I must be assured that all is being well managed, and that everything there is in good, competent hands. Once I am confident that I have capable people carrying out the work there, I will need only to visit Derbyshire perhaps three times each year.'

'I shall miss you so much,' said Kate. 'But at least while you are away this time I shall know that you are not involved in fighting, and that you are no more than a day or two's journey time away from me.' She put from her mind all thoughts of highwaymen and other robbers who roamed the roads and set upon travellers.

'I have asked Thomas to look around in the woodlands while I am gone, and find a young oak tree that can be moved and planted in front of the house,' said Richard. 'So as soon as I come back, we will plant Dickon's tree.'

Richard took two men with him and the small party set off soon after first light the next morning. As Kate clung to Richard she was tempted to tell him that she thought she might be pregnant again but she did not. Although there were some signs that made her think that she must indeed be with child, she wanted to wait another month to be sure, before telling Richard.

Just two days after Richard had left for Derbyshire, Kate awoke feeling queasy. She lay in bed, hoping that the feeling would pass but it didn't. She got out of bed, found a bowl and leaned over it, retching. Her forehead broke out in a cold, clammy sweat, and she was just getting back into bed when Beth came in.

'I thought that might be the case,' she said.

'What? What case? Oh Beth, I think perhaps some of the meat I ate last night must have been tainted. It has made me feel so ill …' She stopped talking and rushed to the bowl, leaned over and retched again.

'Madam, it isn't any sickness from meat. You are with child again, I am quite sure. Two weeks ago, you had the look about you that women get in those very first weeks of a pregnancy. It's something in their eyes. I recognised that look and I was certain you are expecting another child. Just the other day I said to Thomas "we shall be getting out the old cradle again soon".'

'Oh Beth, I do hope so,' said Kate. 'I have had some signs that make me think that I am again with child but I said nothing to my husband before he left, because I am not yet sure. I so much want us to have another child. No baby will

16

ever replace Dickon, but both Richard and I want more children.'

'So, if I'm right …' Beth thought for a moment, then continued, 'if I am right, you would have started this child soon after the beginning of the year. That means that the new baby will be born next October.'

Kate suddenly retched again, then lay back again on her bed, the sweat glistening on her forehead.

'I will go and speak to Meg,' said Beth. 'She will make you a posset to drink each night so that you will not awake feeling this queasiness.'

Old Meg had been living on the estate for many years, perhaps longer than anybody. Nobody knew how old she was because nobody could remember a time when Meg wasn't there. Her knowledge and skill in the uses of herbs for almost any sickness was highly respected, and she was the first person called upon when there was illness. And when men who worked on the land were injured and had bad wounds and cuts, she would also treat these by binding up their cuts with comfrey leaves that speeded the healing. In a small garden plot she grew many of the plants and herbs that she used in her treatments – marigolds, feverfew, lavender, rue – and some whose names she did not know but she knew how and when to use them. Meg had been present at Dickon's birth, just as she had helped deliver almost every child born on the estate for many years. She had been delivering babies for so long that now she was helping with the birthing of the children and grandchildren of women she had brought into the world. Kate lay on her bed thinking that Meg would, God grant that she was still alive, deliver this next baby too.

Meg's husband, Edgar, who was even older than she was, was the rat catcher and was as valued as his wife. Everyone knew that plague and other diseases were carried by the fleas that lived on mice and rats, and Edgar's skill in setting traps to catch them meant that he, too, helped to keep everyone healthy.

Chapter 4

Richard was gone for longer than he had expected – almost four weeks – but he sent a rider with a message for Kate to allay any anxiety she might feel when he was gone so long. His message told her that there were no problems, but there was far more to see and do than he had expected.

When he eventually came home he told Kate, 'I have so much to tell you, it will take days. I didn't imagine that there would be so much to see, so much to do, and so many people to meet. The land is in a very hilly area so the ways of farming are rather different from the way we do it here, and the sheep and cattle are breeds I don't know but they have been bred for the hill land and the colder winters there. Also, of course, I have no knowledge at all about the lead mining.

'Luckily,' he went on, 'there is an excellent man in charge of everything; he oversees all the farming work, as well as managing the lead mine and miners. His name is William Bailey, an educated man who can read and write and he keeps the accounts, collects rents, buys supplies, arranges to sell everything that is produced on the farmed land and he also sells the lead at the best market price. He has been doing all this for several years, working as the King's administrator there, and I can safely leave him to carry on. He was happy working for the King but he tells me he will be happy to stay on and serve me. He and I had many long talks about what should be done and the manner in which it should be done and we are in complete agreement that all the workers should be well housed and well cared for. As you know, the land and mines are at a place called Matworth and it will take me a while to tell you everything but I want you to know everything. In fact, I *need* you to know everything, so that if I fall ill, you and Thomas and William Bailey can work together and continue all the work of running the estates both here and at Matworth, and also carry on the work of the lead mines there. I have asked William to visit us here later this year and while he is here we – that is Thomas and you and I – can talk fully about all these matters.'

Richard put one arm around her shoulders and said, 'Kate, I would like to talk to you about the gravestone for Dickon. In Derbyshire there are several men working on the Matworth estate who are expert stonemasons and stone carvers, and I would like one of them to come here and fashion the headstone for Dickon's grave. You may prefer to use a stonemason from this area, but I have seen some of the work done by the Matworth men and I admire their skills and workmanship. Would you mind if I send to William Bailey and ask him to choose the man he thinks best suited to do this?'

'Of course, I won't mind,' answered Kate. 'But I do not want anything elaborate. I would like it to be a very simple stone, because I think that would be most suitable for a small child such as he was.'

And so a messenger was sent to William Bailey, and in just three weeks, the stonemason, Hal Digby, arrived from Derbyshire. Richard talked to him, and then he and Kate went with him to the grave. Richard explained that they wanted only a small headstone, and it was to be engraved only with Dickon's full name, and the dates of the years of his birth and death.

The stonemason said that he understood fully what was

wanted, then he paused, hesitated, and went on, 'Sir, and My Lady, may I make a suggestion?'

'Of course,' said Richard, 'continue.'

The stonemason pulled something out of his pocket and said, 'This is a piece of stone that was mined on your Matworth estate. It is a kind of stone found only in certain parts of Derbyshire, and there we call it Derbyshire Bluejohn. My suggestion is that I cut it into a round shape and polish it, and then set it into the headstone just above your son's name.'

Richard took the piece of stone that Hal held out, and showed it to Kate. The stonemason went on, 'When it is polished, you will see that it is a rich cream colour, and there are streaks of several shades of greyish-blue in it.'

Kate said softly, 'I think your idea is a fine one. It will look beautiful, and will be something unique, something that is special for Dickon that will be like no other gravestone.' She inclined her head, near tears with emotion at the kind thought and said, 'I thank you for your suggestion. It will make a headstone that is unlike any other, and I like that.'

Before the stonemason arrived, Richard had spent time going around the Fortune estate with Thomas, checking everything that had happened while he was away in Derbyshire, talking about the spring sowing, the lambing, and checking the new calves that had been born. Together they inspected the sheep and cattle and decided which should be sold, which should be kept for meat for feeding everyone on the estate, and which should be retained to breed and increase the herds.

When he had been home for almost a week, one day Richard said, 'Come Kate, I have scarce spent time with you or talked to you since my return … let us walk together for a little while.'

As they walked out of the front of the house Richard paused

and looked around and said, 'I have long wanted to enlarge this house, and I have many ideas for adding to it. I want more rooms, and perhaps another floor, and here at the front I would like to have an area of flagstones laid in the style of something I saw at the house at Matworth. The flagstones will form a large terrace that runs across the whole width of the front of the house, and there will be wide steps leading down to the drive.' He pulled her close and said, 'We will make this into a fine house, Kate …' He stopped speaking, still standing with his arms around her. 'Kate? Kate? Your body feels fuller …'

She looked at him, her eyes shining. 'Oh Richard, I am so pleased and so happy. I am pregnant again. I didn't want to tell you before you left, because although I had some signs, I wasn't sure. Now I am completely sure; we are going to have another child.'

Richard's shout of joy was so loud that several men working in the fields closest to the house straightened up from their work and looked up towards them.

Richard waved to them and shouted, 'It's all right. There is nothing wrong.' And they turned back to their work.

'Oh Kate!' he said, 'I want to shout to them that nothing is wrong, and everything is right! Kate, Kate, my Kate, I am so happy I want to leap about and pick you up and swing you around … but I won't. I don't want to do anything that might harm the baby.'

As they continued their walk neither of them could stop smiling, both thinking of this wonderful news.

'When do you think it would be right to tell people about the coming child?' Richard asked. 'I want to tell the news to the whole world right now but perhaps you want to wait a while?'

'If we want to wait a while, we can do so because my full

skirts will conceal the swelling of my belly, but I don't see why we shouldn't tell everybody immediately,' said Kate. 'Beth already knows. She came into my chamber when I was ill one morning, and she said straight away that she was certain that I was with child. I know that she told Thomas of her suspicions but I know that they never talk about our affairs. And I'm sure nobody else will have guessed.'

While Beth supervised the maids serving their meal later that day she looked at Richard and Kate's faces, glowing with happiness and she knew that Richard had been told about the coming child. But, being a very discreet woman, the perfect servant to have in the house, living close to the family at all times, she said nothing. She did not even allow herself a secret smile to Kate but kept her face a mask of deferential blankness.

After the serving maids had withdrawn and they were alone again, Richard said to Kate, 'You must have counted the months and know when we will have our new child?'

'Yes, of course,' said Kate. 'The baby will be born between the middle and the end of October.'

'Aaah,' Richard mused. 'Last October I was away fighting in France. The main battle was at Agincourt on St Crispin's Day, 25th October.' He turned to Kate, his face serious, 'If this child is another boy, have you thought about a name for him?'

'No,' said Kate. 'I am so happy that another child is coming that I have given little thought to whether it might be a boy or a girl. If it is a boy, I would not want to call him Richard. We have had our Richard, our Dickon, and this child will be different. Is there a name you particularly like?'

'Kate, if it is a boy, I would very much like to name him Crispin. Not only was the great battle fought on St Crispin's Day but, along with all our men, I prayed to St Crispin asking

23

that our lives might be spared and that we would all return home again. So I feel that my safe return was thanks not only to God, but also thanks to St Crispin and the prayers we offered to him.'

Chapter 5

Now that Richard and Kate knew that another child was expected, and they both hoped to have more children, Richard
decided to start building the additions to the house straight
away. He went into York to talk to some builders there, and
arranged for them to come to Fortune House to discuss ideas
and plans for the extra rooms to be built.

Two builders came and they spent a day walking around
the house, talking to Richard about his ideas, making suggestions
themselves, and making some basic drawings that could be
developed into more detailed plans for the work to be carried
out. Richard wanted to keep the main central hall as the
centrepiece of the enlarged house, and plans were drawn up
to add cross wings, each with three floors, on both sides of
the central hall. The wing that faced north would have new,
larger kitchens and sculleries on the ground floor, and the
builders suggested adding a dairy or buttery on that cool side
of the house. On the floor above there would be bedrooms
for the family and the top floor would house the nurseries.
The other wing, on the south side of the house, would have
rooms on the ground floor for dining, and receiving and
entertaining guests, and there would be more bedrooms on
the floor above. On the top floor of that wing there would be
the solar, a long room with large windows all around that would
have views across most of the estate. Kate would use this
room to entertain her women friends, away from the main
part of the house, and the solar's big windows would give her

excellent light for working on her embroideries. In this room, too, Kate would have daily meetings with Beth to discuss and oversee the running of the house.

Richard also planned to build a second, lower courtyard close to the house to provide more lodgings for an enlarged household staff. One day, while he was deep in discussions with the builders and going over their drawings, Thomas appeared at the door and waited till Richard looked up.

'Yes, Thomas, do you need to speak with me?' asked Richard.

'Yes, Sir Richard. If I may, I would like to make a suggestion for you to consider which would require the addition of another section of building.'

'Of course you may make a suggestion. You know this house and the work carried out on the estate, so your suggestions may be useful. Come in and join us and tell us your ideas,' said Richard.

Thomas joined them at the table where the building plan drawings were laid out and Richard introduced him to the builders, explaining that Thomas was very knowledgeable about the business of the house and the estate.

'So,' said Richard, 'tell us your thoughts.'

'During the past year or so, every time I have taken goods or animals to the market,' said Thomas, 'I have walked around the market stalls and I have noticed that there is a growing demand for the cheeses made locally. There are two cheese makers in this area, and both of them always sell everything they bring to the market and there are always more customers than they can satisfy. So, I was wondering if we should add an area of buildings where we could make our own cheese. There,' he pointed to the wing on north side of the house, 'on the cool side of the house. That would be ideal, near to where you plan to have the dairy.'

'It is certainly an idea with possibilities,' mused Richard.

'We have a good-sized dairy herd, and we often have more milk than we can sell. Perhaps making cheese would be a good way to use the excess in a profitable manner. But, wait, I know nothing about cheese making, nor do you Thomas, and there is nobody among our workers who has that knowledge.'

'I hope you will forgive me, Sir,' said Thomas, 'but in the hope that you might think it a good idea, I have already talked to two young men who have just finished their apprenticeship to the biggest cheese maker in this area. They can stay on working there, but both of them have said that they would really like to start their own new cheese making business. They are well trained and they have some ideas for producing several new flavours of cheeses.'

Richard turned to the builders and asked, 'Do you think it would be possible to add buildings for cheese making, if we decide to do this?'

They both said that it could certainly be done, and the four men, Richard, the builders, and Thomas, turned to study the drawings. One of the builders pointed to the area near to the new dairy that Thomas had suggested, and said that he thought that would be the ideal location. After a little more discussion, Richard told Thomas that when he went into the market town next week, he should seek out the two young cheese makers and bring them back to Fortune House.

'I would like to meet them myself, and talk about their ideas, and find out from them just what the building should be like and what would be needed to start making cheese.'

The builders stayed on at Fortune House for a few more days, going over the building plans several times with Richard, discussing ideas and making changes and redrawing the plans. At last the plans were finished, ready for building work to start. As soon as Richard gave his final approval the builders would hire workers they had used in the past, and bring them to Fortune House. There would be stonemasons, roofers and tilers, carpenters, glaziers who made the windows, plasterers, and the men who painted decorations on the plaster, and they would set up a camp for their own temporary living quarters just out of sight of the house.

One evening, as Kate and Richard sat together, Kate with her head bent over her needlework, Richard said, 'Kate, ever since I came home I have been thinking that I would like us to have our portraits painted.'

'Portraits! Richard, who would paint them? I know of nobody around here or even in York who paints portraits. Whatever gave you this idea?'

'On my journey back from France, in the days waiting for a ship to carry us back across the Channel, I talked with several men who told me that they had had portraits of their families painted, and I found out the name of the artist many have hired. He is called Petrus van der Weld, he is Flemish, and lives in Flanders though he spends much of his time in England. I will send messages to some of the men I travelled with and make contact with Mr van der Weld through them. From what I've been told, once he starts working on the portraits it will take him some two or three months to paint our two likenesses so we will arrange for him to stay in the courtyard housing, near to Beth and Thomas for that time.'

Chapter 6

As the days grew warmer with the approach of summer, the crops in the fields were flourishing and the fruit trees showed that there would be an abundant harvest of apples, pears and plums this year. Kate felt that the child inside her body was part of this richness, this growing time.

Every year on the first day of May the whole estate celebrated May Day with a maypole, and dancing, and on that day there was a fair on the village green. Everyone who worked on the estate was given a free day, so that they and their families could enjoy all the delights of the fair. The only people who had to do any work that day were the dairymen and the milkmaids because, whatever the day, the cows had to be milked morning and evening, but after the morning milking was finished they, too, joined with everyone else.

A group of mummers, musicians, jugglers and jesters, who travelled all over England going from fair to fair, came to the village. Some stall keepers came with them and they set up tents to sell their goods. There were some stalls selling cheap jewellery, some sold ribbons and laces, and some sold small ornaments. Young men bought gifts for young girls, husbands bought gifts for their wives, and parents indulged their children by buying small toys for them.

The priest disapproved of the May Day celebrations and complained to Richard when he allowed the festivities to be held every year.

'May Day is a leftover from the old pagan festivals in

Roman times,' he said, 'and as good Christians we should not continue this folly.'

But Richard had no intention of discontinuing what had been a longstanding tradition and told the priest that he thought everyone who worked so hard throughout the year deserved one day when no work was done.

'And I certainly like seeing everyone enjoying themselves with their families on this day of fun,' he added.

Every year, when the maypole was erected on the common green area, just beyond the gatehouse of Fortune House, the priest voiced his disapproval of this too, saying that it was another pagan relic, and was a symbol of offerings to the gods of fertility. But despite his grumblings, the maypole was always erected, bedecked with coloured ribbons and all the children would skip and dance around it, weaving the ribbons into patterns. After a little while, the ribbons would become entangled and the children would all have to weave in and out of each other trying to untangle them.

One young girl from the estate was always chosen as May Queen, and she would have garlands of flowers around her head, and would sit on her 'throne' that was a chair that had been decorated with flowers. She took no part in the dancing, but watched in dignified queenly fashion while all the other girls and boys danced.

On the afternoon of May Day all the men of the estate took part in an archery contest and there was great rivalry between the younger men and the older men. The older men would jeer and shout to the younger men, 'You'll never be as good as we are,' and the young men would shout back, 'We'll show you that we are better than you!' Archery training and practice was compulsory every Sunday after church for all males, and all of them, young and old, took pride in their skills. They all knew that it was the English bowmen who, just last year at Agincourt, had turned the tide of battle in favour of England despite being greatly outnumbered by French bowmen. In the weeks leading up to the fair, the younger men and boys spent extra time practising, hoping to prove that they were as good as any of the older men. Each year Richard presented a prize, a small sum of money, to the winner of the archery contest. This year the contest was won by one of the men who had gone in Richard's army to France, but Young Ben lost by only one shot.

Richard called to the winner to come up and receive his prize of a groat, four silver pennies. Then he also called out to Young Ben to come up to him.

'As the contest was so close and because I know he hopes to marry soon, I am also going to give Young Ben a prize. He shall have half the amount that the winner received.' He held out the two silver pence to Young Ben and added, 'This will, I hope, encourage all the young men to sharpen their skills with bow and arrow.'

The jesters, in their brightly coloured clothes, were entertaining the crowd by performing magic tricks. One of them seemed to pluck a hen's egg from a man's ear, and then just as mysteriously he made the egg disappear. Several of the jesters carried sticks with a pig's bladder filled with water tied to the end, which they waved around, hitting people on their shoulders and heads. One of the jesters approached Richard and waving the water-filled bladder around, hit Richard on the shoulder. The crowd gasped as the bladder burst and showered Richard with water.

Richard pretended to be angry and called out, 'Seize that man and put him in the stocks.' Once the man was fastened in the stocks, the children were encouraged to pelt him with water-soaked lumps of fleece. A small barrel had been filled with these wet balls of wool in readiness, because every year

Richard picked one person and pretended that he had committed some misdemeanour, and deserved the punishment of being put in the stocks and pelted. For the children this was the best part of the fair day, and they squealed with delight as the man in the stocks cried out and yowled, pretending to be hurt by the wet woolly balls.

After some minutes Richard called out, 'Stop! He has paid for his misdemeanour. Release him and bring him ale!'

The music and dancing continued late into the night and so did the ale drinking. Richard knew that many of the men would be holding aching heads next morning as they went about their work, and some might even do a little less work than usual but, he thought indulgently, this is just one special day in the year. The only people who left the fair early were young lovers who slipped away to be alone, and Richard and Kate themselves, as Kate found that she tired easily at this stage in her pregnancy.

Chapter 7

Once the fair was over, Richard wanted to have Dickon's oak tree planted as soon as possible because, as he explained to Kate, at this time of the year he had workmen available. The busiest time of the year lay ahead and in the months of June, July and August, nobody could be spared for such a task.

The next quarter day fell on June 24th, which some people still called Midsummer Day. Both Richard and Thomas would be busy for a whole week at that time collecting rents and any other money that was due to be paid, and also paying all accounts that had accumulated since the last quarter day in March.

June 24th was also St John's Day, and Old Meg, too, would be busy on that day, gathering St Johns Wort flowers. She always gathered her supply for the whole year on that day because folklore and tradition said that the St John's Wort flowers were at their best and would be most potent if picked on the saint's day. She took sacks full of the flowers back to her cottage and then she spent days making some flowers into infusions which she kept in large covered pots. Some flowers were steeped in jars of oil, and some of them were hung to dry so that they could be stored for use throughout the winter. During the coming year, Old Meg would use the preparations she made with the flowers to treat many different ailments – the oil as a balm for burns and insect bites, and sometimes earache could be cured by putting a few drops of the oil in the affected ear. Many of the children of the estate had been cured of bedwetting by drinking Old Meg's St John's Wort infusions, and she also offered it as a healing drink to cure the depressions that young mothers sometimes suffered.

As Richard was pointing out to Kate all the tasks that would have to be done in the next few weeks and months, he went on to remind her that in June many fruits would be ripe and picking would start. In July there would be more crops to gather, and in August the harvest would be ready and he would not be able to spare any men for the non-essential work of planting the tree.

So Richard and Kate went together to look at the tree that Thomas had found in the woodlands that he thought would be suitable to dig up and replant near to the front of the house. They were both pleased with the tree Thomas had found; it looked healthy and sturdy, less than four feet tall, and with a good shape already.

Then they went back to the house to decide on the exact spot for the tree to be planted. They chose a place to one side of the drive near to the house but then Richard reminded Kate that a terrace would soon be built in front of the house with steps leading down to the drive. Because of that, the tree should be planted a little further away from the house. They walked back about 30 paces and chose a new spot for it, and then they asked Thomas to stand on the spot while they went into the house. Looking at Thomas from the house, Richard waved him to move further away from the drive. Thomas moved a few paces and Richard waved him to move on again.

'That's it! That's exactly where I would like the tree,' exclaimed Kate. 'It is perfectly placed to see it from the main door, from the windows of the central hall, and also from the rooms on the upper floors. And because it is near to the drive, every time we come home and every time we leave, we shall see it. That is just what I want – to be able to see it from many different parts of the house.'

As July wore on, the weather turned very warm. Kate's morning sickness had passed but now she found the hot weather oppressive. Beth assured her this was normal.

'I've noticed,' she said, 'that when women are with child, they seem to make their own heat.'

Beth found that the coolest place was a room on the ground floor on the north side of the house. Kate sat there for hours every day, sewing clothes for the coming infant. She still had the clothes that she had made for Dickon but she had packed them all away, carefully wrapped in linen. The new baby, she decided, would not wear Dickon's clothing. Everything would be new for him or her. One day as she sat sewing, Richard came in and asked to look at her stitching.

'What are you making now? I hope it is a new shirt for me, Kate. I swear that the shirts you make for me are the very best I have ever had.'

Kate laughed and held up the tiny garment.

'I think you would find it difficult to fit into this, Richard!'

Richard took the garment from her hands. 'It is so tiny!' he exclaimed. 'It is hard to believe that any baby is so small, even when it is newly born!'

Every day Old Meg brought up a pitcher filled with a cool drink for Kate. She used elderflower and several herbs to make an infusion, which she sweetened with honey, and then put it into a large lidded pot that she lowered into the deep well. By keeping the pot in the well, the drink stayed cool. Every day, when Old Meg brought the pitcher of drink to her, Kate would thank her profusely, and she'd often say, 'Meg, this drink is like a magic potion. As I drink it, I feel that the coolness and the sweetness are doing me good.'

In fact, Kate found that as the pregnancy went on she had

a great liking for sweet things and to please her the cook adapted many dishes to satisfy her palate. Ducks were brushed with melting honey as they turned on the spit, and fruit and honey were added to stews of lamb or pork. The estate had its own pond where the ducks bred, and fish was bought from a monastery about three miles away where the monks had a carp pool. In the heat of July, the fish was poached in wine and herbs, then left to cool and it was eaten cold. In winter, the fish and winter root vegetables would be made into pies or steaming stews.

The hot weather made both Richard and Thomas apprehensive and each day they would watch the sky, looking for any approaching thunderclouds. They hoped that there would be no storms with their heavy rains battering the crops before they could be harvested. The estate grew wheat and barley and oats, and also grasses which would be cut and stored to make hay for feeding all the animals in the winter.

Jack, the beekeeper, was having a busy summer. Although he did other jobs around the estate as needed during the year, in late summer Jack spent all his time tending the hives, stripping the honeycombs and putting the honey into pots and jars.

This year the bees had produced such an abundant amount of honey that several pots full would be distributed to every household on the estate.

In August, when harvest time came, every man, woman and child helped to get all the work done. The crops were cut, then bound into sheaves. Later the wheat and oats and barley would be threshed, and all the grain that would supply the needs of the estate during the winter was carefully stored. Most of the grain would go to the miller to be ground into flour but everything that would not be needed to feed everyone on the estate would be taken to the markets and sold. Grass was cut to make hay, and haystacks were built in fields around the estate. Women searched along the hedgerows and the edges of fields to find the herbs that they used for seasoning and then they dried them by hanging them in bunches from the beams in the ceilings of their cottages.

Suddenly, in September, it seemed that all late fruits were ready to be picked at the same time. Young boys were sent into the orchards to climb the apple, pear and plum trees and pick the fruits, and young girls put all the fruits into baskets. Each family was given fruits for their own needs and the rest of the apples and vegetables were laid in specially built shelves in a barn to keep them dry for use all through the winter. Any fruit that wasn't stored was taken to the kitchens in the big house. All the cook's assistants and kitchen maids worked day after day making the fruits into jams and jellies.

Richard and Thomas were delighted by the crop yields this year. Some years the weather had been bad with too little sun and too much rain to give good crops of the cereals, but this year there would be plenty of food for everyone and a good surplus to be sold at market. The animals would be well fed too, because sufficient hay had been stacked to feed all the livestock for the whole winter.

As the steward of the estate, it was one of Thomas's responsibilities to sell all their excess grain. This year, because the harvest had been so good, he sold to traders in the markets at both York and Beverley. Although Fortune estate was almost entirely self-sufficient, there was sometimes a need for skilled craftsmen to do certain jobs and men of many different skills were available to hire in the market towns. This year Thomas engaged a saddler to come to Fortune House and work for a few weeks repairing all the harnesses and bridles, and making new ones if necessary.

The sales of this year's excellent harvest had made a good

profit and Richard decided that some of the extra money should be spent on buying more breeding cattle to increase the size of the beef herd. He and Thomas went to the livestock market in Beverley where Richard bought a number of cows. The farmer who sold the cows to them agreed to send one of his drovers to accompany Thomas and the cattle on the walk back to the Fortune estate, which would take some days. Richard was anxious not to be away from Kate too long at this stage in her pregnancy, so he spent a night in one of Beverley's inns, then left early next morning and rode straight home, leaving Thomas and the cattle to follow.

Chapter 8

A rider arrived one day in late August, with a message from William Bailey. Richard was concerned that a sudden message might carry bad news, but when he read it he found that William had written saying that, as Richard had asked that he should visit Fortune at some time, he proposed coming in early September. He would then be able to give a full accounting of all that had been happening at the Matworth estate and lead mines.

'Please, Sir Richard, send word back with this messenger if you approve the timing of my visit.'

The messenger stayed overnight and then, having been supplied with a fresh horse, he rode straight back to Matworth with the news that Richard would welcome a visit at the time suggested.

When William arrived, all the news that he brought was good. The farms had been profitable, with good crop yields, and in general all the animals were healthy. The income from the lead mines was steadily rising because many new churches were being built, and older ones were having repairs made to roofs, so the demand for lead was high. William's accounts books were detailed and well kept. Before making this journey to Yorkshire, he had placed most of the money from the estate with a goldsmith in Derby.

'I have deposited money with this goldsmith for all the years I managed the estate's affairs for His Majesty,' he told Richard, 'and I know him to be reliable.'

Richard was pleased to find that William's conduct of

business matters and management of Matworth was so good, and he was even more pleased to find that William and Kate obviously liked each other straight away. Kate told Richard in private that she felt that William was a man they could trust completely.

'I can understand why you felt that he was a good man, a reliable man, to be in charge of all affairs at Matworth,' she said.

Richard invited William to stay for a few extra days so that he could see the Fortune estate and the way that it was managed. The two of them rode out together every day, and for part of each day Thomas accompanied them. At night William stayed in rooms that were near to Beth and Thomas, and he spent the evenings eating and talking with them and their family.

William left to return to Matworth in the middle of September, because he needed to be there for all the business of the quarter day on September 25th. Before he left, William came to Kate and Richard to bid them goodbye. He told them that he would be leaving early next morning but that he would come back again, if Richard approved, early in the new year to give a fresh accounting of Matworth's affairs. Richard was pleased with this thought, and said he would like William to visit Fortune twice every year. In turn, Richard said that he would visit Matworth twice each year. Four meetings each year would enable the smooth running of all Matworth's affairs, thought Richard, thankful that he had such a reliable man to administer all the business of the Matworth estate.

'We will look forward to seeing you again in the early part of next year. As soon as you deem the roads and the weather will make the journey possible.'

Early next morning, as William rode down the drive, Kate

and Richard stood at the main door and Richard waved and cried 'Godspeed'. Beth and Thomas and their family were also standing near the drive waving goodbye to William. This was somewhat unusual, thought Kate, for them to break off from their chores, and then suddenly she noticed that their elder daughter Sarah was waving more vigorously than anyone else and, just as he turned his horse out through the gatehouse, William turned and looked back and waved again. Kate was sure that she noticed that he had directed that last wave especially to Sarah.

'Am I imagining a budding love affair?' she wondered. 'Perhaps pregnancy has made me feel more aware of love all around me.'

Then she thought that if such a love had begun, and if it developed and Sarah and William were to marry, Sarah would leave Fortune. For just a few moments Kate had thoughts of regret. She had watched Sarah grow from a nicely mannered child into an attractive young woman who was being taught by her mother, Beth, the skills needed to become a personal maid to Kate.

Kate gave herself a mental shake. Surely she was only imagining a love between the two. After all, William was several years past 30, and Sarah was but 17 and they had only met a few days ago. Besides, she thought, he might be married already.

'Richard,' she asked, 'do you know anything about William's family? Does he have a wife? Children?'

'No, he doesn't have a wife,' replied Richard. 'When I was at Matworth, I commented that as he was not married, did he not find his solitary life a lonely one? He told me that he had been married, but that his wife had died of the pox some ten years ago. She was only 20, and they had been married scarce a year. After her death, I think he turned all his thoughts and all his energies into his work. Certainly he has never married again.'

Late in September, when all the work of harvest time had been finished, attention was turned to making preparations to store meats for the winter. There were many mouths to be fed on the estate, and although cattle and deer would be slaughtered throughout the winter, some meat was preserved in salt. At the same time, the smokehouse was busy as sides of bacon were smoked and then hung from the beams in the sculleries adjoining the kitchens.

In October a service of thanksgiving for the harvest was held in the church and this year the thanks were especially heartfelt for what everybody said had been the best crops they could remember. In the kitchens of Fortune House, the baker made bread in the shape of a sheaf of wheat, and this stood on the altar during the Harvest Thanksgiving service. Autumn had arrived and the leaves on the trees and hedges changed colour, so that in every direction the view was coloured bronze and gold with only the evergreen trees standing out, starkly dark green. The weather turned cooler, and there was a crispness, almost a chill, in the air. A light mist hung over the fields in the early mornings but as the sun rose, the mist disappeared and in the evenings the air was filled with the smell of wood smoke as fires were lit in every cottage.

Chapter 9

Kate woke up with a nagging pain in her back. She moved around the bed, trying to get comfortable, and then suddenly came wide awake when she realised what was happening. She lay for a few moments, not wanting to wake Richard until she was sure that the baby really was on the way. Suddenly she had a cramping pain, not a bad pain, but it was a pain she recognised.

'I remember ... I remember that pain from when Dickon was born,' she thought and reached over to shake Richard's shoulder.

'Richard, Richard ... wake up ... please wake up.'

Richard turned over, making a grunting noise.

'What's happening? Why are you awake, Kate, it's still dark ...' he broke off and turned fully towards her. 'Is it the baby, Kate? Is the baby coming?'

'Yes, I'm sure it is,' said Kate. 'It will be some hours before the baby is here, but it is definitely on the way. Perhaps you should wake Beth and ask her to come here.'

Richard sprang out of bed, stumbling over the bedclothes, making his way to the fire that still glowed in their room and, lighting a spill from the fire, he lit a candle.

'I'll get Beth! I'll get her now!' He scrabbled to find his clothes. 'I'll get her here straight away.' And he was gone, rushing out of the room.

Kate got up and lit several more candles from the one that Richard had lit. She knew that it would probably be several hours, maybe as many as 12 hours, before the baby was born, but sometimes, she thought, you heard of second babies coming much faster than the first one had done. Suddenly she felt afraid being alone and wanted Beth here. She knew that once Richard wakened her, Beth would be with her in just minutes and she had to calm herself with that thought. Indeed Beth did arrive almost immediately. Kate was surprised to see that she was fully dressed and came in as if this were a normal morning. Kate started to ask her if she had gone to bed fully dressed in case she was called but suddenly her words were cut off as another pain came.

'Come, lie down again on your bed,' ordered Beth, straight away taking charge of the situation. Richard came through the door but as he started to ask Kate how she felt, Beth turned and said, 'Go and tell Old Meg that she will be needed here today.' Richard almost ran out of the room and Kate, who was between pains, laughed and said, 'Oh Beth, you issued an order to him, just as if he were one of your scullery maids. And the funny thing is, he took orders from you promptly.'

Dawn broke, and as the skies lightened, Kate looked out of the window, and looking at Dickon's tree she whispered to herself, 'It will be today. Today, Dickon, your little brother or sister will be here.'

Old Meg arrived, carrying a large pot.

'I've brought you a special drink,' she said. 'All the time you are in labour you must drink and drink and drink. This will taste good, and it will help you through the coming hours.' She had made a drink with plenty of honey in it, and had also added some herbs that would help to dull the pain.

When Richard appeared at the door, Beth went over to him and said in a very low voice, 'Sir, if you will allow me to advise, this is women's business. It would be better if you

44

leave now and go and attend to affairs around the estate. It will be a few hours yet.'

'Yes, yes, I know you're right,' said Richard. 'I will leave now and I'll come back at the middle of the day.'

Kate heard his voice, raised herself and said, 'Beth will take very good care of me, Richard. Go now – I'm sure there are matters that need your attention ...' Her voice trailed away, she gasped and fell back.

'Go, Sir,' said Beth, as she turned to Kate once more. She felt Kate's stomach, and said, 'You'd be better off just now, My Lady, if you get up and we will walk around the room for a while.'

Taking hold of both of Kate's arms, she gently pulled her up, let her sit on the edge of the bed for a few minutes, and then eased her to standing.

'Come, now, come ...' her voice was low and soothing, the voice you'd use to a child that had fallen and hurt itself. 'Come and we will walk around the room, the two of us together.'

Thomas, who had straightaway guessed what the situation was when Richard came in the early morning to call Beth, was waiting near the main front door of the house. As Richard came down the stairs, Thomas removed his cap and came into the central hall. He knew that his job today would be to keep Richard busy.

'Sir, I think you should come and look at the cow that calved late last night. I would like you to give your opinion as to her condition, and if you think that all is well with her.'

Thomas knew that the cow and her newborn calf were both healthy, but his request would serve to get Richard right away from the house. Thomas also knew that Richard was greatly interested in the herd and all matters affecting it and he would certainly want to examine any cow and calf if he thought there might be a problem. They set off at a brisk pace to the penned-off area where the cows who had recently calved and those who were about to give birth were held.

They checked the cow and the calf and Thomas said, 'They both seem very well now, Sir. I had some concerns earlier and I wanted you to come and see for yourself.'

'I would always want you to tell me about any concerns you have, Thomas, whether it is the livestock or the land or buildings. I trust you and your opinions completely,' said Richard. 'Now, as we are over on this side of the estate, let us take a look at those shepherd's cottages that you told me might need some roofing work done.'

After Richard had inspected the cottages he said that he thought any major repair work that needed to be done on them could be handled by the builders who would work on Fortune House, after they had finished all the work there. Usually, the work of repairing farm walls, stone cottages and other farm buildings was done by Joe, the waller. He, like his father before him, built all the dry stone walls on the estate. Being a waller was skilled work, and properly built walls would stand without needing repair for almost a hundred years. Thomas then suggested that he and Richard should look over the sheep that were grazing on the hillside near to the cottages.

By now the sun was high in the sky and Richard said, 'I am getting hungry and thirsty, Thomas, and I'm sure you are too. We are near the edge of the estate so let us walk through the churchyard, and across to the inn and there we will eat and drink together.'

When they had eaten, Richard said, 'Thomas, I must go back to the house. I cannot stay away longer. Even if Kate is still in labour, I want to be there so that I can be called as soon as the infant comes.'

They walked back to the house together at a brisk pace.

It was obvious that Richard felt he had spent sufficient time away, and now he wanted to be home as soon as possible. As they approached the house, Beth appeared at an upper window, waving. Richard broke into a run, and went through the main door and up the stairs as fast as he could. Just as he approached the door to his and Kate's bedchamber, Beth opened the door, smiling widely.

'Come in, Sir, and see your new son!' she cried.

Richard crossed the room in a few long bounds. Kate was lying back on her pillows, cradling the baby in her arms.

'Richard, my love,' she said, 'come and see our new baby.'

Richard bent and kissed her forehead then he reached forward and very gently lifted the tiny child.

'A boy! A son! Our son Crispin!' he said softly. 'And by happy chance, today is St Crispin's Day!' He bent and kissed the baby's head. 'Oh Kate, such happiness, such joy. And I remember, this very day one year ago, I was in the midst of battle and surrounded by death, as many men and boys died around me. Now, today, one year on, I am filled with the joy of a new life.'

The day after Crispin was born, Richard sent for the priest to come to the house to make arrangements for his christening. Kate would rest in bed for the usual lying-in period of about ten days and it was decided that the baby would be christened when he was 12 days old. Richard sent a messenger to Kate's parents to let them know of the safe delivery of their new grandson, and another messenger went to Kate's sister not only to tell her of Crispin's birth but also to ask her and her husband to stand as godparents at his christening.

Richard ordered some of the estate's workmen to build a beacon at the top of the hill just behind the house. As dusk fell, he set off up the hill to light the beacon and was surprised to find that many of the families from the estate were already there awaiting him. As he touched fire to the waiting beacon and it sprang into flame, a cheer went up from the people assembled there. Richard went among the small crowd thanking everybody for coming up the hill, and the men took off their caps and shouted, 'Hooray for the newest Snowwe!' When Richard returned to the house and told Kate, he found tears springing unbidden to his eyes.

'I am touched more than I can say,' he told Kate, 'to know that our people think so highly of our family.'

Chapter 10

Kate's sister Eleanor and her husband Henry arrived during the first week of November, ready for the christening. It had been some time since Kate had seen her sister and though they had never been particularly close when they were children, they had now developed an affectionate friendship based on a new understanding of each other through shared experiences. Eleanor, too, had had a child that had died and since then she had been pregnant twice and had miscarried each time. She was overjoyed to see the baby Crispin, and spent a lot of time either holding him and rocking him gently, or just sitting beside his cradle gazing at him. Kate's heart went out to her sister, understanding her longing for another child, and praying that soon she would have a successful pregnancy and a healthy child.

On the day of the christening, as Kate had so recently left her lying-in bed, Richard insisted that she and Eleanor, along with Crispin, should ride in a litter, while Richard himself and Henry walked to the church. A small group of people from the estate had come to the church and Kate signalled to Beth and Thomas to move forward and stand near to them, as they gathered around the font. The priest poured the Holy Water on Crispin's head, intoning the prayers and pronouncing his names. At the touch of the cold water, the baby suddenly yelled loudly and everyone in the church smiled because there was an old saying that the child who cried while being christened was 'crying out the Devil'.

Eleanor and Henry stayed a few more days and as they

were getting into their carriage for the journey home, Eleanor pulled Kate aside and whispered. 'Don't say a word to anyone. I feel it might be unlucky even to say anything to you but I think, I pray, that I am pregnant again. It is much too soon to be sure, but Kate, remember me in your prayers.'

Kate pulled her sister close and hugged her and whispered, 'I shall pray daily that your hopes are fulfilled, and perhaps months from now, Richard and I will come to visit you and we will be godparents to your new baby. Please God that it may be so.'

As November turned into December, the weather turned colder and the skies had a sullen wintry greyness every day. Some of the farming people said that it would snow before Christmas and started to move the cattle and sheep into their winter quarters in the barns or in paddocks close to the barns. Some of the sheep were of a hardy breed and could safely be left out in the fields and even give birth to their lambs there, unless the winter proved exceptionally cold, in which case they too would be brought into the barns until the coldest weather was over.

All over the estate, branches – especially holly with its red berries – were cut from trees and bushes to use to decorate Fortune House and all the cottages. Mistletoe was a prized find and was supposed to bring good fortune to the person who found and cut it. The priest grumbled again, as he had done about the May Day fair and the maypole, muttering that in olden days the pagans decorated their houses in celebration of the winter solstice. But, despite his grumbling, he accepted that nowadays decorating homes in this way had become part of the Christian Christmas tradition and he even allowed green branches and holly to be used to decorate the church.

The cooks and kitchen maids at Fortune House were busy

preparing the special dishes that were eaten only at this time of year. Fowl of all kinds were cooked, and many small woodcock and several large geese were roasted. The cook followed the new custom of making the goose look even more tasty, by covering it with butter and saffron, so that it glowed golden when it was served.

Many small mince pies were made, filled with chopped rabbit, pigeon, mushrooms and spices, because it was customary to offer a mince pie to every visitor who came to the house. Some people said that if you made a wish with the first bite of your first mince pie, your wish would come true. Others believed that it was bad luck to refuse the first mince pie offered to you over Christmas, so every year the cook came into the dining hall to serve one to Richard, declaring, 'You must eat this for good luck, Sir Richard.' At no other time of the year would she speak to him in such a bold manner, but Richard always took what sounded like a command in good humour and would laugh and say, 'Well, then, Mistress Cook, I must do as you say!'

On the day after Christmas, Kate and Richard followed the custom of giving small gifts to every person who worked for them. All the farm workers and the house servants assembled in the house's Great Hall. Richard took pride in knowing the name of every person who worked on the Fortune estate and he tried – and usually succeeded – to remember the things that had happened to each person during the past year. This was what made everyone who worked for the Snowwe family feel content with their life. As each person stepped up to receive their gift, the men would take off their caps and bow from the waist, and the women curtsied. Richard greeted each person by name, and asked appropriate questions. 'Is the new baby thriving?' or 'Has your father recovered from the fever and coughing?' and each person felt that Richard and his family knew and cared about them and their families.

Richard offered praise to several of the workers. Such remarks as 'The cows have never been healthier' and 'The ale you've brewed this year has been excellent' made each feel that their work was appreciated and valued. At the same time, everybody also knew that because Richard and Thomas noticed everything, both good and bad, they always knew when someone had not done their best work, or had been slack in their tasks.

The feasting continued from Christmas for the whole of the following week, leading up to the celebrations to welcome the new year. There was always special music in the church at Christmas, and everyone attending joined in singing Christmas hymns and melodies. Some years troupes of mummers came and performed the passion plays that had been specially written to form part of the Christmas celebrations.

On the evening of the last day of the year, Kate and Richard left baby Crispin in the care of his nurse so that they could join with the many estate workers who attended the New Year's Eve Mass in the church. Afterwards, they decided to walk back to the house rather than ride in a litter because it was such a bright moonlit night, and they were well wrapped up in fur-lined cloaks to keep them warm.

They walked close together in silence, enjoying the peace and stillness of the night. After a while, Richard said, 'Walking with you, Kate, in this wonderful quietness, towards our house that we both love, I feel that I know the meaning of perfect joy.'

Kate turned to him to answer but before she could speak

they both said in unison, 'Look!' as a shooting star sped across the sky.

'Oh, Richard,' said Kate, 'that is supposed to be a lucky sign, an omen of good things to come. And isn't it especially wonderful to see it tonight! Perhaps it means good fortune for the coming year!'

Richard put his arm around her shoulder and pulled her close to him.

'I cannot imagine that this coming year can be any better for us than the past year has been. Each day, first thing every morning when I awake, I remember that I came home safely after the battle at Agincourt, and so did all the men I took with me, and I give thanks to God afresh. And then, when I think of the blessing of our beautiful new son, Crispin, I also thank God for his birth and your safe delivery. This past year has been remarkable – the gift of land from His Majesty, the King; the title he bestowed upon me; the prosperity of our property and beasts both here and on the farms in Derbyshire, and also the flourishing business of the lead mine there. I am almost overcome. I feel true humility and gratitude for such benefits.'

'I share your feelings,' whispered Kate. 'I think back to the days I spent waiting for you to return, praying that you would be safe and well, and I remember my joy when you came home. We have had our sadness with the death of our first born son, but now together we can look to the future with joy.'

Beth was waiting for them by the main door when they arrived back at the house.

'It is a chill night. Shall I bring you both a warming drink?' she asked.

'That is an excellent idea, Beth,' said Richard. 'Come,

Kate, we will sit before the fire and warm ourselves while we drink.'

As they drank, the slight wind carried the sound of the church clock striking 12 times. Richard stood and stepped over to where Kate sat on the other side of the fire. He bent, kissed her, and said, 'Right now, this minute, we start the new year together.'

Chapter 11

In the third week of January, William Bailey arrived, ready to acquaint Richard with all that had been happening at Matworth since his last visit to Fortune, almost four months ago. He brought with him sets of accounts to show to Richard and the two men spent a whole morning closeted together, talking over all that had happened both on the Matworth farms and also in the lead mines.

'I was very pleased with the work of Hal Digby, the stonemason that you sent over here to fashion the gravestone for my son,' said Richard. 'You chose well. Not only a highly skilled workman, but I liked him personally. Once the builders have completed all the work that I shall have done to enlarge the house, I have some ideas about other work that he could carry out here. One day perhaps I would like to have a very large fireplace built in the Great Hall, and I know that my wife and I would both like some Derbyshire Bluejohn stone worked into the side supports of that fireplace. I shall give more thought to this idea, and if I proceed, I'd like Hal Digby to come here and supervise the work with the Bluejohn.'

'And now,' Richard went on, 'is there anything else that I need to know, anything of importance that we should discuss?'

'Sir, yes, there is …' William faltered, cleared his throat, and then went on. 'Yes, Sir Richard, there is one other matter I wish to discuss. It is nothing to do with Matworth but is a personal matter.' He stopped, looked at Richard, and waited.

'Go on, man,' Richard prompted him. 'It is not like you to

stumble over your words like this. I only hope that you are not going to tell me that you wish to leave Matworth and take employment elsewhere?'

'Oh no, Sir, far from it. That is the farthest thing from my mind. This is, well, you see …' Again he stumbled over the words. William took a deep breath, cleared his throat once more and then went on, 'Sir Richard, last time I was here, in September, as you know I lodged with Beth and Thomas.'

'Yes, yes, I remember that. Go on.'

'While there, I met their daughter Sarah and some evenings we spent time talking together.' There was another pause, then, with the words tumbling out in a rush, William went on, 'She and I have developed a fondness, dare I say, a love for each other, and I now seek your permission to speak to her father, Thomas, and ask his blessing for us to marry!'

Richard laughed out loud, clapped William on the back, and said, 'I can understand your feelings, William. She has grown into a comely young woman and I know that her mother has brought her up to know all domestic skills. She will make a fine wife. And although I am sure her parents will be sorry that she will be living at a distance, they will know that you will make her a fine husband. Go along, man, don't tarry here with me. Go and find Thomas and once you have his blessing – which I am certain he will give – go and speak to Sarah!'

When Richard sat down with Kate to eat their main meal in the afternoon, he told her about the conversation with William and his desire to marry Sarah.

'I thought so!' Kate exclaimed. 'When William left here after his last visit, as we said goodbye and watched him ride down the drive, I thought that he turned and waved especially to Sarah just before he passed through the gatehouse!'

Richard chuckled. 'I'm not sure if you are especially wise,

Kate, or if this is the sort of thing that women notice. I am sure that Thomas will approve this marriage, and that Sarah will say yes to William's proposal, so I shall ask William, together with Beth, Thomas and Sarah, to come to the house this evening so that we may give them our good wishes.'

Late that afternoon, just as the light was fading into evening, Richard and Kate stood in the Great Hall, wishing Sarah and William a long and happy life together. Everyone was smiling broadly, truly happy to see a couple who were so clearly in love.

'We had expected to see you marry in due course and continue to live here at Fortune, Sarah,' said Kate. 'We shall miss you, but I know we will hear news of you from your parents. And, by marrying William and going to live on our estates at Matworth, in some ways you are staying with us still.'

Richard asked, 'When do you expect this marriage will take place? In the summer?'

'If it pleases everyone, Sarah and I would like to marry within the week, so that she can travel back to Matworth with me,' said William. 'If we do not marry now, we will have to wait till my next visit here, which will be next June or July.' He turned and smiled at Sarah, reached out for her hand and held it, and went on, 'We both think six months would be a very long time to wait.'

Richard looked at Beth and Thomas and asked, 'Do you have any objection to the marriage taking place so soon? If I speak to the priest and all arrangements can be made, will you be in agreement?'

Thomas said, 'I speak for Beth as well as for myself when I say that we shall miss our daughter Sarah when she moves away, but we are very happy that she wishes to marry someone we have come to know and to respect. We have a high regard for William and we know that he will make a fine husband for her.'

Beth suddenly burst out, 'And she will make a fine wife for him ... for any man. She is a ...'

'Yes, yes,' said Richard, 'we all understand exactly what you mean. I think they are two good people who deserve each other!'

And so it was arranged that the marriage would take place in just six days time. Kate told Beth to leave as many of her duties to one side as possible, or to delegate some of her work to the maids, so that she could concentrate her time on preparations for the wedding.

As a wedding present, Kate gave Sarah one of her own gowns. It was made of deep blue velvet and had been one of her favourite gowns. She had worn it when she was first married herself, but since her two pregnancies her waist had thickened and now the gown was too tight. Sarah was excited and delighted by the gift.

'I shall wear it for my wedding and I shall treasure it forever,' she told Kate.

Chapter 12

Kate and Richard decided that after the wedding ceremony the newly married couple should return to Fortune House where there would be a wedding feast for them, and Beth and Thomas and any friends they cared to invite. Kate asked Beth to come and see her, bringing the head cook, and together they chose the food that would be prepared. Richard instructed the brewer to breach a cask of the best ale to serve at the wedding feast, and some of a lesser quality ale was sent to the kitchens to be mulled. In the cold January weather many people would enjoy the warm, spiced mulled ale. Thomas decorated a wagon with branches from the evergreen fir trees to take the bride to the church and to carry the bride and groom back to Fortune House after the ceremony.

The night before the wedding, Richard sent for William to come to his room. He handed William a mug of ale, and said, 'I have been thinking that I want to reward you for all the good work you are doing at Matworth.'

William stopped drinking his ale and said, 'But Sir, I am paid for my work and I am happy with that money.'

'Nevertheless,' continued Richard, 'I want to give you extra recompense and I have decided that I will give it to you as a wedding gift. What I intend is to give you a small percentage of the lead mine business. This means that as the business grows – and I hope and expect that under your careful stewardship it will continue to grow – you will have more

money each year. I shall see my lawyers within the next
week and have the documents drawn up.'

The wedding day dawned bright and sunny, though there was
frost shining white on all the grasses and bushes. As Sarah
was dressing in the blue velvet gown, her mother came in.
Excited and happy for her daughter she called out, 'Happy
the bride the sun shines on!' In her hands Beth carried dried
marigolds that Meg had given to her the evening before. In
January there were no flowers in bloom, so Beth had made
the dried flowers into a small nosegay for Sarah to carry.

'Now,' said Beth to her daughter, 'sit down and I will fix
more of the dried flowers in your hair.'

Sarah's hair was hanging long and loose as was the custom,
to signify her virginity, and Beth wove the dried marigolds into
a small wreath across the top of her head. As she finished,
she said to Sarah, 'Stand up so that I can look at you.' Sarah
stood and plucked at the full skirt of the gown to make it stand
out.

'You look lovely.' Beth's eyes brimmed with tears. She
brushed them away quickly and said briskly, 'Almost time to
leave for the church. And remember to sit carefully in the
wagon – don't crease your skirt.' She gave Sarah a quick
hug and hurried out of the room. Sarah did indeed look lovely,
and Beth was afraid that her emotion and tears would come
back.

Everyone walked to the church, except Kate and Richard
who went in their carriage, and Sarah who rode in the wagon
that Thomas had decorated. Thomas walked alongside the
wagon, leading the horses. At the church, as he helped his
daughter to alight from the wagon, Thomas whispered, 'You
look beautiful,' and found himself unable to say more as emotion
swept over him and a lump formed in his throat.

During the Nuptial Mass, William put a wedding ring on

Sarah's finger, then as the Mass drew to an end, the priest conducted them both to a space beside the altar. Documents that the priest had prepared lay there awaiting their signatures. They showed the date of the marriage, and the names of bride and groom. They would be kept with the church's records, which showed all births, marriages and deaths in the parish. William signed his name with the firm hand of someone who is used to putting his name and seal on documents.

Sarah whispered to William, 'I cannot write my name. I can only make my mark,' and she moved to put an X in the space awaiting her signature. William took her hand and said, 'Let me guide you. This is my first gift to you, helping you sign your name. As soon as we are at home, I will start to teach you to write.' And so, in a shaky hand, guided by William, Sarah signed her name.

As they walked out of the church to the waiting carriage, the bells pealed in celebration and the group of people who had gathered at the church followed them back to Fortune House, walking behind their carriage.

The Great Hall had been decorated for the wedding feast with branches from every kind of bush and shrub that bore brightly coloured berries. Over the fire, a large mulling pot filled with ale and spices was gently heating, and long tables were laid with roast fowl, meats, pies and puddings. At first, people were talking quietly as they found places to sit, most of them feeling intimidated to be sitting and eating in the Great Hall of Fortune House with Sir Richard and his Lady. Richard and Kate were seated at the top table with the bride and groom and Beth and Thomas. Gradually, as everyone ate and drank, they relaxed and the talk grew louder as did boisterous laughter.

Richard rose to his feet, tankard of ale in his hand, and called for everyone's attention. His speech was short and simple.

'On such a happy occasion, I ask you all to raise your

mugs and drink to the health and long life of the bride and groom, Sarah and William.'

After everyone had drunk, Richard still stood and said, 'I will add just one more thing. We wish them God speed and a safe journey to Matworth.'

Everyone called out 'Hooray' and 'God speed' and thumped their fists on the tables.

When Sarah and William set off next morning, soon after first light, they were riding on two horses and took an extra horse to carry their baggage. Sarah's possessions were so few that the horse's burden was light. Richard and Kate had said goodbye to them the night before, but Beth, Thomas and a handful of their friends gathered near the gatehouse to wave them off.

The builders sent word to Richard that they would arrive at Fortune House in late February. Work could start then on taking down and demolishing some of the parts of the house that were to be removed. Once there was no more danger of frost and freezing nights, they would start building the new parts of the house and the various outbuildings that were to be added. By March, all the preliminary clearing work would have been done, and the new stone and brickwork would start at the beginning of April.

At the same time, word came from Petrus van der Weld, the artist, who said that he would arrive at Fortune House in late April to discuss the commission of the two portraits.

'Spring,' thought Kate, 'another spring, another year with its regular events, and the work of the farm will continue in the patterns that have been established over more than a century.'

One evening she said to Richard 'Although this year will see many changes made to our house, and the addition of some things that are new – like the cheese making – I like knowing that each year, with the passage of each season, the work on the lands will be repeated. I find myself feeling very comfortable knowing that each year at almost the same time, very much the same things will be happening. And I like to look ahead and think about the future – not just our children and grandchildren, but all the generations of our family, our descendants, who will live in this house. Will they love it as much as we do? Will they enjoy the rooms that we are adding? Will they tear down parts of the house and rebuild in their own style?'

Richard said, 'I feel exactly the same way, Kate. Sometimes I wonder about the people who will follow us. As they are our descendants, will they look like us? And I wonder if they will look at our portraits and think about us. The house and the estate will be here for centuries to come and we, you and I Kate, are just a link in the long chain that will be the story of this house.'

Footnote: Kate and Richard had another son, born just over a year after Crispin's birth, followed by three daughters born during the next ten years.

Part II
1592

Chapter 1

Although it was past eight o'clock in the evening, the setting summer sun still shone a golden glowing light on Fortune House as Edward reined in his horse, just inside the gatehouse. He sat, looking at the house, thinking, 'Every time I come back here, I realise again how much I love this place.'

Edward had been away in London for just over a month, conducting business concerning the Fortune estate and the lands and lead mines in Derbyshire. As he looked down the long drive from the gatehouse, he could see that work on the additional building to the house had made good progress in his absence.

'Sir Edward! Sir Edward!' A shout came from the edge of the nearby woods. A figure was hurrying towards him; it was Will Blundell, his steward. Will called again, 'It's good to see you back safe, Sir Edward. Welcome home.'

'Thank you, Will,' said Edward, 'it feels good to be home, even before I reach the house. I was just sitting here, thinking how glad I am whenever I return. Even if I've only been gone a few days, I'm always happy to be home.' Edward looked at Will, with his two dogs close at heel, and his gun tucked under his arm, 'Were you out for rabbits?'

'Yes Sir, just getting a few for the pot, you know. There's usually good hunting along the edge of the woods at this time in the evening.'

'Looks as if the builders have made good progress while I've been away,' said Edward, nodding his head towards the house. 'I must go on up there now, but I will see you tomorrow. Come up to the house as soon as your early morning chores are finished and we will go over everything that has happened while I've been gone.

Edward kicked his horse into a walk and continued up the drive, while Will and his dogs went back across the field towards the woods. As Edward neared the house, he could see more clearly how much building work had been done in just the last few weeks. 'Not long till it is completed,' he thought with satisfaction. Ever since the break with Rome, and the formation of the Church of England, much work had been done on repairing old churches and many had needed re-roofing. The high demand for lead for the roof works meant that sales from the lead mines in Derbyshire had provided the money for all the changes that had been made to Fortune House.

The work had started almost four years ago in 1588 when Edward had decided to make alterations to the appearance of the house and give it a more fashionable frontage. Many of the high-ranking aristocracy had built houses in the shape of an 'E' as a tribute to the great Queen Elizabeth, who had reigned since 1558. Copying them, some noblemen had wanted to do the same but, unable to undertake the enormous expense of completely rebuilding the house, they were giving their houses the same appearance but at a lower cost. By simply adding a wing jutting forward at each end of the front of the house, and a small gabled porch over the entrance in the centre of the front, they were able to have the desired 'E' shape. Fortune House would now also have this 'E' shape but it differed from all others in one respect; at one end of the front, above one of the new wings, a small tower raised up above the roofline.

When news of England's great victory over the huge

Spanish Armada fleet had reached this part of the country, building work was just about to begin at Fortune House. Edward had consulted the builders who were an old established company in York and told them that he would like to have some feature of the house that would mark this victory in some way. He asked them for their suggestions and ideas. One of them proposed enlarging the great door, and making the gabled porch over it bigger with a model ship carved in wood over it. Another of them suggested putting some extra decorative work along the edge of the roofline, as the Countess of Shrewsbury was doing on the great house she was building at Hardwick, in Derbyshire. Edward liked this idea but then the youngest builder, who had studied architecture in London and Rome, said, 'Sir, why not build a tower at one end of the house? Not a lofty tower, maybe just two storeys above the body of the house but it will be tall enough to be seen for miles around.'

Edward had needed to think for only a minute before he said, 'Splendid idea. Yes, that's what I want to do. Draw up the plans so that the building work can go ahead.'

When he told his wife, Margaret, of this plan, she had immediately exclaimed, 'I really like that idea. I'm so glad you have told them to go ahead with it.' She paused and thought for just a few minutes, 'Edward … what do you think … should we give this tower a name? We could call it The Armada Tower?'

'What a clever idea! Margaret, my love, I've always told you that you have an excellent brain. We shall indeed call it The Armada Tower. The news of what we are building will travel around, and Fortune House will be known for its Armada Tower.' He kissed her on the cheek. 'What a clever wife I have, to be sure!'

Now, as he neared the house, Edward thought that Margaret

69

had probably been sitting in the solar enjoying the last of the summer evening's sunshine and would have seen his approach up the drive. As he thought this, the main great door was flung wide open, and his wife stepped out on to the terrace.

'Edward! Oh, my dear, I am so glad you are home safely. I don't worry about you when I know you are in London but I do worry all the time when I know you are travelling home. The roads can be so dangerous; the stories we hear about robbers and highwaymen …'

'But I'm here safely now, my love,' Edward interrupted her. A stable boy, alerted by the sound of the horse's hooves, appeared around the corner of the house, and came at a run to hold the bridle of Edward's horse.

'Give him a good rub down, and good bedding as well as food,' said Edward. 'Magic and I have been on the road many days.'

Edward dismounted, and turning, gave the horse an affectionate pat on the neck. 'You've never let me down, Magic. I bless the day I bought you as a foal.'

'You can be sure I will give him every care, Sir,' said the boy. 'You know how I love all our horses and care about their well being.'

'I do indeed know that you care very well for all the horses. That's why I am so glad to have you working in my stables,' said Edward. 'I will come to see all the horses in the morning and check that all is well.'

Edward put an arm around Margaret's shoulder. 'Come,' he said. 'I am weary from my journey and my legs are stiff from riding, but I am so glad to be home. Let us go inside and sit together, and you can tell me all that has happened while I've been gone.'

As they went through the Great Hall, Edward said, 'Margaret, my legs are aching so much. Let's just sit here for a while, and drink some wine while we talk. Time enough to climb up the stairs when we go to bed.'

As they went inside, Becky, the housekeeper came hurrying through from the back part of the house. She had obviously been alerted to Edward's return by her husband, Will, and now she dropped a low bob saying, 'It's glad I am to see you home safely, Sir Edward.'

'Thank you, Becky. As I told Will not ten minutes ago, I am always so happy to come home to this place. And I will be an even happier man if you bring up a bottle of that good French red wine.'

'Certainly, Sir, 'twill be here in minutes.' Becky hurried out, calling to one of the serving maids as she went.

Edward and Margaret sat together near the fireplace in the hall as the sun's last rays streamed through the windows.

'I have so much to tell you about my stay in London – it will take a long time to tell you about all the things I saw, and all the changes that have taken place in London since I was last there five years ago. And now that the builders have almost completed their work here, we can start thinking about decorations inside the house. I have been thinking that I would like to hang tapestries on some of the walls.'

As they sat sipping their wine, Edward talked about his time in London, how many new theatres had opened, the lengthy journey home, and the hazards on the roads. Letting him talk now, she thought there would be time enough in the coming days to tell him all that had been happening here at Fortune House while he was gone.

While he was still talking about many of the sights he had seen in London, Edward's chin dipped towards his chest. Gently, Margaret removed the goblet of wine from his hand and set it down on the table.

'Come, dearest, you are falling asleep. Let us go up to our bedchamber so that you can sleep in the comfort of our bed.'

Chapter 2

Edward awoke and stretched. As he opened his eyes and realised that he was at home in his own bed he felt a wave of happiness come over him. Beside him Margaret stirred and he leaned across, kissed her on the shoulder and said, 'Good morning, my love.'

'Mmmm … I'm still half asleep … but oh, I'm so glad you are home again. And how do you feel this morning? You were exhausted last night.'

'Apart from some stiffness in my legs, I feel remarkably refreshed. It must be the peace and quiet here, and breathing the good clean Yorkshire air. London is so noisy all the time, it seems that the city is never still, never quiet, and the smells aren't pleasant.' He moved out of bed. 'And now, I shall eat and then I shall meet Will to talk over all that has happened in my absence.'

'I know you need to hear all about estate matters from Will and afterwards I am sure you will want to see what the builders have accomplished while you've been away. Perhaps then you and I can talk together about the ideas we both have for decorating the rooms. Last night you said that you thought we might have some tapestry hangings.'

'I do have some ideas about the way we should decorate the inside of the new rooms,' said Edward, 'and I want to tell you about some of the things that I saw in London. As soon as I have finished my talks with Will, and the builders, I shall come to you and we will talk together so that I can describe some of the things that I have seen and admired.'

It was almost noon when Margaret descended to the Great Hall. As he saw her coming down the staircase, Edward held out a hand to her and said, 'You have arrived at the perfect time. Of course, you know Mr Cobden, the master builder who is in charge of the team of builders here?' Mr Cobden bowed to Margaret and she inclined her head to him and murmured, 'Yes, we have met.'

Edward went on, 'I am glad you are here because I was just about to tell him of what I would like here in this main entrance hall. I would like to have the fireplace rebuilt and very much enlarged, and I would like it decorated with the stone they call Derbyshire Bluejohn. I know that one of my ancestors had the idea to do that, but the work was never carried out. This stone called Bluejohn is mined in good quantities on our land at Matworth, and the stonemasons there are skilled at working with it. We can get the stonemasons who are already working here under you, Mr Cobden, to build a much larger fireplace, and then we can get the steward at Matworth to send over a quantity of Bluejohn stone and some men who are experienced in working with it. They can then carry out the decorative work on the newly enlarged fireplace.'

'I think that will be a very pleasing appearance and I like to have the connection to our Derbyshire land,' said Margaret. 'I have only seen Bluejohn in one place, and that is on an old gravestone in the churchyard where an infant Snowwe boy is buried. A small piece of Bluejohn decorates the gravestone.'

'I'm glad that we agree that it will be a pleasing decoration. I shall send a messenger over to Matworth within the next day or two so that a quantity of Bluejohn can be cut and the stonemasons can be chosen to come here,' said Edward.

The steward at Matworth was Richard Bailey, a descendant of the William Bailey who had been steward at the time the estate had been given to Edward's ancestor by the King. The stewardship of the Matworth estate and lead mines had been handed down, generation after generation, close to 200 years. 'It must be rare,' Edward had mused to Margaret at one time, 'for two families to be closely associated for as long as my family have employed members of the Bailey family.'

The whole family came together for the day's main meal, which was served in the largest room on the first floor. Edward and Margaret had five children: Margaret, named after her mother, but always known as Meg; William Crispin; Henry Crispin; another daughter Ann; and the youngest child was their third daughter, Jane. All the male children in the Snowwe family had borne the name Crispin, ever since the first Crispin had been named to commemorate his father's participation in the great battle at Agincourt, which had been fought and won on St Crispin's Day. The only member of the family who was missing today was Edward's mother, Eleanor, the Dowager Lady Snowwe. Sometimes she joined them for meals but often, as today, she preferred to stay in her own rooms where she was cared for by her personal maid and a serving girl.

As Edward looked around the table at his family, he realised that at 18, Meg would be marrying soon and leaving the family. 'Time is going by so quickly,' he thought, 'and the boys are growing up fast too.' William was 17 and was already being trained in all matters of the estate. Edward thought that soon he should send William to Matworth, to stay with the Bailey family, and learn about the management of the farmlands and the lead mines there. Henry was now 16, Ann was 14 and Jane, the youngest child, was almost ten. There had been two other children, born between Ann and Jane, but both had died in infancy.

'Now,' said Edward, looking round at his children, 'starting with Meg, tell me what you have been doing while I've been gone. I'm sure you have all been good or your mother would have told me!'

'I have been spending quite a lot of time with Grandmother,' said Meg, 'and together we have been teaching Becky's and Will's two daughters to read and write. They both learn quickly and they work hard so it is a pleasure to teach them.'

'That is a very good thing,' said Edward. 'As you know, I believe that it is right for girls to have some education. It should not be confined to boys. That is why I have had you and your sisters taught to read and write, and each of you will have sufficient knowledge to be able to keep some household accounts.'

'Actually, Father,' Meg went on, 'Grandmother is so pleased with the way the two girls are learning, that she has said that she might like to endow a small school for all the children of the estate. I think she wants to talk to you about her ideas.'

'I will go along and see her after we have eaten. I know she will like to hear about everything that I have seen and done in London.' Turning to his wife he murmured, 'I know that you, too, want to hear about my stay in London; we will be able to talk at length later today, after I've spent an hour or so with my mother.'

'Father, may I be next to tell you what I have been doing? Do I have to wait until everybody else has told you?' The youngest child Jane was obviously anxious to tell him something, so Edward who was more indulgent with this child than with any of the others said, 'Well, I should make you wait your turn, but perhaps just this once …'

'Father, I shall both tell you and show you what I have been doing.' Jane slipped off her chair and crossed the room, picked up something, and brought it back and laid it on the table beside Edward. 'Look, Father, I am learning some embroidery stitches!'

Jane spread out the piece of linen and said, 'Grandmother

showed me the embroidered hangings at each side of her bed, and she said that they were worked by somebody in this family long, long ago. It must have been a very long time ago, because Grandmother didn't know her and Grandmother is a very old lady.'

'I hope you didn't say that to Grandmother,' Margaret admonished Jane. 'You must never tell her that she is old.'

Margaret and Edward exchanged glances. Edward's mother was indeed old, having turned 65 early this year.

Edward hugged Jane and said, 'I am glad you are learning to make some embroidery stitches. Perhaps when you have learned a few more, you can make a sampler to show your work, and you will put your name at the bottom and then everybody will know who made it. Now, go back to your place and finish eating. I want to hear what everybody else has been doing.'

Turning to the others he said, 'William … it is your turn, tell me what you have been doing.'

In turn, each of the children told Edward what they had accomplished while he was away. William had, as usual, worked with Will, the steward, studying the management of the farm, and learning how to make sales of surplus crops and animals. Henry had continued his lessons with the teacher that Edward had brought to live at the house two years ago. The teacher reported regularly to Edward that Henry was an excellent student, who worked hard and constantly asked questions. Whatever the subject, he always wanted to learn more.

'I think the time will come,' the teacher had said, 'when you should consider sending him to one of the great universities. I am sure he will have an excellent career, perhaps in law.'

Ann told her father that she had been spending time in the

kitchens with the cooks, learning about baking and preparing foods for the table.

'I see,' Edward's eyes twinkled. 'So perhaps one day soon we may all have the pleasure of eating a meal that you have prepared?' Ann looked apprehensive at the thought of cooking for her brothers and sisters as well as her parents. Edward guessed that she felt nervous at such a prospect and added, 'and if anybody eating food that you have prepared makes any unkind remarks, then I will insist that they go to the kitchens and learn to prepare a meal themselves! We shall see if they can do any better!'

Chapter 3

When the meal was finished, Edward said to Margaret, 'I will go and see my mother and talk with her for a while. Then afterwards, as I've said, I will tell you everything that happened in London, and we shall discuss plans for the interior decorations of Fortune House.'

Edward climbed the shallow stone stairs that led to the next floor and made his way along to the western end where his mother, the Dowager Lady Eleanor, had her rooms. He tapped softly on the outer door so as not to wake her if she was sleeping as she sometimes did in the afternoons. Her personal maid opened the door and cried, 'Oh, Sir Edward, Lady Eleanor will be so pleased to see you. She knew you had come home last night but thought that you would be busy with estate matters for some days.'

'Edward, is that you? Oh my dear son, how good it is to have you home again!' Lady Eleanor was sitting in a large, comfortable chair pulled up to the windows that commanded a view over miles of the surrounding countryside. As he came to her side Edward took her hand and kissed it, then bent and kissed her on the cheek.

'Mother, you look well! I am glad you are not resting because I have just heard interesting news from Meg. She has been telling me that you and she have been teaching the steward's two girls to read and write. And Meg said that you wanted to talk to me – something about starting a school for estate children?'

'Yes, that is something I have been giving some thought to,

though the thoughts are not yet formed into real plans. For some years I have been hearing that around the country, small schools have been set up by people like me, women who have some financial means. Because they have been founded by women, the schools are usually called 'Dame Schools' and the purpose of such schools is to teach all children in the area – the children of farm workers and others who would not normally have any lessons. These children are taught basic reading and writing, and maybe some numbers skills so that as they grow up even the girls will be able to conduct their own business selling eggs, and cream, and other produce.'

'Go on,' said Edward. 'Even though you say you haven't formed any real plans yet, tell me more about what you have been thinking. For example, where could such a school be put here on the Fortune estate? There would need to be a small building set aside for the purpose. Where would you find a teacher? And the teacher would need housing, and would have to be paid.'

'As to where the school could be housed – Edward, at the very end of the dairy and creamery, beyond the cheese making building, there is a portion of the building that is little used. In fact, I don't think it is used at all nowadays. There are, I believe, four rooms there and, with a little work, two rooms could be made ready to be used as a place for a teacher to live and the other two rooms could be used for the children's classes.'

'It seems to me that you have moved quite far along in your thoughts and plans, Mother!' said Edward. 'But so far, I think your ideas are good ones.' He stopped and gave her a gentle hug. 'Mother, you and Margaret are both women with good minds. What's a man to do when his wife and his mother are both clever women?'

Eleanor enjoyed it when he joked with her, so she quipped

back to him, 'Edward! A clever wife and a clever mother ... and aren't you forgetting that you have a clever daughter too in Meg? You are surrounded, my dear boy, by clever women!

'Actually,' she went on, 'it is partly because of Meg that I have been giving the idea of starting a school more thought recently. I first had the idea a year or more ago, but it is only since Meg and I have been teaching the two girls that I have given it more serious thought. Meg will not be living here much longer, I suppose. She will be marrying within the next year or so but by then the steward's two girls should be advanced enough to be able to give simple, basic lessons in reading and writing to other, younger children. And, as long as Henry is living at home, I thought that perhaps he would give some instruction in simple numbers work. When the time comes for him to go off to university for higher level studies, we will be able find a young man or woman to take his place. And if we are able to offer a place for a teacher to live in the building I have suggested, I don't think we will have any problems finding someone suitable.'

'Mother, I say again, you are an amazing woman! You really have given this idea a great deal of thought and I think the plans you have in mind are excellent. There is only one matter that you have not mentioned thus far – how are you going to pay the necessary expenses of this school?'

'I have been thinking about the costs, but until I had talked to you and asked if you agreed that the building at the end of the dairy block could be used for the school, I could not progress very far. I do not, of course, have much actual money of my own because when your father died, this estate – the land, the house, and all its contents – passed to you. However, I do have some jewellery and some items of silver that I think have good value.'

'Mother! Surely you do not propose selling some of your

personal belongings? I do not care for that idea at all.'
Edward's face was set and he looked quite stern.

'No, I am not planning to sell any of my possessions. What
I propose, and oh I do hope you will agree, Edward, is that
you will fund the school for the time being. That you will
provide the necessary money to get everything started and
that you will continue to pay all the expenses until I die. When
I die, I would like my personal items to be sold then and the
money raised could be used to pay all the school's costs and
expenses.'

'I don't even like to think ahead to the time you die, Mother
…' Edward started to say, but his mother interrupted him.

'You may not like to think about it, but it is, I'm afraid, a
fact. One day I shall die, and I would like to know that any
items of value that I leave will be used for a good purpose.
And it would be even better if that purpose could be brought
about while I am still alive. Also, there is a little of my vanity
involved too. I would very much like the school to bear my
name and to be known not just as a Dame School, but as the
Lady Eleanor School.'

'Now,' she continued briskly, 'in the hope that you would
agree to fund my school until such time as my possessions are
sold, I have compiled a list of all that I possess. I have made
two separate lists: one shows certain items that I would like to
bequeath to my grandchildren and the other lists all my goods
that should be sold to fund the Lady Eleanor School.'

Edward took the papers that she was holding out to him.
His mother still wrote with a firm hand, and so her writing
was easy to read. On the first page she had shown the names
of each of his children, with a detailed description of a piece
of jewellery or silver beside each name and it was obvious
that his mother had put much thought into deciding which pieces
should go to each child. Beside William's name she had shown

81

'Six silver goblets, given to me by my father at the time of my marriage'. Alongside, she had written a note saying that she hoped that, in his turn, William would pass these on to his eldest son, or eldest daughter if he did not have a son survive him. Henry was to have 'a silver-gilt belt that belonged to my father, his grandfather' and each girl was to have a piece of jewellery that their grandmother thought appropriate for them.

The next pages showed a list, with detailed descriptions, of all Lady Eleanor's personal possessions. There were more pieces of silver, some that she had inherited from her own mother, and there was jewellery that his father had given to her during the many years of their marriage. Rings set with emeralds and diamonds; brooches set with rubies and emeralds; and several necklaces of pearls. The Queen had made the wearing of long pearl necklaces very fashionable, and Edward's father had enjoyed giving his wife jewellery that was both beautiful and fashionable.

As Edward looked over these lists, his mother said, 'I have taken some time to make those lists and I am sure that I have included everything that I have in my personal possession. Now, I think it would be wise if you would arrange for the family lawyer to visit me and review these lists and discuss with me my wishes for the disposition of certain items. I would also like him to draw up any documents that are necessary to enable you to sell the items not specified as bequests. I will also want to amend my will so that it reflects my desire that the money raised from the sale of my possessions should go into a special fund to pay the expenses of a school that is to be known as the Lady Eleanor School.'

Chapter 4

The late afternoon sun was flooding into the solar when Edward made his way there. Margaret was sitting near the tall windows, as she often did when working at her embroidery.

'Time at last, my love,' said Edward, 'for us to sit and talk and I can tell you about all the things I did and saw in London. I shall start right at the beginning,' he went on. 'As you know, I stayed with our friends, the Pyms. It has been some years since we saw them, but the whole family was staying in their London house so it was an excellent opportunity for me to see them and hear all that has happened to them.'

'Oh yes,' said Margaret, 'I want to hear all about each member of the family.'

'Hubert Pym is making a great success as a lawyer and it seems he is becoming well known and is in much demand in London, though sometimes his work brings him to this part of the country. I have asked him to visit us here next time he comes north. Their eldest son, Harry, is now a lawyer and he, too, is making quite a name for himself. Their eldest daughter, Mary, was married almost two years ago and she is to have a child within the next few weeks. Both Hubert and his wife are excited at the thought of being grandparents for the first time. When Hubert asked about our family, I mentioned to him that the teacher that I hired to tutor our son Henry is well pleased with him and has suggested that he might make a career in law. Hubert immediately said that if Henry does wish to study law, he would be happy to have Henry live with him and his family in London during his studies. That would be a very good opportunity for Henry because Hubert is very highly regarded in the legal profession and well connected to many of the important people and businesses in London. Through him, Henry's career would have an excellent start.'

Edward paused and poured himself a tankard of ale. 'I'm thirsty after talking for so long to my mother, and I have so much more to tell you.'

He went on, 'During my stay, several times the Pyms invited some of their friends to come to the house, so that I could meet them and, Margaret, I have met people from such varied fields of interest. One day, one of the guests was a man who had sailed with the great Sir Francis Drake on his voyage around the world. That voyage took three years and of course, upon their return, the Queen knighted Sir Francis on board his ship the Golden Hind.'

After another gulp of ale, Edward continued, 'Another day one of the guests was none other than Lord Burghley, the Queen's chief adviser and Lord Treasurer. Do you remember, dear, if you cast your mind back 20 or more years ago, I think you met him when your father had some dealings with him? He was then Sir William Cecil, of course, before the Queen ennobled him. We had heard that he has built a great house for himself and his family, at Stamford in Lincolnshire. Hubert mentioned to him that our house is being remodelled and Lord Burghley said that in that case I might be interested to visit his chambers and see some sketches of his house. I did so one afternoon, and the house is very beautiful. In fact, with its many decorative chimneys and cupolas placed on the roof, I told him that I would venture to say it has the most beautiful roofline of any house in England.'

Edward stopped talking and walked to the windows, stretching his back as he did so.

'I'm not boring you, am I, my dear?' he asked.

'My goodness, no! Everything you're telling me is so interesting! How I wish that I could have visited London myself!'

'Actually, in some respects you can be glad that you were not in London,' said Edward.

'Why? I should dearly love to visit London again. I have not been there since I was very young, before we even met,' said Margaret.

'I know that you found London fascinating then, and certainly it is a city full of interest, but it does have some unpleasant characteristics. For instance, whenever guests visited the Pyms they always came at noon and after they had eaten they stayed only during the afternoon, so that they could travel back to their homes while it was still light. It is folly to venture on the streets of London after darkness because there are so many robbers and thieves, and the streets are full of drunkards too. Another thing, Margaret, you would not believe how bad London smells! As always, there is a runnel down the middle of every street carrying all the waste matter, but to me it seemed to smell worse than ever before. Many people carry pomanders filled with sweet smelling herbs and dried flowers and they hold them to their noses all the time they are in public places.'

'Such a shame,' said Margaret. 'I have always had the happiest memories of my last visit to London.'

Edward went on, 'And the noise! I am surprised that people who live and work in London all the time do not suffer from continuous headaches! There are hundreds of churches and their bells seem to be ringing all day long. Those and the street vendors' cries, the shouts of coach drivers – not to mention the arguments they get into – all contribute to the noise! But I must confess that I did enjoy many things in London. Going to the theatre is all the rage now, and new theatres and playhouses are being built all over London. Until more new theatres are ready, plays are often performed in the courtyards of inns and people throng to see them. The Pyms took me to a play at The Rose theatre, and another day they took me to The Globe, which is one of the newest theatres. It was at The Globe that I saw a play by the young man everyone is talking about, William Shakespeare. The whole of London flocks to his plays and they do say that the Queen herself is a great admirer of his work.'

'Oh, Edward, you know how I enjoy going to see a good play. Smells and noises or not, I do wish I could have been there with you!'

'One thing that is new to me,' said Edward, 'is the great interest people have in planting gardens. A lot of the great London houses now have a formally planned and laid out garden, and from all I heard, it seems that many people are employing specialist garden designers to plan and lay out gardens for their country houses too. I saw and heard of many different kinds of gardens, and I have been thinking that I would very much like to have something specially designed for Fortune House.'

'Edward! What an amazing coincidence! While you were in London my sister Matilda came and visited us here, and when she was admiring the changes and additions we have made to Fortune House, she said that she wondered if we would be adding some formal gardens. She said that the area right in front of the terrace is smooth and level and would lend itself to a garden with a geometric plan, and the big old tree known as Dickon's oak would be a central feature of one side of it.

'My sister also told me that people are laying out gardens with separate sections for different purposes,' Margaret continued. 'There are special herb gardens and also walled gardens are being built within which there are beds filled entirely with roses. She said that the new roses called Damask roses have a beautiful scent and I should very much like to have those. Don't you think that a rose garden would be a particular joy?'

'I like all of those ideas – a formal garden to the front of the house and a walled area to one side of the house where we would plant many rose bushes.' Edward paused and pondered for a moment. 'In fact, I think I have an even better idea! What if we planted roses in beds and other roses climbing up the walls, and also put lavender hedges around the edges of some of the rose beds and along the paths between the rose beds, so that the whole area would become a scented garden?'

'I think that is a most delightful idea. Oh Edward, yes do please see if you can find one of these garden designers and arrange for him to come here as soon as possible.' Margaret broke off as their daughter Ann came into the solar.

'May I join you, Mother and Father, or are you talking privately?' she asked.

'Of course you may join us,' said Edward. 'Your mother and I are talking about the possibility of having gardens designed especially for us.'

'Oh, Aunt Matilda was talking about gardens when she visited while you were in London,' said Ann.

'Yes, your mother has told me that and I was telling her that everyone in London seems very taken with gardens now. I think there is so much interest because so many new plants are now coming into England from all over the world. One other thing,' Edward continued, 'that I have not yet had an opportunity to discuss with your mother,' Edward turned to Margaret. 'I hope you will forgive me for going ahead without first talking to you, but I have engaged the services of a young portrait painter who is much in favour in London and he will be coming here as soon as he has fulfilled the commitments he had already made before I talked to him. I want to have our family group painted, especially as the children are all growing up so fast, and before we know it, they will have left home and gone about their own lives. I do apologise for not waiting to consult you, my dear, but this young man is so much in demand that if I did not engage his services immediately, we would probably have to wait two years or more for him to be able to undertake our commission.'

'I like the idea,' said Margaret. 'I like to look at the paintings we have in the house of two of your ancestors. In fact, I believe they are the parents of the small boy whose gravestone is marked with a Bluejohn decoration. Who knows, perhaps in hundreds of years' time, maybe some of our descendants will look at our portraits.

'And another thing I would like,' she continued, 'would be to have a landscape painting of Fortune House and its surroundings. I think that when the gardens we plan are in place we should have a painting made, showing the house, with its new appearance, and the gardens.'

'I think that is an excellent idea, Margaret. I shall certainly write off to Hubert Pym. I am sure he will be able to give me the names of good landscape painters. And now,' Edward changed the subject, 'what I would like most is to have my mother join us, along with all our children, and the children shall play some music for us. Ann, go and find your brothers and sisters, and tell them to come here and play for us.'

Each of the children had been taught to play several musical instruments and the two older girls were quite accomplished players of the virginal and the lute. The two boys preferred to play the trumpet and drums but, as all five children played that late afternoon, Edward thought that even as a fond father he had to admit that neither of the boys had any musical skills at all.

Chapter 5

Serenity and calmness descended on Fortune House after the builders finally completed all their works and departed. For the next weeks, work was done on the interior of the house, but those workers did not make nearly as much noise as the builders had done. Plasterers made all the walls smooth and, once the plaster had completely dried, painters who specialised in painting on plaster started to decorate the walls. Several carts full of Bluejohn arrived from Matworth and with it came the stonemasons who were skilled at working with it. They would to cut it into pieces of different sizes and shapes, polish it, and then set the pieces into sections of the enormous fireplace that had been built in the Great Hall. Oak panelling was put on the walls of two rooms that led off the central hall; one was a small room that Edward intended to use for conducting estate business and the other was a small withdrawing room. Carpenters who were skilled in carving oak set to work making a design on the panelling that was called 'linen fold' because the finished appearance looked like folded cloth. The last workmen to arrive were gilders. These men applied real gold leaf to the decorations on the top of columns in the hall and on the pediments over all the doors in the Great Hall.

Edward had ordered tapestries from the English makers at Mortlake. For many years the finest tapestries had been woven in Brussels, but while he was in London, Edward had seen some Mortlake tapestries and decided that he would prefer to have pieces that were made in England. He had ordered a set of four very large tapestries, depicting the four seasons, and they were to be hung on the walls on each side of the great staircase.

Fine weather continued through August and September and all the crops were harvested. Some were stored for feeding everyone who lived on the Fortune estate, and some were sold. Surplus animals were sold at the livestock markets and when Will and Edward sat down and went over all the accounts and receipts for sales, they found that Fortune had had a good, profitable year.

'It's fortunate indeed that we have had a good year,' Edward pretended to scowl and look grumpy, 'all this work on the house will have eaten up a great deal of the profits we've made.' Then he turned and clapped Will on the shoulder. 'But not all the profits will be spent on the house and the gardens we are planning. I have a small gift for you, Will, a token of my thanks for all your work throughout the year.' Edward handed him a leather purse in which he had placed several gold coins.

Will pulled the drawstring, and looked inside the purse. His face froze and he looked stunned.

'Sir Edward … Sir Edward…' he stumbled over his words. 'To say thank you is not sufficient! I have done my job to the best of my ability, and I am paid a wage for doing it. I do not expect more!'

'I know you don't, Will. And it is because you always do everything to the very best of your ability that I am happy to make you this gift. In centuries gone by, under the feudal system, you would have worked here in return only for housing and food and perhaps a small gift occasionally. Those days have gone. I no longer have to raise men from my estates to

91

fight in the army and you are not tied to working for me. I pay you for the work you do, and you are free to leave here and work somewhere else if you ever choose to do so.

Will started to protest that he would never leave, that he could not imagine living anywhere else, but Edward stopped him.

'Will, I believe that you won't ever leave here. You are young enough that perhaps you will still be steward when my son William takes over after I am gone. In the meantime, as long as you work for me, allow me to mark your good work with a small gift.'

The two men continued talking about the business of the estate for a while longer. Edward was particularly impressed with the work of the cheese makers.

'Ask them both to come in and see me when you leave, Will. I want to compliment them on the increased amount of cheese produced this year, and also the varieties of different flavours they have introduced. Sales have risen a great deal.'

'Yes, Sir Edward, it is noticeable at the markets that the Fortune cheese stall always has a crowd around it and however much is taken to market, the whole amount is sold. The new sage flavoured cheese is proving to be very popular, and so is the softer, creamier cheese that they started making this year.'

Just as the gilders were finishing their work, a letter arrived from Sir Hubert Pym. He said that he and his son Harry were both travelling to York Assizes where a legal case needed their presence, and at the end of the trial they would visit Fortune House.

'This summer you invited us to visit you if ever we came to Yorkshire and I did not expect to be able to act upon your invitation so soon. We think that the trial and all matters connected with it will be completed by the end of September and we would like to visit Fortune House at that time,' said the letter.

Margaret was delighted and excited at the thought of having visitors from London and she whisked the maids into a frenzy of activity, cleaning the entire house, even all the newly decorated rooms, and making bedchambers ready. She spent hours with the cook discussing meals that would be prepared and served to their guests.

'These people are from London and they are probably used to everything that is newest and most fashionable,' she worried. The cook (always known as Mrs Cook, though she wasn't married) was not perturbed.

'I will use our own meats and vegetables and fruit from the estate,' she said, 'together with our own cheeses, and I have all our own herbs and also the newest spices to make food that will pleasure them, I'm sure.'

'What a pity that the tapestries from Mortlake are not yet here,' Margaret said to Edward. 'I know you told me when you ordered them that they would not be ready for some three years, which seems such a long time. And I do wish that the gardens could have been made in time for visitors to walk in them! What a joy it will be when we can show visitors our plantings.'

When Sir Hubert and Harry arrived, they were both so charming that Margaret relaxed. She knew immediately that entertaining the two of them would be a pleasure and no problems would arise.

On the first evening, the whole Snowwe family sat at the table, along with their two guests. The youngest daughter, Jane, had been allowed to eat later than usual, so that she could meet their special visitors. Margaret was anxious for all the news from London.

'I feel we are in a backwater here, Sir Hubert, and we

never hear news until it is a year or more late!' she complained.

'Well,' Sir Hubert asked her, 'what sort of news do you want to hear? News from the world of business and finance? News from the political world? For that you must speak with my son Harry, he is quite involved with the politicians in the City of London. Or perhaps you would like news from the Court?'

'Oh yes,' said Margaret. 'Yes please, tell us about the Court, what Her Majesty is doing, and what her ladies at Court are wearing …'

Sir Hubert laughed, 'I'm not sure either of us is qualified or able to tell you about Court fashions, but I can tell you that there is the usual gossip that Her Majesty will soon choose a husband!'

'A husband!' Meg burst out. 'But she has always said that she is married to England and will take no husband!'

'Ah yes, she has indeed said that. Mostly, I think, she used that phrase as a political ploy so that she could keep several foreign suitors waiting and hoping. An alliance through marriage to England's Queen would be most advantageous to any foreign country. However,' Sir Hubert continued, 'since our defeat of the Spanish Armada, the Queen feels that her Royal Navy can keep England's coasts secure against foreign invaders. The gossip now is that she teases her advisers by saying that she might be minded to take one of her English favourites as a husband!'

As the meal drew to an end, Jane, protesting that she really wasn't tired, was taken off to bed by her nurse, William and Henry drew nearer to Sir Hubert, and Harry moved his chair closer to Meg and started talking to her. Margaret looked across the room and saw that very quickly they were deep in conversation, and when she looked again later, it was clear that they were still absorbed in each other. Meg's face was slightly flushed and her eyes were bright.

'Well, well,' thought Margaret, 'now that is a surprising, and not displeasing, turn of events.'

Edward suddenly called across the room, 'Come, Meg, before we all retire, play something for us. Play that pretty melody by William Byrd that I like so much.'

Meg crossed to the corner, picked up her lute and sat down and started to play. When she finished, everybody applauded, but Margaret noticed that Harry applauded more enthusiastically than anybody else.

'Play on, Meg!' called Edward.

'Yes, play more!' cried Sir Hubert. So Meg played again and, looking directly at Harry, she played and sang the love song 'Greensleeves'.

When they were in their bedchamber Margaret started to ask Edward if he had noticed how engrossed Meg and Harry had been in each other, then she decided to say nothing. 'Time enough to talk about it,' she thought, 'if anything comes of it.'

Chapter 6

The fine autumn weather continued beyond September into October and Edward was able to take Sir Hubert and Harry out riding around the Fortune estate. All three men were excellent shots and on several days they were able to bag a number of pheasants. Mrs Cook regretted that she could not cook them immediately and serve them to the guests as they would have to be hung for at least three weeks. But Sir Hubert said that they completely understood and he paid her the compliment of saying that he thought he was already getting fat on her excellent meals.

'I am sure my waist has expanded since I arrived here,' he joked with her.

Suddenly, just before the two Pyms were about to set off on their journey back to London, the weather changed and heavy rain fell for a whole week.

'I fear we must stay with you for longer than we had anticipated,' said Sir Hubert one morning. 'Obviously the rain will have made the roads impassable for another week or two, so I am afraid we must impose on your hospitality for a little longer.'

Margaret caught a look that passed between Meg and Harry, and she noticed that neither of them looked displeased at the thought of the enforced longer stay at Fortune House.

The bad weather continued, many fields were flooded, and most of the cattle and sheep had to be brought into their winter barns. By the end of October even the oldest inhabitants were saying that there had never been such a long wet spell in their memory.

One morning, Harry approached Edward and asked if he may speak to him.

'Of course, my boy. What do you wish to speak about?'

Harry's face went slightly pink, he stumbled over his words, then drew himself upright and said in a firm voice, 'If I may be so bold, Sir Edward, may we speak privately in the room you use for conducting business?'

The two men went into the newly panelled business room, and Edward said, 'Sit down, Harry, and tell me what you want to talk about.'

'I will not waste your time, Sir, I will come straight to the point. During our stay here at Fortune House, you may have noticed that your eldest daughter Meg and I have spent quite a lot of time in each other's company. I have very much enjoyed conversing with her, and I venture to say that she has enjoyed my company too. Forgive me if I appear bold, but I ask you, Sir, to consider me as a husband for Meg. I would very much like your permission to speak to her and ask her if she would consent to marry me.'

'Well, now, I won't say that this comes as a complete surprise,' said Edward. 'I have noticed that the two of you draw together each evening and spend much time in conversation. Meg is very young but I realise that she is at an age when many girls marry. As her father, it is of course my duty to ensure that if and when she marries, it should be to a man who can provide well for her and offer her a life at least as comfortable as the one she has here at home.'

'Sir, with respect, I think you know from my father that I have made a good start in my chosen profession. I am building a good reputation for myself as a lawyer. Also, I have become friendly with some of the gentlemen, mostly politicians, who conduct all affairs governing the City of London. I have been carrying out business on their behalf for two years now and I find that the affairs of a great city like London interest me greatly. In course of time, I hope I will become an Alderman of the City, and perhaps, if I apply myself diligently, eventually I may even become Lord Mayor of London.' Harry paused then went on, 'But I hope you will understand and forgive me, Sir, if I say that what is most important to me is that I have the highest regard for Meg, and that it would be my sincere desire to make her happy and be a good husband to her.'

Edward's expression was serious. 'Harry, will you understand if I say that I would like to consider all that you have said for a day or so? I will think carefully about all you have said, and also what I think will be best for my daughter. I do not treat this matter lightly, and nor, I think, do you. Let us speak again tomorrow or the next day. I will let you know when it is convenient.'

Within the hour, Edward sought out Margaret. She was alone in the solar and he drew a chair alongside her.

'Margaret, I want to discuss with you a matter that usually would be something resolved by me alone. But as it concerns our daughter Meg, I think that it would be discourteous – nay, unfeeling – if I did not discuss this with you and hear your thoughts. Young Harry Pym has just been talking to me, and it appears that he and Meg have developed a fondness for each other. In fact, it goes beyond mere fondness. It seems that they hold each other in such high regard, that Harry has asked for my permission to marry Meg. He has not yet, he says, spoken to her of marriage, but …'

'Oh, Edward! I am surprised that you have not noticed the growing friendship and affection between the two of them,' said Margaret. 'Right from the very first evening, it was clear that they enjoyed each other's conversation and company. I said nothing to you because I thought that the Pyms would be staying here for only a few days, then they would leave and return to London, and that would be the end of the matter.'

Margaret continued, 'And what have you told Harry? Have you given your consent?'

'No, not yet, my dear. I told him that he and I would speak again in a day or two. I wanted time to set matters clearly in my own mind and also I wanted to talk it over with you and hear your views. It would, of course, mean that after her marriage Meg would live in London. Such a long distance from us ...'

'Edward! It is normal for a young wife to go to live where her husband lives. I moved quite some distance from my family home when we married. Of course, we shall miss her, but ...' Margaret turned to him with a wide smile, 'just think, my dear, I told you that I would like to visit London again. Well, if Meg is living there I would have good reason to journey there!'

'So ... just so that you can pay visits to London, you think I should tell young Harry that my answer is "yes"?'

'Edward, I know that you are making fun and so was I. It is a serious matter, but really, my dear, could we ask for a nicer young man as a son-in-law? And it seems that he is already highly regarded in his profession, and would be able to provide a comfortable home and manner of living for her.'

'You are right. To tell you truly, Margaret, even before you and I talked, I had it in my mind to say yes to Harry tomorrow. I shall talk to his father too, and discuss with him the dowry or what they are calling nowadays "a marriage portion" that I shall make over to Meg upon her marriage. Luckily, I can afford to be quite generous in that regard. And before the Pyms leave for London we should think about when this wedding is to take place. Perhaps it will be early next summer?'

Next morning, after Edward had talked again to Harry and consented to him speaking to Meg about marriage, he and Margaret did not have to wait long until the young couple came to them. Meg's face was shining with joy and Harry looked as if he had grown two inches in height, he held himself so proudly.

'Sir Edward, Lady Snowwe, I am overjoyed to tell you that Meg has agreed to be my wife! I promise you, as I have promised her, that I will try always to make her as happy as we are today.' Harry turned and took Meg's hand and said, 'After I have returned to London, I will send you a betrothal jewel and I hope you will wear it always as a token of my enduring love for you.'

At Edward's request, the vicar came to Fortune House that afternoon and all the Snowwes and both the Pyms were awaiting him in the Great Hall. When he arrived and they told him of the betrothal and forthcoming marriage of Meg and Harry, he immediately gave the couple his blessing.

'Has any thought yet been given to the date for this happy occasion?' he asked.

Sir Hubert said, 'It is entirely a matter for the bride and her family to decide upon a date but of course, our family party would not be able to travel until the roads are in good condition after the winter and spring rains. So that would mean perhaps towards the end of April, I suppose.'

'But you must not forget,' said the vicar, 'that the marriage cannot take place during Lent, and next year Easter does not fall until late in April. So it will not be possible to have the ceremony until at least the beginning of May.'

Meg said, 'If it pleases everyone, my choice would be to

marry in June. It is always such a lovely time of year, with fair weather and there are so many flowers in bloom that can be used to decorate the church.'

And so it was decided, before the two Pyms left to travel south to London, that the wedding would take place in June 1593.

Chapter 7

As if to make up for the terrible weather in the latter months of 1592, the weather in the new year was good. Although January could be a bitterly cold month, day after day, week after week, it was bright and clear. Although the nights were cold there were no heavy freezes and only a dusting of white hoar frost lay on the fields and hedges each morning, and even the weak January sun dispersed this by mid-morning. When Margaret looked across the Fortune estate from her bedchamber windows each morning, and saw how bright and clear it was, she thought that it almost looked as if someone had taken a cloth and polished the sky. One day she said this to her mother-in-law, Eleanor, who said that was a perfect description.

'I would not dare say such a thing to Edward,' said Margaret. 'He always says he regards me as a sensible woman and if I made a remark such as that he would ask if my mind was addled!'

The two women laughed together. Right from the time when she had come to Fortune House as a young bride, Margaret had liked Eleanor, and Eleanor in her turn was pleased to have Margaret as a daughter-in-law. Over the years a warm friendship had grown between them.

Because the bad rains had made the roads impassable for such a long time, nobody had been able to go to the markets. The good weather in January meant that Will was now able to go to the nearest market town, along with the cheese makers, and he came back telling Edward that they, at Fortune, had been lucky compared with the misfortunes suffered by many other local estates and farms.

'I've heard shocking stories of land owners and farmers who have lost much of their livestock because there has been flooding in many areas,' he told Edward. He went on, 'Many fields were flooded when rivers burst their banks and in some places the waters rose so fast that it was not possible to move the cattle and sheep to higher ground and so they were drowned.'

'This is indeed grim news,' said Edward, 'and will cause much hardship I am sure. Once again it seems that Fortune has lived up to its name.'

A letter came from the gardener that Edward had engaged to design the gardens for Fortune House saying that he would arrive in February and would bring with him his assistants who would help with the planning of gardens.

'This all sounds very interesting and exciting,' Edward said to Margaret as he read the letter from the gardener. 'He says he will bring with him drawings and paintings of some of the new plants that are now being brought into England, so that we can choose the ones we like best.'

When Thomas Wilkins, the landscape gardener, and his assistants arrived, Thomas himself was accommodated just off the main courtyard of Fortune House, and the three young assistants he brought with him, stayed at the inn beside the church. The night after they arrived the wind started to blow strongly in the late afternoon. Because of the strong winds, Will sent men to go all over Fortune estate and ensure that all gates were closed and all barn doors were shut, and to check that no farming equipment had been left lying out in fields where it could be blown about and damaged.

About two o'clock in the morning, Margaret woke up

suddenly. The wind was blowing so strongly now that she could feel the old house shuddering under its force.

'Edward, Edward, wake up … please wake up.' Edward came awake, grunting a little, still half asleep.

'What? What's the matter?' But as he came fully awake he heard the wind howling and the creaking sounds that the house was making.

He got out of bed and went to the windows, pulling back the heavy drapes that covered them at night. Margaret got out of bed, too, and went over and joined him at the window, looking out into the darkness.

'I can't see anything at all, it is so black,' she said, then suddenly the heavy clouds parted and bright moonlight lit the scene. Both Margaret and Edward gasped as they could see that the wind was so strong that it was bending large trees and then, as they watched, a branch that must have been wrenched off a tree was blown against the window where they stood.

They both jumped back in fear. Luckily the branch had not broken any of the small diamond-shaped panes of glass in the windows.

Through the windows they could see that candles were being lit in several of the farm workers' cottages that were visible from the house. Then there was the sound of movement on the floor below them, followed by a light tapping on the door of their bedchamber.

'There is someone at the door,' said Margaret. 'Quick, Edward, you go and see who it is. There may be some problem that needs your attention.' Margaret fumbled to light a candle.

Edward opened the door to find Becky standing there, holding a candle aloft.

'Are you both all right, Sir?' she asked. 'I came across because I thought you might need me.'

'That's good of you, Becky,' said Edward. 'You must have

104

been nearly blown off your feet in this wind! We are perfectly all right here, but I would like you to go up to make sure that my mother and her maid are all right. I have never known a wind of such ferocity and they may be frightened. I will come up and see my mother myself, as soon as I have dressed.' He started to put on some clothing, and Margaret pulled on a loose robe.

'I am going up to make sure that my mother is all right. Perhaps I should suggest that she comes down with her maid, and we all sit together in the Great Hall …'

As he spoke, the wind blew more strongly than ever and there was a huge gust that shook the house.

Edward and Margaret both turned back to look out of the window again and they both gasped. As they watched, Dickon's Oak was blown over and fell as easily as a child's skittle in a game.

'Dear God,' cried Edward, 'that oak has been there for almost 200 years! I will go out as soon as there is daylight enough to see. Probably several more big trees are down all over the estate.'

In Fortune House there were a number of documents detailing certain events that had taken place in the house's history. One of them told of the death of the first-born son of one of Edward's ancestors, a death that had occurred while his father was fighting in France in the year of the great battle of Agincourt. It was this child's grave that was marked with a stone that had a Bluejohn ornamentation, and the oak tree had been planted as a memorial to him.

As dawn broke, it was evident from all they could see that the storm had done damage not only to trees, but also to some of the buildings. Some roofs were damaged though the ones that had been tiled had fared worst. The older roofs that were made of thatch had fared better. As Richard walked out of the house and across the terrace and started to go down the steps to the drive, Will appeared from his own cottage.

'Good morning, Will – though just how "good" we shall find things, I don't know,' called Edward. 'Is your house damaged?'

'Good morning, Sir Edward. Our house has fared well, I think. There may be some slight damage but nothing to worry about.'

'I want to walk over to see Dickon's Oak,' said Edward. 'We were looking through the window and saw it blown down. It seems impossible that a tree that has been standing for nearly 200 years can be blown down – though of course it was a wind of huge force.'

'I will go with you, Sir,' said Will, 'then I will take several men and we will check all the fields, and make sure that the cattle and sheep are all safe.'

As Edward and Will reached the fallen great oak tree, a voice called 'Good morning' from behind them, and turning, Edward saw that it was Thomas Wilkins, the garden designer.

Edward and Will both called 'Good morning' and Edward added, 'But in truth, not a very good morning, I fear. I am just going to inspect the damage that has been done.'

Thomas joined them and the three men walked in silence towards the fallen oak tree.

'It is sad to see something that has stood so long, and seemed so strong, fallen and lying there,' said Edward. 'Of course, you don't know the history of that tree, Mr Wilkins,' said Edward and then he told him why the tree had been planted.

Thomas said, 'May I suggest, Sir Edward, that you get some of your men to remove all the side branches, and then have the trunk taken to an empty barn. Place it on trestles, and leave it to dry and season. Of course, it will take several years for the wood to become properly seasoned but then it could be made into a piece of furniture for your house so that it will continue, albeit in a different form, to be a memorial to that small boy.'

'Ah, Mr Wilkins, here come your three assistants,' said Edward, as the three young men hurried up the drive.

After they had greeted Edward and Thomas Wilkins, and they had viewed the sad sight of the huge oak lying on the ground, one of them said, 'In the churchyard, next to the inn where we are lodged, a great yew tree was also blown down in the storm.'

'That is another tree that has stood for centuries,' said Edward. 'All the rain we had a few weeks ago must have soaked the ground around the roots of these big trees, or they would not have blown down.'

'Sir Edward,' one of the young assistant gardeners spoke, 'that yew tree is blown on to its side, but some of its roots are still in the ground. I have heard of this happening in another place, and the tree was pulled upright and it rooted itself firmly again and has continued to live and grow.'

'Come, Will,' said Edward, 'let us go down – and you Mr Wilkins, and all of you,' he indicated the three assistant gardeners. 'We will all go to the churchyard and look at this fallen yew. It would please me greatly if we could rescue that tree. It has stood there for centuries, and wood from it was cut to make bows. I daresay some of the bows that men from here took to Agincourt were made from that tree.'

When they reached the churchyard they saw that although the great yew had blown down, as the young gardener had said, a portion of its roots were still firmly in the ground. Two or three farm workers were in the churchyard and Will sent

107

one of them to bring as many men as he could find and tell them to bring strong ropes. When about 15 men were gathered in the churchyard, Will had ropes placed around the trunk of the yew tree, and then all the men pulled and heaved on the ropes and finally, after much effort, the tree stood upright again. Will then told three of the men to get spades, and dig earth and put it around the roots of the tree, and the other men trod over the earth so that the tree's roots would hold firm.

The young gardener who had said that he had heard of a yew being righted and continuing to live and grow, said that he had heard the other yew referred to as 'the miracle tree' because it had survived after being blown down.

'Well,' said Edward, 'I daresay that this tree will be considered a miracle too if it does indeed survive.'

Chapter 8

All the farm workers on Fortune estate were kept busy for some weeks after what became known as The Great Storm. All over the estate, branches had been broken off trees, some of the barns and storage sheds had been damaged and needed repairs, and there was damage to several of the cottages where the workers lived. As Will had said, the thatched roofs had survived best but tiles needed replacing on the roofs of many cottages, the dairy, and some of the courtyard buildings. The ancient dry stone walls had not been damaged at all, but some of the hurdles that formed pens for the sheep and kept the pregnant ewes apart from the others had been destroyed. Some of the farm workers had had experience making hurdles and they set to work straight away to make new pens for the animals that needed them.

It seemed that all the animals had survived the storm without any harm except two cows that had been killed when a large tree fell on them as they huddled in the corner of a field. The normal spring business of the farm needed to be done, so Will had to take some men away from doing repair work, and set them to working in the fields. Some fields had been roughly ploughed last autumn but they now needed to be tilled again so that the soil was ready for seeds to be sown.

In the midst of all this activity, a rider arrived with a packet, which he said was for the daughter of the house. It was addressed to Margaret Snowwe. The gatekeeper told him that Margaret was the name of Lady Snowwe, and then he thought and said, 'Oh aye … that's right, the elder daughter is named Margaret too, but we always think of that young lady as Meg.' The rider was kept waiting at the gatehouse while a message was sent to Will. When he arrived at the gatehouse, the rider told him that the packet he carried was a gift from Sir Hubert Pym's son, Harry, to Margaret Snowwe. Will escorted the rider to the house and when they reached the Great Hall, he sent one of the maids to fetch Lady Snowwe.

When Margaret arrived, the rider swept off his hat, bowed, and explained again that he carried a package that contained a gift to Margaret, the daughter of the family, from Mr Harry Pym. Margaret sent the maid off again, this time to fetch her daughter Meg. When Meg came into the hall, the rider bowed again, and handed her the small packet. Meg took it, and when she broke the seal and started to unwrap it, a note fell out and fluttered to the floor.

She read it quickly and then said, 'Oh, Mother, I'd like you to read this note from Harry.'

Margaret took the note over to the window where the light was better for her to read it. The note said:

'As I promised, I send you a betrothal jewel. My father gave this to my mother when they were betrothed, and he had it from his mother who had worn it all her life.'

Margaret felt sentiment sweep over her and she held out her arms and embraced Meg.

'Oh my dear, he has given you a jewel that has been in his family for two generations already. Do open that small package so that we can see it.'

Meg tore open the wrapping and found something wrapped in cloth. When she removed the cloth she found a pendant hanging from a gold neck chain. The pendant was a knot shape, made of gold, and set with pearls and diamonds.

'Oh Mother,' she gasped. 'I think this is the most beautiful jewel I shall ever possess! I can't wait for Father to come back to the house so that he can see it too!'

Then, remembering her manners, she turned to the rider and said, 'Oh, thank you, thank you for bringing this package to me. This is something I shall treasure all my life! But you must be tired and hungry from your long ride, and your horse will need refreshing too. I will call one of the servants to take you to the inn just outside the gatehouse and you shall stay there as long as you need, until you are ready to return south again. Before you leave on that journey, please come back to see me so that you can take with you a note from me to Mr Harry Pym.'

Holding up the pendant again, Meg said, 'Mother, when the artist comes to paint our family group portrait, I shall wear this pendant. When people see the painting of our family together, I want them to see that I am wearing this beautiful jewel.'

As Meg had wished, the wedding was to take place early in June and preparations started soon after Meg's betrothal gift arrived.

Edward needed to talk with the family's lawyer who would draw up the documents pertaining to the money he would settle on Meg at her marriage. The lawyer had his chambers in York and Margaret decided that she and all three daughters would go to York too, and visit the dressmaker there. They would be able to look at all the fabrics that the dressmaker had available, so that they could choose what they wanted for their new garments. Meg would need not only a wedding gown but also other gowns, ruffs, a new travelling cloak for her journey to London after the marriage, and another cloak of finer material for more special occasions. Ann and Jane were to have new gowns to wear on the wedding day, as they would be bridal attendants to their sister, and Margaret was determined that her own new clothes for the wedding would not be outshone by the London fashions that Lady Pym would be wearing. Edward would visit his tailor in York and have new garments made for him and both his sons. Each of them would have new breeches, a new doublet and a ruff, and new shoes.

After the marriage ceremony, there would be a wedding feast for both families in the Great Hall of Fortune House, and Margaret and Mrs Cook spent many hours talking about the foods that should be prepared. As there would also be a wedding feast for the household staff and farm workers and their families which would be held in the courtyard, Mrs Cook and Will were both instructed to bring in more workers to help with all the extra work.

In the midst of all the bustle of wedding preparations, Thomas Wilkins told Edward that he had made preliminary sketches of the gardens he proposed and was ready to show them.

'We will need several tables so that I can spread out all the drawings for you to look at them and at the same time I will show you the drawings and paintings of the new flowers that are available,' he said. So several tables were pulled into the Great Hall, and Thomas Wilkins and his assistants laid out the sketches of garden designs, for Edward and Margaret to review them. What was proposed for the front of the house was a garden on each side of the drive, with geometric shapes of beds and paths, and a small fountain in the centre of each bed. The proposal showed a walled rose garden, to one side of the house. This was divided into four main sections, with a wide path going across the garden in each direction, meeting in the centre.

Thomas said, 'You told me that you would both like this to

be a scented garden. So, as you will see from the sketches, I have suggested that each of the four quarters is planted with rose bushes, and that along each side of the paths there should be a low lavender hedge.'

Margaret said, 'Mr Wilkins, we had also thought that we would like to have roses climbing the walls of the rose garden, too.'

'I have already thought of that, Lady Snowwe, and I have sketched in climbing roses here and here,' Thomas indicated places on the inner walls, 'and I have also suggested that there should be honeysuckle interspersed with the climbing roses to give another scent. Additionally, I would like to add some edgings of pinks – another highly scented flower.'

Margaret couldn't restrain herself from clapping her hands with joy.

'Mr Wilkins, I don't have to study your designs any further. I am already delighted with all your suggestions. What do you think, Edward? Are you as pleased as I am?'

Edward said that he found the designs completely satisfactory and he would be happy for Mr Wilkins and his team to start to lay out the gardens, exactly as shown in the sketches.

'So that is all settled and agreed,' he said. 'By this time next year, we should have our new gardens in place. They will be in their infancy, but we shall watch them grow to maturity over the coming years.'

Both Margaret and Edward were happy because all arrangements for the forthcoming wedding were going ahead smoothly. Their new garments had been ordered and the seamstress and the tailor would both come to Fortune House so that each item could be tried on and adjustments made. Final plans were made for the dishes to be served at the wedding feasts and it had been decided that the main dish at the family's own meal would be roast peacock. Margaret and Mrs Cook had both heard that it was the fashion to serve this bird decorated with its own colourful feathers and Margaret wanted to be sure that all the dishes served would equal anything that was being served in the grand houses in London.

The priest at the church just beyond the gatehouse, where the marriage would take place, arranged for the banns to be called at the church, which meant that the couple's names and their intention to marry was announced from the pulpit in the church. This had to be done on three consecutive Sundays before the marriage ceremony could take place.

One day when all the family were gathered for their meal, Jane produced a piece of embroidered cloth, which she gave to Meg, telling her that this was a wedding present.

'I have been making it for weeks,' she said, 'but I have been keeping it a secret until it was finished.'

Meg was touched by Jane's thoughtfulness and told her that she would treasure it always.

'But I thought you were working on a sampler?' she asked.

Jane said, 'Yes, I am still working on the sampler but I put it aside until I had finished your wedding present. I wanted to give this to you before you leave Fortune House because I hope you will use it in your London home. However, my sampler is almost finished,' Jane added. 'I have worked all the main part, and the date at the bottom. The only thing still needed is that I shall stitch my name underneath the work.'

Edward looked at the gift she had made for Meg and said, 'This is beautiful work, Jane. I am sure the sampler will be just as lovely, and when it is finished, I will get one of the estate carpenters, one who does the finer woodwork, to make a frame for it and we shall hang it on the wall in the Great Hall.'

Suddenly, the last days before the wedding seemed to go by very fast. The Pyms arrived from London and Margaret's sister and brother-in-law arrived the same day. After all the planning, preparation and hard work, everything was ready.

The wedding day dawned bright and sunny, and all the members of both families gathered in the Great Hall ready to walk to church. Resplendent in their new finery, they admired each other's clothes until Edward suddenly said, 'It is time for us to leave,' and he offered Meg his arm. He leaned towards her and said very quietly, so that only she could hear, 'You look very beautiful. A daughter any father would be proud to escort to her marriage,' and then the wedding party walked out of the Great Hall and across the terrace. As they started past what would soon be formal gardens, a group of musicians came alongside the group and played them down the drive, out through the gatehouse, and into the church, which lay just beyond.

Chapter 9

The whole Pym family (now including Meg as Harry's new wife) set off together for London. Although normally the newly married couple would be alone when they left on the journey following their wedding, this time the entire party, which included Sir Hubert's manservant and Lady Pym's personal maid, travelled together in two coaches. At nearby towns they would join up with other coaches travelling south and make the journey to London as a group of six or seven coaches. Highwaymen and robbers were always a danger to coaches travelling singly on the roads between Yorkshire and London, and going in a group of several coaches was safer and they were less likely to be attacked. On the same day that the bridal party left, Margaret's sister and brother-in-law also set off for their own home, and suddenly Fortune House seemed very quiet.

'I suppose we shall get used to Meg not being here, though it seems strange that now only four children live at home. And I suppose that it won't be long before William goes off to Matworth to work with Richard Bailey and learn about the business of the estate and lead mines there, and then Henry will be going to university, and ...' Margaret's voice trailed off. A lump formed in her throat and she swallowed hard.

Edward, glancing at her, realised the emotion she was feeling and came over and put his arms around her.

'I shall miss Meg dreadfully, too,' he said softly, 'but we knew she would marry soon, and we could not ask for a better husband for her. It is obvious that they both care deeply for each other and he will provide well for her.'

Margaret nodded, 'Yes, I know you are right, and I know I'm being foolish.' She took a deep breath, then went on, 'It's just that the house seems so quiet now, after all the hustle and bustle of the past weeks. But it's just as well, I suppose, that we get back to our normal routines, and the servants take care of their usual tasks.' But she couldn't help her mind going back to Meg again.

'I do hope that Meg writes us a letter and tells us about their journey to London, and I want to hear all about their house there. How glad I am that she writes a good hand. We shall both enjoy hearing about her life in London.'

Later that day, when Margaret was sitting in the solar, Ann came and sat beside her and said, 'Now that I am the eldest daughter still living at home, I should like it very much if you would teach me more about the running of the household, Mother. I would like to sit with you when you discuss food with Mrs Cook, and when you give instructions to the housekeeper. And I would also like to learn about keeping the household accounts.'

Margaret looked at Ann fondly. 'Of course you shall spend time with me learning about the running of the house. I am pleased that you wish to learn these things. It will be good for you to know such things before you marry yourself, and besides, it will be nice for me to have your company more of the time.'

'There is another thing I should like to talk to you and Father about,' Ann said. 'When you first talked about having gardens made for Fortune House, I remember hearing you talk of formal gardens to the front, and a walled garden for roses, and also a herb garden. But although I know that you and Father have approved the designs and work will soon start on the formal gardens, and also the walled scented garden where the roses will be, I have heard nothing more about the herb garden.'

'You are right, Ann. That was mentioned, and I shall bring it up with your father today.'

'It is the herb garden that particularly interests me,' went on Ann, 'because I would like to learn more about herbs and their different uses – all their uses, for cooking, for treating ailments – everything. I would like to become really know-ledgeable about the subject.'

'We can certainly talk to your father about a herb garden, and I see no reason why he would not agree to having one. As you say, it was discussed at one time, and while Mr Wilkins is still here he can draw up plans for the plantings there. Perhaps you would like to be with us when we meet with Mr Wilkins when he has the herb garden plans ready?'

'Thank you, Mother, yes that would please me very much.'

Later that day, while the whole family was gathered for their meal, Margaret brought up the subject of having a herb garden.

'We talked about it at one time, but somehow it seems to have been forgotten,' she said to Edward.

'You are absolutely right, we did talk about it. I will see Mr Wilkins this very day and ask him to draw up some plans, and I will ask for his suggestions as to which plants we should have in that garden.'

A few days later, Edward called to Margaret and said that Mr Wilkins had some ideas about the herb garden and had drawn out plans for their consideration and she should come and look over the suggestions. Margaret sent a maidservant to find Ann and tell her to join them, and soon they were all gathered round Mr Wilkins and the plans he had spread on a large table.

Mr Wilkins had suggested that this garden, too, should have

a high wall around it because some of the herbs would benefit from the protection of a wall.

'I had some dealings with a Mr John Gerard, in London,' said Mr Wilkins. He has made what he calls "a physic garden" because all of the plants there can be used to treat ailments of many different kinds. He treats physical ailments, of course, and he has many different plants that he uses for what he calls "calming purposes", and some for what he terms "restorative treatments".'

Ann's face glowed with enthusiasm. 'Oh Mr Wilkins,' she said, 'I find all you say so very interesting! Will it be possible to have the same plants in our herb garden that this Mr Gerard has planted in his physic garden? I mean, would such plants grow and prosper in this area, which is so far north of London?'

'I see no reason why not,' answered Mr Wilkins. 'In fact, I understand that there is another such garden in Edinburgh, even further north than you are here.'

'And how can I find out more about the uses of all these plants, and how to prepare them for medicinal use?' Ann asked.

'Ann, Ann,' Edward interrupted. 'Mr Wilkins is a gardener, not a herbalist! He knows about planting and growing a herb garden, not about how to make use of all that grows there!'

'Sir Edward, I can, I think, be of assistance. Books that are called "herbals" have been published and pamphlets have been printed which explain these plants and their uses. And as well as the pamphlets and books on this subject, there is one large book that has been translated from the Dutch by a gentleman who has made a botanic garden at Oxford.'

'Oh father, I should so much like to have such a book if it will be possible.' Ann broke off as Jane's nurse came to the door. None of the servants would ever normally approach the family when they were meeting and talking with someone, but now the nurse stepped into the room and her face looked serious.

'Sir Edward, Lady Snowwe, I do beg your pardon, but I am very anxious about Jane. She does not seem at all well, and as you know, she did not eat with you today because she said she was not hungry.'

Margaret excused herself from the group, saying, 'I will come up at once.'

When she returned about 15 minutes later, Mr Wilkins had gone, leaving his plans for the herb garden lying on the table.

Edward and Ann both turned as Margaret came into the Great Hall. 'How is our smallest daughter?' asked Edward. 'Has she been eating too many sweetmeats and is feeling sickly?'

'No, Edward,' Margaret's face was grave. 'I am very worried. I fear that it may be something serious. She has, I think, a high fever and she says that her head aches and parts of her body hurt.'

'Perhaps she has caught a bad chill? Or, do you think …' he broke off, looking at Margaret's face, which was creased with worry.

'I'm afraid it might be something more serious than a chill. I think, and so does her nurse, that we can detect the beginnings of a rash. I would like to send a man on a fast horse and tell him to bring back a doctor. If a doctor is not available straight away, he should bring the apothecary from the nearest town.' She stopped, then turning to look Edward full in the face, she said, 'I am so afraid that she might have smallpox.'

Chapter 10

Margaret sat alone in the solar, as she did for hours every day and for many hours through sleepless nights. Her grief was beyond anything she had ever felt before, beyond anything she could ever have imagined. Her baby girl, Jane, was gone. She kept repeating to herself over and over, 'Jane is dead, Jane is dead,' and still she could not believe it. Sometimes she would go into Jane's room and stare at the bed, as if willing the small child to be there.

Margaret's first instinct that Jane had smallpox had been right and the disease had moved with a swiftness that left the whole family, and all the servants, stunned. Then, on the day that they had taken her body in its tiny casket to the church for the funeral service and burial in the churchyard, Ann had suddenly fainted. Everybody thought that grief had overtaken her, but within hours the dreaded rash had appeared and it was evident that Ann, too, had smallpox.

Now Ann was recovering. She was still confined to her bed, still very ill, but the doctor who had attended both Jane and Ann assured the family that she was not going to die. 'But, although she is not going to die,' thought Margaret, 'Ann, on the threshold of young womanhood, has been terribly marked by the disease and will bear the scars all her life.'

One day Edward came to Margaret and, sitting down beside her, he noticed that she had Jane's sampler on her lap. Taking one of her hands in both of his he said, very gently, 'My dear, I know you are grieving dreadfully for little Jane, and of course

I share that sorrow. But I think the time has come that we both must think of Ann and her need of us. I may sound harsh, but I think it is time that you gave some thought and comfort to Ann,' he said.

'Edward! How can I give comfort to Ann, when I cannot comfort myself?' Margaret was in tears. She clutched at Jane's sampler. 'One daughter has gone from the house in marriage and one, our baby, has gone in death, and …'

Very gently Edward took the sampler from her hands.

'Margaret, I promised Jane that I would have this framed and that we would hang it in the Great Hall. I will arrange for that to be done.'

'But it isn't completely finished,' Margaret cried. 'Look! At the bottom, she had started to embroider her name and … and …' tears choked her.

Edward looked at the sampler and across the bottom was embroidered the date and then the words: 'Me name is Jane S'. Jane had died before she could stitch her full name. He swallowed hard and when he spoke again his voice was husky.

'Nevertheless, I will have this framed exactly as it is. It will be something very personal of Jane's that will hang in this house.' He cleared his throat and went on, 'I go back to what I was saying. Our daughter Ann needs you now. She has desperate need of your love and comfort. Although she is alive, she is so badly marked by the pox that she feels her life is over and she is in low spirits all the time. Becky, the housekeeper, came to me because she is so worried about her, and you know that Becky would never interfere in, or comment on, what is so clearly a family matter if she didn't feel it absolutely necessary to talk to me.'

'Why did she talk to you?' asked Margaret. 'As the housekeeper she should have come to me with any concerns that she has.'

'She didn't come to you, my dear wife, because she did

not want to lay yet another burden on your sorrowing shoulders. But I come to you now and, as I have already said, I may appear harsh but I say to you that you have to accept that all your sorrowing and all your tears cannot bring back Jane. She is gone. But as a mother, you are now very much needed by Ann. Instead of grieving for something that cannot be, can you not raise the strength to put aside your sorrow and help Ann back to a normal life, back to the way she used to be?'

Margaret looked at Edward as if for a moment she did not understand what he was saying but suddenly her brow smoothed, and she stood and gathered her skirts, and as she did so she seemed to gather her strength and resolve.

'Yes, Edward, you are absolutely right. Ann needs me, and perhaps as a mother I need her too. Together, as mother and daughter, we can try to look forward, instead of grieving for what is past. I will go to Ann now.'

As she stood, Edward stood too.

'Yes, my love, go to Ann. And go with the knowledge that I have always admired your many strengths, but I have never admired you as much as I do now, seeing the resolve on your face.' He kissed her cheek, patted her shoulder, and said, 'Go to Ann, and take with you my love for you both.'

During the days and weeks that followed, Ann and Margaret were inseparable. Margaret tried to be brisk and said that Ann should try to summon the strength to work with her on some household matters. 'You asked to work with me on such things, my dear,' she reminded her. Ann spent time with Margaret when she was discussing household business with Becky or with Mrs Cook, but she felt so ashamed of her appearance that she said she did not feel she could ever again go outside the house. Margaret told Edward how Ann felt and said that she despaired of ever being able to get her to walk outside, even on the terrace at the front of the house and look at the work that had started on the formal gardens.

'You've given me an idea,' said Edward, and that afternoon he appeared in the solar where Ann and Margaret were sitting sipping an elderflower cordial that Becky said had restorative qualities and would be good for them both.

'Ann,' he said, 'I need you in the Great Hall. Please come down with me right away.'

When the two of them reached the Great Hall, Mr Wilkins was already there. As soon as she saw him, Ann tried to pull back through the door and mumbled, 'Father, I can't ... I can't go in ... I can't let him see me. My scars make me look so ugly.' But Edward grasped her arm firmly and pulled her with him.

'Come along, Ann. Mr Wilkins has been telling me some fascinating things about the proposed herb garden, but we both want to discuss some aspects with you.'

Mr Wilkins swept off his hat and bowed to Ann.

'I offer my congratulations on your recovery from your illness. It is good to see you again and I have need of your opinion.'

'My opinion? But you are the expert gardener, I do not have the knowledge to offer any opinions, I'm afraid.'

'Ah, but you expressed so much interest in herbs and their uses,' said Mr Wilkins, 'and I mentioned to you that pamphlets have been printed with instructions for the preparation and use of many herbs. So now that we are ready to start planting, I would like to suggest the herbs that I think should be included, and I would like to know if my ideas meet with your approval.'

'But I have no knowledge as yet, Mr Wilkins,' Ann repeated. 'I must be guided by you ...'

'Oh forgive me, I should have told you immediately.' Mr Wilkins produced something from the far side of the table.

'This has arrived by special messenger. It is one of the pamphlets that I mentioned and your father asked me to procure it for you. Perhaps I should ask that you read it, and then we will meet again in a few days and together we can decide what you think would be of most interest and use to you. I shall then plan the arrangement of the plantings in accordance with your ideas, and also keep in mind what will be most pleasing in form and colour.'

Ann took the pamphlet that Mr Wilkins held out to her, and turned to her father. For the first time since she had fallen ill, her face was wreathed in smiles.

'Father. You are the kindest, dearest, father imaginable. I am sure these printed works are very expensive, and I am so grateful that you have indulged my wish for one.'

For the next few days Ann was completely absorbed in reading the pamphlet and making notes of things to speak about with Mr Wilkins. They met several times, and together they agreed on the plants to be grown in the herb garden, and also on the way they would be placed so that all the colours blended well together.

Edward and Margaret both commented on Ann's enthusiasm for the whole subject of herbs and herbalism, and both were overjoyed to see her face so animated when she talked to Mr Wilkins. As weeks passed, and the planting of the herb garden was started, Edward asked Mr Wilkins to get any other pamphlets that were available.

'Or,' he added, 'I believe you mentioned that there is a book that has been written on the subject?'

'Ah yes, that is the book by Henry Lyte, the man with the botanic garden near Oxford. I am sure that I can send to London for a copy.'

It took some weeks for the book to arrive but when it did, Ann would sit and read for hours at a time, then talk with

Mr Wilkins, or one of the gardeners who was planting out the herbs, and then go back to reading again.

Margaret said to Edward one day, 'When she is reading or talking about herbs, Ann completely forgets her disfiguring scars, and she becomes the old Ann that we have always known. For one so young, she is becoming very conversant with the subject, and says that once the plants are growing and ready for their flowers or leaves to be harvested, she wants to try to make the various recipes that are in the book.'

When a year had gone by, and the herb garden was flourishing, it was obvious that Ann was becoming more and more knowledgeable about herbs and their various uses. But there was so much she wanted to do, that she could not accomplish all that she planned and talked about. Margaret decided that it would be a good idea for one of the young maids to work with Ann, and she asked Becky if she thought there was one who would be suitable for such a task.

Immediately Becky said, 'Oh yes. There is a young maid, just a little older than Ann, called Lettice. She has always been interested in herbs and their uses and, in fact, she already has some small skills.'

'Send Lettice up to talk to me, and ask one of the servants to find Ann and tell her to come here at the same time,' said Margaret.

When the three women were together, discussing the subject of herbs and the possibility of Lettice working with Ann, Margaret asked her how she had acquired the knowledge that she already had.

'Oh, My Lady,' said Lettice, 'my mother has taught me some things, and her mother taught her. And I am told that my great, great, great … I don't know how many "greats" … grandmother was a woman who lived here at Fortune estate a very long time ago. Her name was Meg, and she is said to have been very skilled in the uses of herbs, and she treated most people living here for many of their ailments.'

And so, out of Ann's misery and despair after surviving smallpox, came the interest in herbs that was to last her a lifetime. Some years later, when her knowledge and skills had become well known not only at Fortune, but in the villages and towns nearby, a young herbalist called to see her one day. He introduced himself as Edgar Culmaine, and he explained that he had a successful herbalist shop in Beverley. In the shop he sold herbs, and he also used them to make up ointments and tinctures and distillations that were used to treat many ailments. He said that he had come to see Ann, hoping that she would sell him herbs, especially some of the unusual ones that she grew at Fortune. He suggested that perhaps they could work together on developing new products that could be sold in his shop. This idea interested Ann and the two of them started to work together regularly.

The young man came more and more often to Fortune, and he and Ann spent many hours together. At first their talk was of their shared interest in herbs, but gradually they found that they talked about more and more widely ranging subjects.

Watching them together one day Edward said to Margaret, 'Do you think there is an attachment growing between Ann and that young herbalist?'

Margaret said nothing, simply smiled and nodded. But she thought to herself, 'Have you only just now noticed, Edward? Oh well … women do notice such things more quickly than men, I am sure.'

Footnote: Ann and Edgar worked together for several years, and eventually married. They had no children but their shop became very successful and together they published a book on herbs and herbalism that was considered the definitive work on the subject.

Part III
1679

Chapter 1

The date for William Snow to marry Elizabeth Austin had been set, and all the arrangements were in place for the wedding to take place in two weeks' time, when William's father died suddenly while out shooting pheasant one day. Normally, the wedding would have been postponed for some months out of respect and because of family mourning. But upon the death of his father, William, then aged only 24, inherited the large Fortune estate in Yorkshire, as well as the lands and lead mines in Derbyshire that the family owned. Although he had been educated and trained all his life in readiness for the day when he would assume control of the properties, it had never been expected that he would have to take over so soon and so suddenly. He knew that he still had a great deal to learn, and he knew just how hard he would have to work. So, as he explained to Elizabeth and her family, he felt that if they did not marry on the date that had already been arranged, the wedding plans would have to be postponed for some considerable time – perhaps as long as a year. William also added that as his own mother had died some years ago, he did not have to consider her period of mourning before the wedding could take place.

Elizabeth's parents were concerned that, because of all his responsibilities, he might find that he had little time to spend with his new wife. But Elizabeth said that she was in agreement with William that the wedding should go ahead as planned.

'I know that William will be very busy and will not be able

to spend as much time with me as would be normal for a newly wed couple, but I hope that perhaps I may be of some help to him in his work. And if that is the case, we will work together,' she said.

'But, Elizabeth, you will be living in a strange place, with no friends nearby, and you will have to learn to run a large house and its staff,' her mother pointed out, 'and my feeling is that you may be very lonely.'

'Mother, as you say, I shall be learning about running Fortune House and as I read and write well, and know something about keeping household accounts, I think I shall be too busy to be lonely,' was Elizabeth's firm answer.

'Also,' William added, 'since my mother's death, the housekeeper, who is a very able woman, has been in charge of all household matters and the staff. She has organised everything so efficiently that I think Elizabeth will be able to take over the reins quite smoothly.'

And so the wedding took place as planned in late October and when Elizabeth and William arrived at Fortune House as a newly married couple, all the staff, both the farm workers and the household servants, lined the drive to greet them. The housekeeper, waiting just outside the main door, bobbed a curtsey to them both.

'On behalf of all your staff,' she said, 'I welcome you, Lady Snow, to Fortune House, your new home. We all wish that you will find great happiness here.'

As she said this, a cheer went up from the assembled staff that had now gathered at the foot of the terrace steps.

'My new wife and I thank you very much for your welcome,' said William. 'During the next days and weeks Lady Snow will meet all of you and I am sure that in time she will get to know you and your families as well as my mother did. Thank you all again.'

The housekeeper said, 'I have had the main suite of rooms

prepared for you and your bride, Sir William. I hope everything will be to your liking.'

'I am sure everything will be suitable, Mrs Eggars,' said William, (the housekeeper was not married but had the courtesy title of 'Mrs'), 'and I know that Lady Snow will wish to spend time with you, so that she will become familiar with the way you have arranged the running of the house.'

As William and Elizabeth went through the main door, they entered the Great Hall, the beautiful panelled room with its huge fireplace that had been embellished with Derbyshire Bluejohn stone. Elizabeth stopped and looked around.

'William! This is beautiful, and the portraits on the walls must be your ancestors. I shall very much look forward to finding out exactly who each person is, and how they relate to you.'

Some of the paintings that Elizabeth was looking at were individual portraits, and some were family groups. William pointed to one family group and said that he always felt that this was a most poignant group picture. It had been painted in the winter of 1592 to 1593.

'It was fortunate that this painting was made during that winter, because a year later the family group had changed completely,' said William. 'In June of 1593 the elder daughter married and went to live in London, and very soon after the wedding the youngest daughter died of smallpox. The middle daughter ...' he pointed, '... that one, whose name was Ann, also caught the disease but although she didn't die, she was very badly scarred by it.'

'Oh,' said Elizabeth, 'this is just the sort of detail about your family and your ancestors that I want to know! I am afraid I shall be a nuisance to you, asking for stories about your family.'

'My dear, you can discover much about my family for

yourself. There are stacks of papers and documents, all relating to the family and giving details of people and events
right back to the time of the Battle of Agincourt,' William told
her.

'I should so much like to see and read all those documents,'
said Elizabeth.

'You can do more than just read them, my love,' said
William. 'If you find the subject of real interest, you could
take on the task of sorting them and putting them in some kind
of order. As things stand, they have all just been put into
drawers and cupboards in several places around the house.'

Elizabeth had taken him up on his suggestion, and within days,
she had started collecting papers and documents from the
various places they had been kept for years. Some were
over 200 years old and had to be handled with great care as
they were brittle with age. She spent some months bringing
order to the chaos of the family documents and when William
complimented her on her dedication, she said that the task
was giving her great pleasure.

'It is taking me a long time to have everything in order
because I keep coming across a story that is fascinating, and
I stop to read it and learn about those people before I continue
with the sorting of the papers. Some of these stories are just
small family matters, but some of them connect the family to
important events. When all the documents are in order, and I
have the people and their stories clear in my mind, I think I
shall write down the story of the family thus far.

'By the way,' she went on, 'did you know that until fairly
recently, only about two generations back, your family name
was spelled Snowwe? I just read about that today.'

'Oh yes, I knew that,' said William. 'My father told me
that his father – or was it his grandfather? – had told him that

134

the family changed the spelling for simplicity, and also because some people pronounced the name as Snowy instead of Snow.'

'You see,' said Elizabeth, 'there is so much that should be written down and recorded so that future generations will know these details about their ancestors.'

William drew her closer and, smiling, said, 'Well, we have done our best to ensure that there will indeed be future generations. I am so happy to have you as my wife, and it adds so much to my happiness to know that you are with child.'

One evening, after a day spent working with the documents, Elizabeth asked William if he knew why the house and surrounding estate was called 'Fortune'.

'Hmmm, I'm not sure,' said William. 'I think I have heard some story. I think it is because long, long ago many men who went from this area to fight a battle in some foreign land, all returned safely.'

'That is exactly right!' exclaimed Elizabeth. 'That is something I discovered among the old documents today. Long ago, one of your ancestors took a small army of men from here to France to fight under King Henry V at the battle of Agincourt. It says in the documents that not one man was killed, and as they had all returned safely, your ancestor changed the name of the house and estate to Fortune because he felt that this was indeed a fortunate place.'

'And,' she continued, 'that same ancestor of yours, Richard, was given his title by the King in gratitude for his contribution of men to aid in that battle. He became Sir Richard, and that is how your title originated.'

'My goodness, Elizabeth, very soon you are going to know more about this family and its history than I do myself! And

135

now that I think of it, this house has indeed been fortunate in many ways. I know that when I was a boy of about ten, there was the last terrible outbreak of plague. I remember hearing stories about a village called Eyam in Derbyshire, not too far from our lands there. When plague came to that village, all the inhabitants bravely decided to stay in their village and not flee, hoping for safety in some other place, and thus taking the disease with them. About two thirds of the people in Eyam died during that self-imposed isolation. And that was another time when the Fortune estate lived up to its name. We did not have a single case of plague here.'

Before long, William's dearest wish was granted and they were both delighted when Elizabeth gave birth to their first child, a boy. He was born just a few weeks before their first wedding anniversary and given the names Charles Crispin.

One year and a month later another son, James Crispin, was born. William felt that, having two healthy sons, it seemed almost too much to wish that the next child would be a girl. His desire was fulfilled when they had a daughter whom they named Henrietta, after Elizabeth's mother.

But their joy at her birth was short-lived; she died when she was just two months old. It was another two years until Mary was born, a healthy robust little girl who, by the time she was five years old, wanted to try to do everything that her older brothers could do.

Chapter 2
1702

It was a perfect late spring day at the very end of April. The sun shone but it was not hot, and the sky was a bright blue with just a few puffy white clouds. William and Elizabeth stepped out of Fortune House, crossed the terrace, and went down the steps to walk in the formal gardens where the tulips were now in bloom.

'They really are splendid this year, aren't they? And the head gardener told me that in another week or two there will be even more blooms. Some varieties bloom slightly later than others,' said William.

'It's hard to imagine how there could be even more blooms. Everywhere looks so perfect right now,' said Elizabeth. 'Before we came out, I stood at the windows of the solar and looked out across all the gardens. You can see the geometric patterns of the formal gardens at the front of the house so clearly from those high windows. And when you next speak with the gardeners, would you compliment them on the way they have put lower-growing plants between all the tulips. Just look,' she exclaimed, 'look at these beds – the rose-pink tulips standing proud above the bright blue of the forget-me-nots, and there in the next bed, the bright yellow tulips above the rust coloured wallflowers.'

'You're right, Elizabeth. I sometimes think that our gardeners are not just good plantsmen but are clever artists too, when I see how skilled they are in presenting the plants to show all their different colours to best advantage.'

As the two of them continued to walk among the beds filled at this time of year with tulips in full bloom, they talked about William's great-grandfather who had bought hundreds of tulip bulbs in 1637 when the bulb market had suddenly crashed. In the years before the crash, tulip bulbs had become a craze all over Europe, and it was said that there had been occasions when a single bulb had changed hands for a sum of money that would have bought a good size house. Then, quite suddenly, rumours spread that the flood of willing and extravagant buyers was drying up, and the sellers dropped their prices to attract new buyers. Almost overnight the price of tulip bulbs fell dramatically. That was when William's great-grandfather had bought so many of them. Most of the ones that were blooming now had come directly from those first bulbs. Each year beds were planted out, and each year, after the flowering period was over and the leaves had died back, the bulbs were lifted and carefully stored away ready for planting again the next year.

When William and Elizabeth walked back into the house they went into the Great Hall where, every afternoon, they drank tea. Some of their children preferred the new chocolate drink but Elizabeth often said that although tea was an expensive luxury, she felt that nothing refreshed her so much as a dish of tea in the afternoon.

William looked around and said, 'I love this room. I always enjoy the feeling that here I am surrounded by my family from the past.'

'My dear, you are indeed surrounded by your family from several generations back. Look at all the portraits, showing many of your ancestors, and look at the bench.' Elizabeth pointed to a very long, heavy oak bench.

'Oh, Dickon's Bench. Yes, that one piece of furniture really has a family story of its own, doesn't it?' In the early days of their marriage, William had told her about the bench that had been made from a big oak tree that had blown down in the storms of 1593. Originally, the tree had been planted in memory of a young son of the family who had died in 1415, and when it blew down it was decided to save the trunk, let the wood season, and then have it made into a piece of furniture. The bench had been made by an estate carpenter in about 1603.

This particular afternoon, Elizabeth and William found their three children, Charles, James and Mary, awaiting them in the Great Hall. It was usual, if all three children were at home, for the whole family to meet and talk about the happenings of the day. As soon as William and Elizabeth arrived, two serving maids brought in trays to serve both tea and chocolate. Now, as the family sat sipping their drinks and talking about the various matters that had occupied their day, William said suddenly, 'I have been thinking that although your mother and I had our separate portraits painted soon after we were married, we have never had our family painted as a group. I think that is an oversight that should be rectified as soon as possible. After all in just two or three years I shall be 50, and I'm vain enough to feel that I don't want to look like an old man when I'm painted! When I was last in London I heard people talking of a portrait painter called Michael Ahmson. I saw some of the paintings he has made of several well known people and I would like to commission him to come here and paint all of us as a group.'

'That's a splendid idea, Father,' said Charles. 'After all, one can see by looking around this Great Hall that it is a family tradition that almost every generation has had either individual portraits or family portraits painted and I think it would be a good idea for us to continue that tradition.'

William looked at his elder son fondly. 'You really care

about the family and tradition, don't you?' he said. 'I am so glad, and I feel so happy to know that when I am gone, you will continue to run this estate and the Matworth estate and lead mines, in the way they've always been run.'

'Father! You will be alive for many years to come. As you have just pointed out, you may be approaching 50 but I hope I shan't inherit Fortune until I am an elderly man myself. And when I do inherit, it is lucky that if I ever need legal advice about the estate's affairs, I shall have my young brother here to consult!' Charles clapped his hand on James's shoulder.

'You might find my fees too high, big brother,' James joked. 'Anyhow, I still have more than another year of study before I will be a fully qualified lawyer, and …' He broke off.

His mother looked at him questioningly. 'Yes? What else were you going to say, James?'

'Oh nothing, nothing, Mother. I've finished drinking my chocolate so I think I will walk over to the stables, and take a look at the mare that foaled two days ago.'

He bent and kissed his mother on the cheek and left the room.

Elizabeth looked after him, pondering, 'Hmmm, I wonder what he started to say. Is it a mother's intuition that I feel that he is not happy at the prospect of spending his life working in the law? Or am I just being an over-anxious mother?'

Her thoughts were broken by her daughter Mary saying, 'Mother, I don't believe you have heard anything I have said to you!'

'I'm sorry, my dear, my thoughts were travelling. Now, what was it you were saying … something about your gown for the ball we shall be giving for you this summer? Oh Mary, it is so difficult to realise that you are now grown up, and that you will be presented to society at the ball. Suddenly so many years seem to have flown by so quickly.'

Charles, listening to this exchange, had a wide grin on his

face as he said, 'Yes, Father, now that I realise that Mary is also getting old, it is indeed a good idea to have that portrait painted as soon as possible, before she becomes wrinkled and … ouch!' He ducked as his sister threw a cushion at him.

'Mary, Mary … you have been a tomboy all your life. Even as a very small girl you wanted to do everything the boys did. But now that you are about to enter society, you must conduct yourself in a more seemly manner! Throwing a cushion indeed!'

'Oh, Mother,' Mary came across, and sat down next to Elizabeth, putting an arm around her shoulder, 'you are not truly cross with me, are you? Please, Mother, let's talk about my ball gown. You say you want me to behave in a more feminine way and you must agree, nothing could be more feminine than discussing gowns, could it?'

Standing up, she went on, 'I know that fashion dictates that every girl wears a white gown for her first ball but I have had some ideas about how I would like my gown to look, and I have made some sketches. May I show you my ideas now? I have put my drawings on the table.' She walked across to the large table.

Elizabeth got up and walked over to join her.

'You see, Mother, the gown is the traditional white, but I would like to have some roses made of pink silk, and have two or three tucked into the scoop of the neckline, here …' She indicated where the roses were sketched, '… and I would like the hem of the skirt caught up in several places with a pink silk rose. Oh Mother, tell me what you think. Do you approve of my designs? And do you think the dressmaker in York will be able to make the gown from my drawings?'

'I am sure she can carry out your designs, dear.' Elizabeth was still looking at the sketches Mary had made. 'You have made these drawings beautifully. I had no idea that we had such a talented artist in the family!' She turned to William.

'Come and look at these drawings and see if you agree with me that Mary has a talent for drawing.'

William came over and looked. After a few seconds he turned to Mary and said, 'Your mother is right, you do indeed have a talent for drawing. But,' he had a twinkle in his eye as he added, 'I don't think I shall ask you to paint our family portraits! I think I still prefer to have a professional artist come from London!'

'Oh Father! You know that I could not paint a portrait!' For a moment she looked quite horrified. Then she realised he wasn't serious, and said, 'Oh, you are joking!'

James was to leave Fortune in a day or two to return to his studies at the university in Oxford and Elizabeth gave no more thought to her premonition that he was not entirely happy with his choice of career. Instead, she busied herself with preparations for Mary's ball. The ball gown was ordered from the dressmaker in York who had exclaimed with delight when she saw Mary's sketches and said that it would be a real pleasure to make a gown that was so unusual.

Invitations were sent to aunts and uncles and friends who lived near enough to attend the dinner and ball, and those who lived further away were also invited to stay at Fortune House. The dinner menu was discussed with the cook and all the dishes were decided upon, and William chose the wines to be served with each course. When Elizabeth checked all the bedrooms that would be used for guests, she told William that she wished there was more time so that she could have new curtains and bed-hangings made for each room. William groaned and pretended to complain about the cost of "all this entertaining" but really he was very proud of his only daughter and did not begrudge any of the expense.

Chapter 3

The day after James returned to Oxford, William said to Charles, 'I want to talk to you about some plans I have. Come into my business room – it is the only peaceful place where we can talk! The whole house is in turmoil with all the preparations for the ball. The number of maids your mother has cleaning everywhere, you'd think we were preparing for a visit from royalty!'

Father and son settled comfortably in the room off the Great Hall that had been used for several generations to conduct all the Fortune estate business matters, and William said, 'I have been thinking, Charles. The other day I said that I felt comfortable that when you inherit from me, you will continue to run things with the same love for Fortune that I have always had for the place. Then I started thinking about how it was when I took over. As you know, I was only 24 years old when I inherited and although I'd been trained in estate affairs, I was quite overcome with the enormous amount of work I had to handle. I almost felt that someone had thrown me into a deep lake and I had to learn very fast how to swim! You have already accompanied me to cattle sales and auctions, and you have sat with me when I've conducted business dealings with wool merchants, and you've already learned a lot about Fortune's financial affairs. At some time in the future, I shall want you to go to Matworth and live there for a year or so, learning all you can about the estate from Robert Goody, who manages everything there. And you will need to learn as much as possible about the lead mining business. That is a very profitable part of our business and we derive a great proportion of our income from it. But before you go to spend time at Matworth, what I want you to do now, is take over one part of our business here completely. I want you to run the cheese business. As you know, it has always been successful and is already very profitable, but it could be much bigger. In fact, if it grows, as I hope it will under your charge, we will probably have to enlarge the buildings, or even build additional ones, and add more men. But all that will be your responsibility.'

William paused but Charles said nothing.

'Well, Charles, you are sitting there silently. What do you think?'

'I'm sitting silently, Father, because I'm still absorbing what you have said. I am very happy that you feel you can place so much responsibility on me. Of course, I know that I will have a great deal to learn, and that I will be working hard, but I relish the opportunities that I can see already. I think we can expand the business and sell the cheeses in some cities outside this area, perhaps even London. Truly, Father, I'm excited by what seem great possibilities! And I thank you for placing your trust in me.'

'Good. Let's walk over to the dairy and cheese making area right now, and I will announce to the men working there that in future you will be in charge of all matters concerning the dairies and cheeses.'

'But Father, what about Sam Johnson? He has been managing all that business for many years. He is an excellent worker and I know all the other men respect him greatly. I would not like him to feel that I was usurping him.'

'You won't be usurping him, Charles. Sam asked to speak with me a week or so ago and he told me that he feels that the time has come for him to step down from that job. He is over 60, and it seems that he has terrible pains in his joints, and he feels that he can no longer work as hard as he always has done. He will continue to work part of the time, and you could have nobody better to go to for advice whenever you need it. Of course, I have told him that he and his wife will continue to live in their cottage near the dairies, and everything will continue for him as it has always been, except that he will work for only a few hours each week.'

'Well the news that he is ready to stop being in charge makes me feel comfortable about taking on the responsibilities, Father. I'm certainly glad that Sam will be around to guide and advise me until I am more familiar with every aspect of that part of our business. I know that there will be a lot to learn, but I am excited at the prospect.'

'Good! Put on your hat, son, and we will walk over there now. No time like the present!'

When William announced to all the men that, at his own request, Sam Johnson was going to work fewer hours and that his son, Charles, was to take over full responsibility for the cheese business, the news was greeted with approval. They all liked and respected William, and knew that he had the best interests of everything on the Fortune estate at heart. Sam Johnson asked William's permission to say a few words, and he told the men what many of them had already noticed, that he was having difficulty walking and standing for long periods. He ended by saying, 'I am happy to hand over to this young man, and I am sure you will all work as well and as hard for him as you have done for me.'

William shook Sam's hand, and then turned to the workmen and said, 'I know that all of us wish Sam well, and I'd like you all to join me in giving him a cheer.' A resounding 'Hooray' was shouted by all the men. Sam turned away and furtively wiped a tear from his eye.

Charles threw himself into learning all he could and after just a few weeks, he was so absorbed by cheese, that his mother complained: 'At meal times we never have any conversation now. All we hear about is cheese, cheese, cheese! Different flavours and strengths you want to try to make, and selling our cheeses in places beyond just the local markets.'

'I'm sorry, Mother. It's just that I'm so interested in this job that Father gave me, and so anxious to make a success of it, that I'm afraid I've lost my good manners! Just one more thing, then let's talk about other subjects. Father, I shall go to London next week to arrange for certain shops there to sell our cheeses and I shall make arrangements for a quantity to be put on the London-bound coach regularly, every month. I am thinking of restricting sales of our cheeses in London to just two shops, which are in the fashionable parts of the city. By doing that, people will know that our cheeses are something special, and aren't sold in every shop and market.'

'That's an excellent idea, Charles! And now, let's indulge your mother and sister and talk about the ball this summer!'

'Oh William! I like to talk about other things than just the ball!' exclaimed Elizabeth. 'Whenever I go into York and meet our friends there, I hear others talk of so many things that interest me and I don't like to feel that we are in a backwater here, and have no conversation but of Fortune's business and affairs. Important things are happening all the time. For instance, the other day in York, they were saying that travellers from London had brought news that the King is not well and there are fears that his life may be coming to an end.'

'Poor man,' said William. 'He came to the throne quite

unexpectedly and at first he reigned jointly with his wife, Mary, but she died when she was only in her early 30s. It must have been a lonely life for him since then, especially as they had no surviving children. Now, I understand that on his death the throne will pass to Anne, the sister of the late Queen Mary.'

William looked around the table at his family gathered there and went on: 'Thinking of His Majesty's position, as a childless widower for so many years, makes me realise how very lucky I am to be surrounded by my family. As you know, I have often said that the Fortune estate has lived up to its name over the centuries. Right from the beginning, when the name was first given because all the men from this area came home safely from battle in France. Then, when that terrible outbreak of plague ravaged all England when I was a young boy, again Fortune was true to its name, and not a single person on this estate was infected. There were some turbulent years in England during the Civil War and at that time, so many houses of this size were occupied by one side or the other, and some were under siege for lengthy periods. But, once again, no trouble came to Fortune. We must all be thankful and at the same time, we must pray that our beloved house continues to be true to its name.'

'Although all you say is true, William, like all families, yours has had it's share of misfortunes,' said Elizabeth. 'Babies have been born and died in infancy, children have died, and your own father died when he was only about the age you are now. And speaking of children dying, you recall the sampler that hangs in the Great Hall – the one made by the little girl who died before she completed embroidering her own name at the bottom? I have heard of a man in York who is a specialist in caring for old fabrics and pieces of needlework. He has the skill to clean such pieces, and then he frames them and puts them behind glass to protect and help preserve them.

Once behind glass, moths cannot get to the wool stitching, and eat it away. I am minded to have him take care of that sampler. Oh, I know I'm being sentimental and perhaps a little foolish, but I think of the little girl who worked on it, and I would like to ensure that it is preserved for her sake.'

'I don't think that you are being at all foolish. I think it is a kindly thought, and I, too, would like to have that little girl's work preserved as best as it can be,' William told his wife.

Elizabeth then went on, 'And there is another family heirloom that I would like to have cleaned and framed by the same man. It is a piece of embroidery that forms part of the bed-hangings in one of the bedrooms that is not normally used. When I was supervising the cleaning of rooms to be used by guests for the ball, I saw the old bed-hangings and I remembered something that I had read about them when I was going through those old family documents years ago. I believe that the woman who made that embroidery lived in this house in the early 1400s. That is almost 300 years ago, and although the pieces are very worn and have some damage, I think we should ask the man in York what he can do to stop them deteriorating further. The two pieces of needlework can then hang together in the Great Hall as part of the Snow family's history.'

Chapter 4

The flurry of activity, cleaning and preparing the house for Mary's ball was halted, as was work all over the Fortune estate, when everybody took a day off to celebrate May Day. During the time that Cromwell had ruled England, there had been no May Day festivities. The Puritans frowned on all celebrations, and for many years Cromwell had even banned any festivities at Christmas. For over 40 years now, since the monarchy had been restored, all the old customs had been revived. Once again, this year, the maypole was raised, with coloured ribbons attached, and at the Lady Eleanor School the children all learned the traditional dances so that as they circled the Maypole, holding ribbons, they intertwined and wove them into patterns.

Centuries ago there had been archery contests between all the men who worked on the estate, but these had now been replaced with some competitive sports and various trials of strength that allowed the young men to show off in front of the girls. Most of the young men tried their hand at splitting logs, carrying tree trunks, and racing each other, while the older men competed to plough the straightest furrow. Every year Sir William gave a prize to the winner of each contest, usually a small sum of money. This year he announced that he would also give a special award to the person who showed skills in several competitions. The trophy was a pewter platter, and he told the crowd that the winner's name and the date would be inscribed upon it.

When the time came to present it to the young man who

had performed well in several contests, William said, 'This is the first time a trophy has been presented to the man who has achieved the best result in most of the contests. From now on, I shall present a similar platter every year, so today we are all witnessing the start of another Fortune tradition.'

Each year a young girl was chosen to be Queen of the May, and after he had presented the pewter platter trophy, William then went to crown her with a garland of flowers. He made a short speech declaring that he was glad he didn't have to choose the May Queen, adding, 'There are so many pretty girls, I would find it impossible to choose just one.' This remark raised an appreciative cheer from the crowd, especially the young men.

That evening, as they talked over all that had happened that day at the fair, Elizabeth said, 'It seems a pity that the men compete at many different events, and a young girl is crowned May Queen, but the women do not have any opportunity to show their skills. I think I will talk to Annie, the housekeeper, and ask her to talk to the women who live and work on Fortune estate, and see if they would like to have their own competitions. Many of them are very skilled at baking cakes and breads, and making preserves and herbal cordials. And I know that two or three women here make lace, and some do beautiful embroidery.'

'Yes, you are right, the women who live and work at Fortune have many varied talents and we could have a number of competitions for women. Talk to Annie about it and see what she and the other women think of your idea. I think it is something that most of the women would enjoy. If Annie and the other women like your idea, then they shall exhibit their crafts and skills next year.'

Annie liked Elizabeth's idea and said she would talk to the

women and ask how they felt about having their own contests. When she did so, all the women were enthusiastic, and said they would like to exhibit their skills and compete against each other. As well as the lace-makers and embroiderers, some women wove cloth, several made honey, which they flavoured in different ways, and some used herbs to make cordials and lotions and soap. And so, in this way, another new tradition began. The annual May Day festivities became a village Mayfair. The traditional tests of strength for young men were still held, but new competitions for older men were added. They would vie with each other to see who could grow the biggest potato, the longest carrot, or the largest cabbage, and women would exhibit their skills at lace making, needlework and weaving, baking and preserving, and using herbs in different ways. A prize would be awarded for excellence in each different skill.

With May Day behind them, and the month of May drawing to a close, Elizabeth's attention turned back again to the ball which was to be held in July. James would be home for this, bringing some friends from the university with him. Elizabeth had asked him to bring three or four friends because at most balls there was a shortage of young men to dance with the young girls. All the guests who had been invited had sent notes accepting the invitation, and the cook was working with the kitchen maids making and baking everything that could be made in advance. The game larder was well stocked, the still room had all its shelves filled, and several different flavoured whole Fortune cheeses had been set aside. Elizabeth and William toured the kitchens, the larders and the dairies one day and William laughed when he saw so much food, and said that he thought they could feed a small army for some weeks!

'You'll be surprised,' answered Elizabeth. 'All of this will be eaten in a matter of a few days!'

The dressmaker came from York several times so that Elizabeth and Mary could try on the new gowns that she was making, and each time small alterations to the fit were made, so that everything would be perfect. Mary was excited to see her sketches come to life under the dressmaker's skilled fingers, and Elizabeth was delighted when she tried on her own exquisite new gown. William's favourite colour was blue, and as her eyes were bright blue and she was quite vain about the compliments they attracted, she had decided that her gown would be a blue that matched her eyes as closely as possible. It had a silver thread running through it to form a brocade pattern, and the skirt opened at the front to reveal a silver underskirt. The collar was made in a very fine silver lace, dotted with sparkling beads, and it stood up, framing her face.

At last, the day came when the dressmaker arrived, bringing with her the finished gowns. When Elizabeth and Mary had put them on, Elizabeth sent her maid to find William to ask him to come up to their bedchamber so that he could see the new gowns. He came in through the door in a hurry saying, 'I can only spare a few minutes, my dear, I am very busy this ...' He stopped, took in the sight of his wife and daughter wearing their new finery and said, 'You both look very, very lovely.'

He went over to the dressmaker and gave her a small bow, saying, 'You have excelled yourself, Madam. These gowns are beautiful,' and turning to Elizabeth he added, 'I think you look even more beautiful now than you did on our wedding day.'

His voice turned husky, he cleared his throat, and said quite gruffly, 'I must get back to business. I can't stay here chatting about fashions!'

All the guests who were staying at the house were to arrive the day before the ball, except James and his friends who came several days before any other guests arrived. Elizabeth and William were both charmed by the young men that James had invited. They were all good looking and had impeccable manners, and were all interested to go out and about on the Fortune estate with either William or James.

One of them, Walter Banham, was the son of a horse breeder at Newmarket, and one afternoon he said that his father had told him to ask if he could see some of the very fine white or near-white horses that were bred on the estate.

William was flattered and said, 'I did not know that anything was known about our horses, beyond perhaps York!'

'Oh yes, Sir,' the young man said, 'my father told me that you have been breeding a strain of horses that others in the equine business refer to as "the Snow's Snowy horses".'

'Well, it all started quite by accident. We had a silver-grey mare and we put her with a very pale grey stallion, and each time she foaled, the offspring was a very light, near white colour but we always thought that as it matured, as so often happens, the colour might change. In some cases it did, but in many cases her offspring stayed very pale. To avoid inter-breeding, we found another silvery white stallion, and brought him in to service the fillies. And now, over the past 20 years or so, we have established quite a good breeding stock of what you say are referred to as Snowy horses.'

All the young men were intrigued by this story and they all accompanied William to the stables and paddocks to see the horses.

Pointing across a lush green field to where four of the horses were grazing, William said, 'Look! Over there! Quite a sight isn't it?'

'It certainly is, Sir!' exclaimed Walter. 'They almost look like the unicorns that were sometimes shown on mediaeval tapestries.'

'It's interesting that you say that,' replied William. 'Take a look at the Mortlake tapestries that we have hanging on each side of the great staircase. One of those depicts a unicorn, and you're right, it looks for all the world like a Snowy horse!'

Later that day, when everybody was gathered round the table to eat, William said, 'I've been thinking, Elizabeth. As these Snowy horses seem to have gained something of a reputation, we should have some of them included in our family portrait. Instead of the usual formal group seated somewhere inside the house, I think it would be a good idea to have us all seated outside, perhaps on the terrace, and have two or three of our horses in the background.'

Elizabeth started to say she agreed with him, when both Mary and Walter said 'What a good idea' in exact unison. They looked at each other, burst out laughing, and then Walter, blushing very red, said, 'I am so sorry, Lady Snow. Do forgive me for interrupting you. I do most heartily apologise.'

'Walter, thank you for your courtesy, but it doesn't matter. I, too, was going to say "what a good idea" so but for a matter of a second or so, we would all three have spoken together! And,' she added, 'I'm not surprised that Mary thinks well of the idea. She has been very fond of those white horses since she was a small girl. I think she was only two or three years old when her father first lifted her up and put her in front of him when he was riding one day.'

'Father,' Mary said, 'would you allow Walter to ride one of the Snowy horses?' Without waiting for an answer, she turned to Walter and said, 'I ride almost every morning for an hour or so and perhaps you could accompany me tomorrow?'

Walter turned to William and said, 'I would be honoured if you would allow me to ride one of these beautiful horses, Sir, but of course, I will understand if you would prefer that a stranger does not ride one.'

William said, 'You obviously have quite an interest in horses, and must have acquired knowledge through your father's years of breeding them. I can see no reason why you shouldn't ride a Snowy horse. After we've all finished eating, we will go down to the stables and talk to the head groom and ask him to select a horse that would be suitable for you to ride. And tomorrow, Mary can show you some of her favourite rides around the estate.'

'That is most kind of you, Sir. I shall look forward to that very much.'

'And,' continued William, 'at the same time that she is showing you around, perhaps you can try to persuade her not to ride so fast, or take such high jumps!'

Chapter 5

The ball was declared to be a great success by everyone attending. The hired musicians played tirelessly throughout the evening, and everyone said they'd never seen so many attractive young people gathered together in one place. Elizabeth was asked to pass on compliments to her cook who had produced such magnificent food. 'It is worthy of a Court ball in London,' said one elderly dowager Duchess who had attended several such grand events, and many flattering comments were made to William about the wines he had chosen to serve.

As Elizabeth looked around at the dancing couples, she thought to herself, 'I know I'm being hopelessly romantic but I wonder if any of the young men and women who have met here for the first time tonight will fall in love and marry?' Just as she was thinking this, her daughter Mary and the young man called Walter danced past her, both with a look of dreamy happiness on their faces. 'Well, there's one couple who may have found love tonight,' she thought. 'And though we hardly know that young man, he certainly seems very nice and he comes from a good family.' She gave herself a little mental shake and admonished herself. 'You really should stop trying to marry off every young couple,' and she turned to talk to one of the guests sitting near her.

Two days after the ball, when all the guests had left and the house was returning to normal, Elizabeth sat in her solar writing about the ball, and listing the guests. She noted down all family events of importance and intended that these documents should be kept with the family papers that recorded things that had happened in the family for several hundred years. She must have dozed off and woke with a start to find Annie, the housekeeper, standing near her. Annie had replaced Mrs Eggars as housekeeper many years before and was one of the longest serving employees at Fortune.

'I'm so sorry, Milady, I did not wish to startle you, but I wonder if I may crave a few minutes of your time to talk to you?'

Annie's voice sounded troubled and as Elizabeth said 'Of course, Annie. What is it you wish to speak about?' she saw Annie's face crumple and tears started from her eyes.

'Annie, what on earth is upsetting you so much?'

Annie gulped, started to speak, but her voice choked. She wiped at her eyes and started again. Elizabeth pointed to the chair near her and said, 'Annie, come and sit down and tell me what is troubling you.'

Annie hesitated. She had never before sat in the presence of her employer. Elizabeth saw her hesitation and she stood up, took Annie's arm by the elbow and guided her to the chair.

'Now,' she said, seating herself once more, 'now Annie, tell me what's wrong.'

'Oh, Milady,' Annie started, then she gulped. She took a deep breath and the words came out in a rush, 'It's my daughter, Susan. She is pregnant!'

'Pregnant! And unmarried! Oh, dear! Oh, that is a pretty kettle of fish! I can understand your distress.' Elizabeth paused for a few moments, hoping that Annie would go on, but when she didn't, Elizabeth said, 'Tell me, Annie, do you know who the father of the child is? Has Susan told you? If he works

157

on the Fortune estate, Sir William will speak to him, and a marriage will be arranged immediately.'

'Oh, Madam, a marriage cannot be arranged,' Annie burst out. 'You see, Madam, the man is already married!'

'Oh dear. We have a greater problem than I'd thought. Well, who is he? Tell me.'

Annie was now crying silently and dabbing at her eyes with the corner of her kerchief, and said nothing.

'Come along, Annie. You have already told me the worst part of the news. Now you must tell me the man's name.'

Annie wiped her eyes again, straightened up and said, 'It is Henry Woodall, the innkeeper.'

'Henry Woodall! He is not only married but he has six, or is it seven, children!' Elizabeth could not disguise the shock in her voice. She paused for a moment, then went on, 'Annie, let me give this matter some thought and then I will speak with Sir William about it, and see if he can suggest any way in which we can help.'

'Oh please, Milady, please do not tell Sir William,' Annie begged. 'I have suspected for some weeks that my daughter was in this condition, but when I confronted her with my suspicions, she finally admitted it to me but she asked me to swear that I would tell no one but you.'

'Well, Annie, you have kept your promise. You have told only me. Now it will be *me*, not you, who tells Sir William. Believe me, Annie, it is for the best. I am sure that he will think of a way to resolve this situation that will be best for all concerned.'

That evening, Elizabeth asked William to walk in the gardens with her.

'It is such a lovely summer evening. Come, my dear, let us share it.' Before any of their children could suggest joining them, Elizabeth turned with a look that encompassed all of them and added, 'Just the two of us, William; let just the two of us enjoy our walk.'

As they walked, they both turned into the rose garden which was full of blooms in this month of July.

William breathed in deeply, 'Isn't this scented garden beautiful? On an evening like this, with the scent of all these roses and the lavender, it seems that all problems vanish on the perfumed air!'

'I wish you were right, William. But I'm sorry to tell you that I wanted us to walk alone so that I could tell you of a problem right here at Fortune.'

William looked at her. Her face was set in a very serious expression that he had learned over the years meant that she had something important on her mind.

'Let us sit over there, by the wall,' he said, guiding her to a seat where the evening sun shone gently on climbing roses. 'Now, tell me about this problem.'

When Elizabeth told him of Annie's daughter's pregnancy, he immediately said, 'Tell me the name of the father. I will deal with him. He shall marry her as soon as possible.'

'Well, my dear, however you may "deal with him" as you put it, you will not be able to make him marry Susan. The man is already married and has several children!'

'What?' William's voice and face expressed disgust. 'Who is this scoundrel? If he works for me on the Fortune estate, I will dismiss him and send him packing immediately!'

'William, William … please think for a moment. Firstly, if he did work for you, what good would it do to dismiss him from his job? That would put his wife and children out of their home, and leave them without any breadwinner. It would affect them very badly, and they are innocent in this business.

Secondly, he doesn't work for you. It is Henry Woodall, the innkeeper, who is the father of this child.'

'Let me think, let me think…' William muttered. He was obviously shocked by this information and needed time to compose his thoughts. He sat silently for some minutes, thinking.

'Does this young girl have any skills at all? Has her mother trained her in any household tasks?' he asked.

'I believe Susan is an excellent needlewoman. Annie says that when fine linens or good garments need repairs, she always gives the task to her.'

'Hmmm … I am thinking that in view of the fact that we cannot arrange a marriage for the girl, probably the best thing would be for her to leave Fortune as soon as possible and live somewhere else. Perhaps she could describe herself as a young widow? No, that would not be plausible. If she had been suddenly widowed when she was pregnant, she would have gone to live with her parents. Even though she is a good needlewoman, I cannot ask any of our friends to employ her knowing that soon she will be unable to work. But there must be something we can do. There must be something…'

He sat deep in thought for a while. Elizabeth said nothing, knowing that it was best to let him think without interruption.

Suddenly, he straightened up and said, 'I might have a solution. I don't know if it is the right thing. Tell me, Elizabeth, what would you think if I sent her over to Matworth? I cannot do it without discussing it first with Robert Goody, the estate manager there, because he would have to provide lodgings for her and arrange for her to be cared for when the child is born. Of course, I would send a sum of money to pay for the expenses of keeping her there and she would have to be given whatever work is available that would be suitable.' He turned to her and said, 'Oh Elizabeth, tell me what you think. I want so much to do the right thing. I feel that I am suddenly responsible not only for her well being, but also for that of the child she carries. And her parents are good employees of ours, who have worked here for many years. I would want them to be satisfied with any arrangements I make.'

'I think it is a sound idea, William, but I think we should sleep on it and think it over again in the morning. Sometimes a night's sleep clarifies the mind wonderfully. And if, upon reflection tomorrow, we both still agree that we think this would be the best course of action, we will talk to Susan and her parents, and suggest the plan to them. Of course, as you have said, you will have to send a messenger with a letter to the estate manager at Matworth and ensure that he will be willing to have Susan there.'

Chapter 6

The meeting with Annie and her husband, Jack, was tense and difficult at first. It was obvious that they both felt awkward and were embarrassed to talk about their daughter's situation but as William explained his suggestions for Susan to be sent to live at Matworth, suddenly Annie burst into tears and sobbed, 'I'm so grateful, so grateful, oh thank you.' Her tears eased the tension and all four of them, William and Elizabeth, and Annie and Jack, relaxed and talked more easily.

'Well, as both of you are in agreement with my suggestions,' said William, 'I think we should now bring Susan in here with us. I want to be sure that she fully understands the plans we have in mind before I send a messenger with a letter to Matworth.'

When Susan came in to join them it was clear that she was intimidated by William. He tried to put her at ease by getting her to sit down between her mother and father.

'Susan, we have some plans that we think will serve you well in your situation,' he said in a gentle voice, 'but we want to talk to you before proceeding further.'

He explained that she would go to live at Matworth, that she and her child would be cared for when she gave birth, and that later she would be found suitable work.

He continued, 'I understand that only your parents know of your condition, and I hope that we can arrange for you to go to Matworth before it becomes obvious to anybody else. That will spare you and your parents embarrassment.' He looked directly at her and said, 'I am doing this not only for you, but also for your parents. They have worked here at Fortune for many years and I value them and their work.'

When he said this, the tears started to flow down Annie's cheeks once more and, seeing this, Susan started to cry too.

Dabbing at her eyes she said, 'I am not crying because I am unhappy, Sir William. I am crying because I am so relieved that I can go away and never see that man again. I know that this situation is my own doing and I know how foolish I've been. But,' she gulped, 'he said he loved me, and I believed him, and I truly thought that I loved him too. I feel so ashamed and I have been so worried that my parents would suffer embarrassment because of the way people would gossip about my condition.'

Elizabeth intervened and said in a brisk tone, 'Susan, you aren't the first girl to find herself in this predicament and you won't be the last.'

'That's perfectly true, my dear,' said William. 'A very practical point of view. And now that we are all agreed on what is best for not only Susan, but for all concerned, I will write a letter to Robert Goody, the Matworth estate manager.'

He turned to Jack and said, 'Go to the stables and tell them to prepare a good, fast horse. I want a rider to leave for Matworth within the hour. He will get a fresh horse there and bring back the reply to my letter immediately. The weather is fine and the roads are good at this time of year, so with luck, it may be possible for Susan to move to Matworth in just a few days' time.'

As Jack went off to the stables, Elizabeth shepherded Annie and Susan out of the room, saying, 'I will let you know as soon as we hear from Matworth. Meanwhile, Susan, start to get your things together and be ready to travel.'

Later that day William said that he was sure Robert Goody would agree to have Susan go to live at Matworth and that he would travel there with her.

Elizabeth said, 'I don't think that would be a good idea. If you go, and eventually the word spreads that Susan was pregnant when she left here so suddenly, I think it might cause some gossip. Some people may say that they think you escorted her to Matworth not merely as an act of kindness, but because she is pregnant by one of our sons. Far better if you send the Fortune estate steward with her.'

'I hadn't thought of that, but I realise that you are probably right. You have a shrewd mind, Elizabeth, and great clarity of thought.' William smiled as he complimented her, then went on, 'I suppose we must be very thankful that neither of our sons have ever given us cause for such concerns. Certainly it is not unknown for one of the sons of a family – or even the father – to get a servant girl pregnant.

'And now,' he said, 'I am going to ride down to the inn. I intend to tell Henry Woodall that I think his behaviour is reprehensible, and that my only reason for not exposing him as a scoundrel is out of concern and consideration for his wife and children. I will not have them embarrassed through no fault of their own.'

As he went out of the door he looked back at Elizabeth and said, 'Tis a pity that I have to consider his wife's position, when what I'd really like to do is horsewhip that man!'

Elizabeth looked at him in amazement. 'William, in all our life together, I have seldom seen you so angry. And I love you the more for your concern for this foolish young girl.'

A coach went from Fortune to Matworth frequently, as members of the two estates conducted business concerning both places, and just three days after William had suggested his plan to Annie and Jack, Susan slipped aboard the coach without anyone seeing her leave.

When William travelled to Matworth himself a few months later, he spent a day discussing business matters with Robert Goody and looking at the accounts for the lead mines. That evening, he and Robert dined together as they usually did when William visited.

'You will remember the girl Susan whom you asked me to care for here?' Robert asked William as they were eating. 'I must tell you that I have found her a most pleasant young woman, and very willing to do any work that can be found for her. She has fitted in well with the house servants, minds her own business, and does not involve herself in gossip.'

'I am glad to hear that,' said William. 'As I told you when I asked if you would house her, her parents are loyal, longstanding employees of mine. I was moved to help the girl Susan for their sakes. I cannot remember … is her child due soon?'

'The child is due to be born in about two months, I understand,' said Robert. 'Susan has expressed her willingness to continue working right up until the birth, and she has already told me that as soon as possible after the baby is born, she will gladly accept any suitable work that I find for her. I think this bitter experience has taught her some practical lessons about life.'

'I am sure she is most grateful that she could come and live here, and I'm glad that she has proved to be something of an asset to you. After the child is born,' said William, 'if it is convenient, I would like her to work closely with your housekeeper and be taught some basic skills of household management. My wife, Lady Snow, and I have had some thoughts as to useful employment for Susan in the future which would mean that she must be able to manage a small house and supervise a few servants.'

William and Robert sat for a long time over their ale that evening as William told him about an idea that Elizabeth had had soon after Susan had gone to Matworth.

Elizabeth, he said, had started by saying to him, 'You may remember that I remarked that Susan was not the first young woman to find herself pregnant and unmarried, and she would not be the last?'

'Yes, I do remember you saying that, and I remember thinking that it was a sensible comment.'

'Well, after Susan had gone to Matworth,' Elizabeth continued, 'I started thinking that although we had been able to resolve her situation satisfactorily, many other young women do not have the benefit of such help. Abandoned by the father of their child, and often cast out of home by their parents who feel shamed by the situation, these young women have nowhere to go and are forced into lives of begging or crime or worse. I started to wonder if somehow there was a way that we could help such women and their babies in a practical way, as we had been able to help Susan.'

'Go on,' said William. 'I know you … when you start thinking about something that needs to be done, you don't stop until you have thought through to a solution!'

'I have an idea, and I have given it some thought, although the plans are not yet fully formed, but I would like to hear what you think. You are so good at taking an idea, and turning it into a practical plan.'

Elizabeth explained that the more she thought about young, pregnant women, who were alone and with no proper home, the more she felt that she wanted to do something to help them. And then her idea came to her.

'I would like to set up some kind of home where they can

live until after their babies are born. While there, they would be given useful training so that once they have given birth to the child, they will have enough skills to find work. In the same way that just over 100 years ago an ancestress of yours founded the Lady Eleanor School, which has been of such practical use to children in this area, such a home for these young women would be of equal practical help.'

'I can understand your purpose, and on the whole I think your idea is a good one,' said William. 'We should discuss the whole thing thoroughly and decide exactly what would be required and how best such a place should be organised and run on a day-to-day basis. Then we can decide if it is a practical proposition.'

For two days, William and Elizabeth talked of little else and gradually some new ideas were added, and others were dropped as impractical. The first step would be to find a suitable house and for this purpose, they thought it should accommodate at least ten young women at any one time. They pondered over the best location for such a house; it should be easily found by young women who had need of it but it should also give them some privacy, away from prying eyes. If they converted one of the spare buildings on the Fortune estate into such a house, would it be easily found by women in need of its help? Or would it be too hidden away? If they set up the house in the heart of York or Beverley, it would be more easily found, but would it offer the privacy they felt was needed?

William decided to go into both York and Beverley and talk to some lawyers and land agents that he knew in both places. This proved to be a good idea, and when he came home he said that he thought he had found the perfect place.

He took Elizabeth to see the house; it was large enough for their purpose, standing off on its own just outside the city centre of York, but near to one of the main roads that led into the city. Elizabeth was delighted by the house.

'Its location is perfect,' she declared, and, with her practical mind already running ahead, she went on, 'and there are sufficient rooms to house at least ten young women, and in addition there are rooms that can be kept separate for the housekeeper's private use. We would need only one or two maids to be hired to come in on a daily basis, because I intend that most of the daily work of cleaning and running the house will be done by the young women residents, in return for their board and lodging. In fact,' she added, 'if Susan is taught something about housekeeping and running a house while she is at Matworth, I think it is possible that she might be suitable as the housekeeper there.'

'And that,' said William to Robert, when he had finished explaining their plans, 'is why I would like Susan to be trained by your housekeeper in the skills of managing a small house.'

Elizabeth and William were both glad that something beneficial and useful had come about because of what was originally an unhappy situation and both felt that it was fitting that they should use some of their wealth to endow the house. William insisted that it should be named Elizabeth House. 'After all, the whole plan originated with you, and I think it is fitting that this place should always bear your name.'

Chapter 7

The day after William returned from Matworth, he spent the morning going around the Fortune estate, checking that all was well. So it was afternoon before he went into his business room, and opened the pouch of letters that had arrived by coach from London in his absence.

Most of the correspondence was routine business and accounts matters but there were two letters that he carried up to the solar where Elizabeth was sitting.

'I always enjoy sitting here on a day like this in late autumn,' she said. 'I really do think that this is my favourite season. Just look at the trees and the wonderful colours of the leaves!'

'I was looking at the autumn colours when I rode around the estate this morning, and I thought what a perfect day it was,' said William. 'Each year, around April and May, I think that spring must be the most beautiful season, when all the fruit blossom is on the trees and all the new crops are showing fresh green in the fields. Then when autumn comes and I see the golds and bronzes and reds of the leaves, I change my mind and think that this is the most beautiful time of year. And there is something almost magical when there is a light mist on a sunny autumn morning.

'However,' he went on, 'I didn't come up to discuss the seasons with you but to tell you of two very interesting letters I have just received. One is from Michael Ahmson, the portrait painter. He is working on portraits he is doing for a family who live in Derbyshire – by chance, he is not too far from

169

Matworth – and he says that he should have finished that work by the end of November or the beginning of December. He would then be free to come here to start painting our family portrait, if the time is convenient for us.'

'Oh, that will be excellent timing,' said Elizabeth, 'because James will be home from university for the Christmas holiday. Of course, James will have a limited time to stay here, so perhaps Mr Ahmson will paint him first, and then he can paint the rest of us after James has returned to Oxford. But, oh dear,' her face fell, 'in one way it is not such good timing. You had said that you wanted us to sit outside so that some of the horses can be in the background of the painting and I fear that it will be much too cold at that time of year for us to sit still outside for long periods.'

'That is something that we can ask Mr Ahmson to work around, I'm sure,' said William. 'I will explain what I want and I imagine that he will be able to paint us as a group, while we sit in comfort in the house, and then he can paint in the background of trees, paddocks and horses just by looking out of the windows. But I will write to him immediately and tell him that we will be delighted to see him here when he has finished work on his present commission.'

'And you said there is another letter you wanted to tell me about?'

'Yes, Elizabeth. This is a great surprise. You remember Walter Banham, the young man who was so interested in our Snowy horses as he called them? He told us that his father is a horse breeder and when I've been at the livestock sales in York, I have asked people if they know the name Banham and I have discovered that his father is a breeder of some repute. He has his breeding establishment at Newmarket, where he also trains some horses for racing. This other letter is from him. He says that he has always been intrigued by what he has heard about the Snowy horses that we breed here and his son has talked enthusiastically about them since he visited here last summer. Now Mr Banham asks if he may visit us and see the horses for himself? If we agree, and it is convenient, he would also like to come here around the end of November.'

'Well, I see no reason why he shouldn't come then,' said Elizabeth. 'We shan't all be sitting for our portraits all of the time, and I'm sure you will enjoy showing our special horses to someone who is so knowledgeable. I wonder, do you think he will want to bring his son Walter with him?'

'He doesn't ask that, but I think when I reply to his letter I will suggest that if Walter would like to come with him, we would be pleased to welcome him back to Fortune.'

When the family was together, eating their meal later that day, William told them that the portrait painter would be arriving in another month or so to start work on their painting. Mary immediately said that she thought that she would like to be painted wearing her ball gown. 'Because,' she said, 'it is the most beautiful gown that I possess.' Elizabeth said that she, too, had been giving some thought about what she would wear for the portrait, and she had also decided to wear the beautiful blue and silver gown that she had worn for the ball.

William looked at Charles and grinned. 'And what about us, eh, Charles? What shall we wear? Shall I wear my best grey coat, or my second best brown coat?'

'Mmmm ... I just don't know, Father! I shall have to think long and hard to decide which of my coats to wear, and ...'

'Stop! Stop teasing!' cried Mary. 'Mother, make them stop teasing us. Father would not be pleased if we did not bother to look our best!'

'All right, Mary! I will stop teasing you! Instead I will tell you another piece of news. We shall have another visitor at the same time as Mr Ahmson. You will recall the young man, Walter Banham, who took such an interest in our special breed of horses? And you and he rode together one morning?'

'Actually, they rode together on three mornings,' murmured Charles under his breath.

Mary coloured and hissed 'ssshh' at him.

'What? Were you saying something?' William asked. Then he went on, 'Today I received a letter from the young man's father, Matthew Banham, and he has proposed visiting us himself if it is convenient, as he would very much like to see our Snowy horses. I have heard from a number of people that Matthew Banham has bred some outstanding horses, and also he has trained several winners of the races they hold at Newmarket.'

'Surely you will agree to him visiting us?' asked Mary. 'You know how much I've always liked our special horses, and I am so pleased that their fame has spread and that someone so well known in the equine world has heard of them and wants to see them.'

Elizabeth was sure that Mary would like to ask if Mr Banham would bring his son with him when he visited. Although she knew it was William's intention to include an invitation to Walter in the letter that he was going to write to Matthew Banham, he had not mentioned this to the family around the table. But she remembered the look on their faces when Mary and Walter had danced together at the ball this past summer and decided that she must say something.

'When you write to Mr Banham, will you suggest that his son Walter accompanies him on his visit here?' she asked. 'The visit could be timed so that Walter will be home from university for Christmas. After all, it is because of Walter's enthusiasm for our horses that Mr Banham has proposed himself.'

Elizabeth stole a quick glance at Mary under lowered eyes. Mary was concentrating very hard on her food and did not look at her father as he answered, but Elizabeth was sure she could detect just the slightest heightening of the colour in Mary's cheeks. William realised why his wife had broached the subject in this indirect way, and instead of saying that he had already told her that he would suggest that Walter should join his father, he said very casually, 'Yes, I think that would be a good idea. It would be courteous as Matthew Banham says that his son talked so much about our horses, after he saw them and rode them while he was here.'

The letters from William Snow to both Michael Ahmson, the portrait painter, and Matthew Banham were sent off by the next coach that carried mail. They would have to go all the way to London, and then be put on the appropriate coaches to go to Michael Ahmson in Derbyshire, and Matthew Banham in Newmarket. As four of the family members settled down in the quiet time of late autumn, three of them were anticipating December with great pleasure, but for different reasons. Elizabeth was always overjoyed to have James home, so that all her family was together in the house; William was looking forward to hearing Matthew Banham's expert comments on the Snowy horses; and Mary was counting the days until Walter Banham would arrive.

Chapter 8

Michael Ahmson arrived in the second week of December, a little later than had been expected. As a courtesy, William accompanied the housekeeper to show him the room he would be occupying.

'Sir William,' said Mr Ahmson as they went up the broad staircase, 'May I ask a favour of you? During the next few days, before I even make preliminary sketches for the painting, I would like to sit with you and your family so that I can observe each of you as you talk between yourselves, conversing in your normal manner about everyday affairs. In that way I can study not only the faces, but also the character of the people I am to paint,' he explained. 'By doing that, I feel that I can make a portrait that tells you something about the person, and does not just depict their face.'

'That is exactly what I liked so much about the portraits you'd painted when I saw them in London, and that is why I wanted you to paint our family. I don't want just faces on canvas,' said William. 'I'd like to feel that when future generations look at the portraits, they will know something about us, something of our characters, as well as our features.'

William went on to tell Mr Ahmson that as well as the family being shown in the portrait, he would like the background to show some of the land around the house and also some of their horses.

'We have always been very proud of the horses that we've been breeding here since my father's, or indeed my grandfather's, time and recently I've discovered that our horses have become quite well known to people outside this area. We had thought that we, as a family group, could sit for you outside on the terrace so that some paddocks and horses would be visible in the background, but obviously, the weather is not suitable for us to do that. Mr Ahmson, I know you are not a landscape artist, but we very much hope that you will be able to paint a view of some of our land, with two or three of the horses included, and have that as a background to our group portrait.'

Michael Ahmson said he understood exactly what William was describing and that he would be happy to paint a picture in the style described.

'Although I paint only portraits now, when I was at the art school in Sweden, my training did of course include painting both landscapes and animals. In fact,' he went on, 'your ideas excite me. This painting will be quite different from anything I've done before, and now I am intrigued to see these famous horses and also to look around at the views from the house and decide which I shall incorporate into the painting.'

A few days after Michael Ahmson arrived, the Banhams – father and son – also arrived. Walter had left the university a little ahead of all the other students, so that he could accompany his father on his visit to Fortune. William and Matthew Banham spent several hours together every day, both in the stables with the horses, and in William's business room going over the breeding records. The two men found that they had several interests in common as well as horses, and a good friendship was fast developing between them.

'I do hope that you will come and visit my establishment in Newmarket soon. Perhaps you will come next spring, when the weather should be fine. There is excellent riding all around the area, and we can go up to the gallops early in the morning and watch the racehorses at their training,' said Matthew.

'I should be delighted to come,' said William. 'As you know, although we have successfully bred these Snowy horses for some time, I really know very little about the general business of horse breeding and I know nothing about training them for racing.'

'In addition,' added Matthew, 'when you visit us you will meet my elder son. He has always worked hard alongside me and has acquired great expertise on all matters of breeding and training. I am very lucky because I know that he will take over from me successfully when I decide that I no longer want to work the long hours that are needed every day.'

'I know exactly what you mean about feeling happy that you have a son to take over from you who will carry on all the work you have done. I am blessed with just such qualities in my elder son, Charles. He loves Fortune, the house and the estate, and he has worked diligently so that one day he will be a responsible and capable owner. But what about your son Walter?' asked William. 'He, too, has worked hard and is obviously very knowledgeable about all matters concerning horses. Will he become an assistant to his elder brother, or will he perhaps want to start his own establishment?'

'That is something I do not know,' replied Matthew. 'Of course, if he wished to make his own place, I would help him financially at the start. As long as he is working with horses, I think he will be happy wherever he is.'

Walter usually went with them to the stables, and also sat with them as they looked at the stud books. Mostly he listened to their conversations but occasionally he would make a remark about some point of breeding, or would comment on some event connected with their own horses.

'Would you like to ride one of our Snowy horses again

while you are here?' William asked Walter. 'I remember that you said how much you enjoyed riding one on your last visit here.'

'Oh thank you, Sir, yes, I would certainly enjoy riding here again. Thank you very much for suggesting it.' The words almost tumbled out of Walter's mouth in his enthusiasm and from that day on, first thing every morning, he rode out, accompanied by Mary.

One day, when William and Matthew were at the stables, Walter and Mary returned from their morning ride. Their cheeks were flushed pink by the cold morning air, and both were laughing at some shared humour. As soon as they saw their two fathers standing there, watching them, both of their faces flushed even more.

Walter immediately sprang down from his horse, handed the reins to a groom, and went round to help Mary dismount.

'Thank you,' she said and quickly turned to her father and Matthew Banham, and said very briskly, 'Good morning Father; good morning Mr Banham. Please excuse me, I must go straight into the house.' And she hurried away, her cheeks still very pink.

'I must go and change too,' said Walter. 'I hope I may join both of you in a little while either here or in the business room?' And he, too, hurried away.

Matthew and William exchanged glances.

'Er ... forgive me if I'm making bold, but I think that my son and your daughter find great pleasure in each other's company,' said Matthew.

'I am sure you are right. And now that I think back, I recall that they seemed to enjoy dancing together at the ball this past summer, and of course, they rode together several mornings when Walter was here then. Well, well, well. Are we just a pair of romantic old men or …?' William did not finish his sentence, but both men smiled widely at each other.

The Banhams left to return to Newmarket on the same day that James came home from Oxford. Matthew Banham had been profuse in his praise for the Snowy horses.

'I can see why my son talked about them so much,' he said as he and Walter were leaving. 'They really are very beautiful to look at and they have good temperaments too. I sincerely hope that you will accept my invitation to come and visit us at Newmarket whenever it is convenient for you.'

William told Matthew how much he had enjoyed having him and his son stay at Fortune.

'I have never had the opportunity until now to meet anyone who has so much knowledge about horses,' he explained, 'and I really value the comments you have made about the ones we breed here. Of course, we have always thought they are rather special but it's good to know that an expert thinks so too.'

All the Snow family came out on to the terrace to wave goodbye to the Banhams. At the last minute Matthew turned in his saddle and leaned down a little to speak to William and said, 'I think my son would stay on a great deal longer if he could!'

Walter, who had been bending to speak to Mary, heard the remark and immediately sat up straight and said in a loud voice, 'Goodbye, Miss Snow. It has been a pleasure to see you and ride out with you again.' And with that he spurred his horse and it went down the drive at a canter.

William and Matthew shared a look that spoke volumes.

Elizabeth, watching the exchange between Walter and Mary, and then catching the glance between William and

Matthew, thought to herself, 'Ah ... at last ... William has seen what I saw back in the summer when they danced together.'

Chapter 9

Michael Ahmson, who had been working on some preliminary sketches for the portrait, showed them to William and Elizabeth. He explained that usually the two of them would be placed in the centre of the painting, with their children on either side of them.

'However,' he said, 'as you will see, I am placing Sir William in the centre of the group, with Charles and James on each side of him. This is because I want to place a lady at each side of the group in order to show the skirts of their gowns, which will be spread out to the sides.'

Elizabeth was delighted and said, 'Most men wouldn't even think of that, Mr Ahmson, but as an artist you appreciate the beauty of the gowns that my daughter and I will wear for the sittings.'

'The background will, as you can see, show some of the Snowy horses as you asked,' added Michael Ahmson, 'and if you approve of the general grouping and style of these sketches, I would like to start work on the painting. As your son James is only to be home from university for a short time, I will start by painting him. While he is here, I can observe his personality, and as well as painting his face, I will also paint his hands. So often I find that the hands contribute greatly to the character of a person's portrait. Then, after he has returned to Oxford, I can paint in his garments and other finishing touches. For that he need not be present.'

To get the best possible light for the sittings, an area at one end of the solar was set aside where Mr Ahmson would work. At this time of year the daylight hours were short but by using the top floor of the house with its very large windows, the best use possible was made of available daylight.

Elizabeth always spent time in the afternoons in the solar, sitting at the opposite end to where Michael Ahmson painted, working on her needlework, or writing in her record of family events. Two days before Christmas, when she went up to the solar, instead of going to the end that she usually used, she turned to the opposite end where Michael Ahmson was painting. James had been sitting for him in the morning, but now the artist was alone. The canvas on which he was working was so large that he had to stand on a small ladder to work on it. Elizabeth approached, and said softly, 'Mr Ahmson?' He was so engrossed in his work that he did not hear her. More loudly she said, 'Mr Ahmson … may I speak to you?'

'Of course, Madam. I have been painting for several hours and I shall be glad to take a short break. But it must be only a short break. The light will go soon.' He stepped down from the ladder.

'I was wondering …' Elizabeth hesitated. 'May I look at the work you have done so far on James's portrait? Or do you prefer that nobody looks at your work at this early stage?'

'There are times when I prefer that the client does not look at the work, because at some stages it does not look good and often the client cannot envisage the eventual result. But I am happy for you to see what I have done so far. Please, come around to this side.'

Elizabeth stepped around so that she stood beside the artist, and looked at the huge canvas.

'Ah, yes. Already you are capturing a wonderful likeness of my son.' She stepped back a little, still looking at the painting. 'Oh, Mr Ahmson, I can see already why you are in such demand. You portray the features in such a lifelike way and also you have captured the expression on his face so well that I find myself wondering what he is thinking. Thank you, Mr Ahmson. I am so grateful that you allowed me look at the work you have done so far and I will take no more of your time. Now that I have seen how you work, I am vain enough to hope that when you paint my likeness, you will flatter me!'

That evening, when the family was gathered in the Great Hall, in front of a huge log fire, Mary went over to the spinet and played a melody that she had just learned. William stretched his legs out and said, 'Isn't this a perfect way to spend an evening? All the family together, and sitting in front of this huge fire. I really enjoy time spent like this.'

Mary had come to the end of the piece she was playing and asked, 'Shall I play more?' but before anyone could answer James said, 'I would like to say something please.'

'My son, you look so serious. I hope that you are not going to speak of bad news?' William's face and voice showed his concern.

'No, no, Father. It is not bad news. It is something I want to tell you, and as we are all together this seems a good time.' James stopped, cleared his throat, then went on, the words coming out in a rush. 'When I have finished my law studies at Oxford, I want to go to live in America.'

Everything stopped in the room. Nobody moved. It was as if a sudden blast of icy wind had frozen everything and everybody.

'I don't understand,' William started to say. 'No, I don't mean that. Of course, I do understand what you said but I am at a loss. I always thought it was your intention to make the law your life's work. Probably not here in Yorkshire; perhaps in London, but ... Are you thinking of practising law in

America? And why America? I'm sorry, James, I am not speaking coherently. I can only say again, I don't understand.'

'I'm sorry, Father and Mother,' James went on, 'I know that this is a shock to you, but it is not a decision I have reached lightly. I have been giving thought to my plans for quite a long time, and I have been wondering when and how to tell you. I did not know how best to explain to you my hopes and dreams, and I'm afraid the words just tumbled out. But as I have said, they did not tumble out without forethought. This is not a sudden whim.'

Elizabeth finally found her voice. 'When you were home last year, I had a feeling that your heart was not entirely in your studies, James. I wondered if perhaps you felt you did not want to be a lawyer, but I did not think beyond that. And even if I had given the matter more thought, in my wildest imaginings, I would not have thought that you might want to journey to America.'

'Not just journey there, Mother. As I have said, I want to go to live there. I have considered this step very carefully and talked to several people who know something of life in the Americas.'

Now Charles spoke up. 'James, I know, as both of us have always known, that as the elder son, I will eventually inherit Fortune and take over the running of everything on this estate. And, because of these circumstances, I've always known that almost certainly your life and work would not be here at Fortune. But I always imagined that you would be somewhere nearby, at least near enough for us to visit each other frequently. I thought that I would always be able to talk to you about any problems I might have, and discuss possible solutions.'

'Charles, as you say, we have both always known that all of Fortune is entailed upon you. The house, the lands, the

183

horses and all the animals that we breed for sale, the Matworth estate and the lead mines there in Derbyshire, they will all be yours. I do not resent or regret this situation for one minute. It is a fact that I've always known and accepted. I thought that I would enjoy the legal profession, and that I would probably live and work in London, and I had even thought that perhaps eventually I might have a career in politics. But a year or two ago I met a couple of young men who were about to leave for America, and they talked to me of their plans. Through them, I met some people who were visiting London who already live there and who have established flourishing businesses there. One of the men I talked to grows cotton on a plantation in the southern part of the country, and another grows tobacco in the part called Virginia, which is on the eastern coast.'

While James was speaking the others sat silently, listening intently to what he said. Now he glanced around them and said, 'My mind is quite made up. I think it is sensible that I finish my studies and obtain my degree in law. And afterwards I intend to go to Virginia and I hope to be able to establish myself as a tobacco grower.'

'My son,' William spoke now, 'I must ask if you have enquired as to the costs of setting up and establishing yourself? How many acres of land would you have to buy, and how would you learn the business? I am sure that, as with any business, there are pitfalls and problems.'

'Yes, Father,' said James, 'I have talked several times to the man who is already growing tobacco in Virginia and questioned him on the subject. He has been established there for several years, and he has advised me how much land and what type of land I should buy. And he has offered to give me as much help as possible. In fact, he has suggested that after I arrive in America I should go to live with him and his family.

I can then work with him for several months so that I have practical experience before I actually purchase land.'

'Well, that is a kind offer and a sensible one too. I presume he will also advise you as to just how much money you will need to buy land, equipment, a place to live, people to work for you, and to live until your first cash crop is sold?' William, as usual, displayed a practical turn of mind.

'Yes, Father, I have all such information written out, and I will gladly go through it all with you so that you can see how I plan to do things.'

'Tomorrow morning we will talk and together we will look at all your plans very carefully. And if I approve, I daresay that you will ask me for the money to get you started?'

'Yes, Father, I know that I shall have to ask you for some capital to start on this venture. But I have some money of my own, as you know. You will remember that my grandmother left me a sum of money that came into my possession on my birthday this year, when I became 21. This is a substantial sum of money but not as much as I shall need.'

Suddenly Elizabeth broke in with a cry, 'You are both talking as if this is already an accomplished fact; a decided move. William,' she turned to her husband, 'James has only broken this news to us less than an hour ago, and already you are discussing investing in his business venture. Surely it is not already decided. Surely, James, you may change your mind? You may decide against this journey to a far land, to do something of which you have no knowledge?'

'Mother,' James came over and put his arms around her. 'I knew that it would not be easy for you to accept that I shall be going so far away, and I understand your anxieties that I am embarking upon something of which I know little. But look …' he pointed across the Great Hall. 'Mother, look at Dickon's Bench. Look at what is carved into the back of it.'

185

He walked across and ran his hand over the words that were carved along the back of the seat. They read: 'He Who Will Not When He May, He May Live To Rue The Day'.

'Whenever I have read that, I have thought that they are excellent words to live by. Words to encourage and inspire. Words that say, whatever is in your mind, do it now, while you can. Later you may find that you cannot do it. I feel that the man who carved those words over a century ago is speaking to me across the years.'

Chapter 10

The next day was Christmas Eve and William and James spent two hours in the business room with the door firmly shut. Elizabeth waited in the Great Hall, impatient to know what they were saying. When the two of them finally emerged, William's arm was around James's shoulder and both of them looked relaxed.

William saw Elizabeth sitting near the fire and said, 'We will join you, my dear, and tell you all that we have talked about this morning. But first have some claret brought here – my mouth and throat are dry after all the talk this morning and I daresay James, too, would appreciate a glass of wine.'

Elizabeth went to the door that led to the main inner hall where she knew there would always be a servant waiting in case anything was needed.

'The claret will be here in a few minutes,' she said as she came back into the Great Hall. 'Now, let us sit and you will, I hope, tell me all about your discussions this morning. Please start at the beginning and tell me everything.'

'In fact,' said William, 'I will start at the end because I can reassure you. I have looked very carefully at the information James has been given by the man who is already living in Virginia and growing tobacco, and I am pleased to tell you that this man has laid out all the facts clearly and thoroughly. I am satisfied that the numbers he gives of estimates of costs for James to set up a tobacco growing plantation are sensible, and he has also included provision for things that can go wrong and delay the start of income from the crops.'

'But, surely,' interjected Elizabeth, 'James's inheritance from his grandmother can't possibly be sufficient money to buy land and everything else that will be needed to make a start? And also it has to be considered that he will have to live without any income for at least one year, perhaps two.'

'Ah,' William said, 'here is the claret.' All conversation stopped while the tray with a bottle of wine and glasses was placed on a low table near to them.

'Thank you, that will be all,' said William to the manservant who had brought it, then he turned and poured the wine and handed glasses to Elizabeth and James.

'I think it is fitting that we should drink a toast to James, and wish him good luck in this venture.' He raised his glass and held it towards James. Elizabeth did the same with her glass. 'Of course I wish you good luck, my dear,' she said, and all three of them drank.

'Now, as to the capital that James will need from the outset, I have decided to give him a substantial sum because insufficient capital has caused many businesses to fail.' William turned to Elizabeth and said, 'I will not bore you with too much detail, but I can make money available from Fortune's businesses. Although, of course, the house and almost all of its contents, and the land, are entailed upon Charles as the elder son, there are some of our undertakings that stand outside the entail. I am free to sell off those portions and do as I wish with the money raised.'

'I did not realise that some parts of Fortune can be sold,' said Elizabeth. 'However, as it seems that you are persuaded that James has sufficient information to pursue this plan, then I am glad that we can give him the necessary financial help.'

'I have considered the several parts that I am at liberty to sell should I wish to do so,' said William. 'I could, for example, sell the part of the estate that is devoted to the breeding and sale of the Snowy horses.' There was a sharp intake of breath from Elizabeth and she murmured, 'Oh ... no' and William went on, 'but I do not want to do that. I can also sell the Matworth estate, and I can sell the lead mines, which form a separate part of that property. I have decided that the most sensible course is to sell the lead mines. I intend to offer the mines first to Robert Goody, the Matworth estate manager. He has been a loyal, hardworking employee, and of course, we recently had good reason to be grateful to him when he agreed to take the girl Susan to live there. He knows the lead mining business thoroughly, having managed it as part of the Matworth estate for many years, and I believe he will be interested in buying the mines.'

'But surely, you will sell them for a very high price? They have always been profitable, and you will want to raise as much money from the sale as possible in order to give it to James. How could Mr Goody possibly afford to buy them? Where would he find that sort of money?' asked Elizabeth.

'I shall ride over to Matworth straight after Christmas and offer to sell the lead mines to Robert Goody and, assuming he is interested in making the purchase, I shall suggest that he talks to our lawyers in York. They can, I am sure, find people who will be willing to lend him the amount of money necessary to make the purchase. His income from the mines can be used to pay off the loan plus the interest on it. He will not need that money as an income as he will continue to work and be paid as the estate manager, and live in the house we provide for him.'

Christmas Day followed its normal routine, with the family and the entire household staff from the Fortune estate attending church in the morning. In the afternoon, the traditional Christmas food was served to everybody, family and servants alike. Elizabeth looked around the table at her gathered family all laughing, joking with each other, admiring the gifts that they had received from each other and she found herself thinking, 'I must remember the way everybody looks and all that happens, for Christmas will never be the same again. In future, one dear member of the family will be absent.' She turned her head away so that nobody saw the tears that sprang to her eyes.

After the meal was finished, Elizabeth and William decided to sit close to the fire but the three younger members of the family said they were going for a walk. 'It is a fine day, though cold,' said James, 'Are you sure you won't come with us?'

'No, no, you go off and enjoy your walk. I am at the age where I like my comfort,' said William, putting his feet up on a stool.

The three of them headed towards the stables, as William and Elizabeth had guessed they would.

Elizabeth said, 'I knew you would not consider selling off the horses, William. They are so much a part of our life here, I cannot imagine Fortune without them.'

'I know,' said William. 'I feel the same. To me they are not just horses that we breed and sometimes sell, they are so strongly associated with our family name, and are a part of Fortune that must remain here. But,' he went on, 'I sometimes wonder how much longer I can manage to take care of everything on the estate. These days I have so many aches and pains in my back and my joints, but as long as I am in charge, I must ensure that Fortune continues to run efficiently. It is lucky that we have an excellent estate manager here who takes over many responsibilities, and Charles has made such a great success of the cheese business that I have every confidence that he could take over more of the work of running Fortune.'

'I think you would be right to hand over more responsibilities to Charles now. Let him take over from you in some matters so that you do not have to work so hard. I am sure that he and the estate manager could take on many of your tasks.'

'Yes, I know you are right. I am sure that, with guidance from me, he could handle things successfully. It is a pity though, that of all the children, he is the one least interested in the horses.'

'Ah, well, if you are judging solely by interest in the horses, then Mary is the one who has always had the most enthusiasm. I've always thought it is perhaps not quite seemly that she takes such an interest in their breeding, but she has become very knowledgeable about everything concerning them. I imagine that you would not consider letting Mary take over responsibility for all matters concerning the Snowy horses?'

'No, I would not consider it at present. She is too young and anyhow I expect she will marry and leave Fortune before many years have passed. But I have thought that perhaps I might let her take on part of the work with the horses. Although she is so young, she has a good head on her shoulders and her keen interest in them compensates for her youth. You know, Elizabeth, the more I think of it, the more I am inclined to let Charles take on much of the day-to-day responsibility for Fortune's affairs. And if I let Mary take on some matters concerning the horses, it would relieve me greatly. It's not easy to know and accept that the time has come to step back and hand over to someone younger.'

Chapter 11
1712

Elizabeth went into the rooms off the inner hall that had been made into a bedroom and a sitting room for William since the ague had made it too painful for him to climb the stairs to their bedchamber. Most days he would make the effort to walk the few yards to his business room which was just along the hall, so that he could sit and talk to Charles about the daily affairs of Fortune. This day, when Elizabeth had tapped on the door of the business room and gone in, only Charles was there working at the desk.

'When Father didn't come in to see me, I went along and put my head around his door and he said that he felt very tired and was resting, but would come along soon,' Charles told his mother. 'He has not been in to see me yet, but I don't like to go and disturb him again.'

'That was a good thought, Charles, but I will go along now and see how he is feeling,' said Elizabeth, and she left the business room and walked along the hall to William's day room and went in. He wasn't sleeping but was lying back on the bed that had been put there so that he could rest at any time.

'Come in, my dear. I'm not sleeping. I felt so tired this morning that I decided to indulge myself by resting all morning.' Elizabeth thought that William's face looked more lined than she had ever seen it, and his pallor was such that he looked quite grey. 'Come and sit near me, Elizabeth, and talk to me.'

As she sat in a chair next to him, Elizabeth silently thanked God that she could bring him some really good news.

'Look, look!' She held up something. 'It's a letter from James! Oh William, so exciting, such good news from him.' In the years since James had sailed from Bristol on his journey to Virginia, correspondence from him had been sparse. One short letter arrived just six months after he had left and it was full of excitement and enthusiasm. He said that the family who had invited him to stay with them had made him very welcome and very comfortable.

'Mr Horton – or Jack as he has asked me to call him – is already teaching me much about life here in general and growing tobacco in particular. I know that I shall learn a great deal from him, and I hope to purchase land fairly close to this plantation so that I can easily call upon him for advice.'

No more letters came from James for two years, though he sent messages through friends who were travelling to England, so they knew that all was well with him. When his next letter arrived, and he told them how his business was progressing, it was obvious that he had written two or three times but those letters had never reached Fortune.

William said, 'Elizabeth, I don't think my eyes can read James's letter today, so please read it to me while I continue to lie here.'

The letter was quite long and full of news. The tobacco crop had been better than ever this year, and as tobacco prices were steadily rising, James said that he was having a very profitable year. He told them that he had saved the income from the past few years, and had now spent it on having what he termed a 'real' house built. His first house had been little more than a wooden cabin with a dirt floor.

'But now,' his letter said, 'my house would not disgrace a house in a small town anywhere in England. I ordered carpets and furniture from Europe and everything has now safely arrived, having come on ships that docked within the past month.'

Elizabeth broke off to say, 'Isn't this all good news, William? I feel so relieved that James seems to be comfortably settled and his business is successful. But wait, my dear, the next part contains some really exciting news.'

She went on reading: "You may remember, Mother and Father, that when I first arrived here and stayed with the Horton family on the plantation that is almost next to where I now have my land, I found them all very congenial. One of their daughters, Harriet, is a most likeable young woman. She is one year older than me, and is, I think, beautiful, with very dark hair, a milky complexion, and the bluest eyes I've ever seen – other than yours, Mother dear!"

William raised his head from the pillow and asked Elizabeth to put more cushions behind him so that he could sit up a little.

'I feel that I am about to be given some really important news?' his voice was questioning.

'Yes, I think you have guessed what is coming,' she said, 'but I will read on. "I have asked Harriet to marry me, and she has made me the happiest man in the Colonies by saying yes to my proposal. Her father has said he could not have chosen a better husband for her and all her family seem pleased and excited that we are to marry."

'Well, I should think so,' said Elizabeth. 'They are right. She could not find a better man as a husband! But I admit that I am prejudiced!'

'When was this letter written?' asked William. 'What date is on it?'

'Oh, I hadn't thought to look. Ah, here is the date. It was written three months ago! Oh William, that means that they are probably already married! So now all three of our children are married! I must write immediately to James and send our love and best wishes to him and his wife. What did he say her name is? Oh yes, Harriet.'

'Don't rush off to write that letter. Stay and talk with me for a while,' said William. 'My mind is going back over the years since James left here. So much has happened in nine years, Elizabeth. So much that is good and happy.' His voice trailed away. Elizabeth knew that he had difficulty talking for long because his breathing became difficult at times, so she took up what he had been saying.

'They have indeed been good and happy years. When I think back,' said Elizabeth, and her eyes took on a far-away look, 'I think how sad I was, so very unhappy, when James left. I tried hard never to cry in front of him because he was so filled with excitement at the prospect of his great adventure. I think he only ever saw my tears once and that was the actual moment of saying goodbye, as he left this house to set off for Bristol to embark on his voyage.' Her face was downcast now at the memory of that time. 'But,' she thought to herself, 'today I must talk of only cheerful things; that is what William needs from me.'

'And then, a few months after James had gone, the Banhams, father and son, arrived unexpectedly,' she went on.

'And what a blessing that visit proved to be!' William's face brightened as he thought of that time.

Matthew had apologised for arriving without first asking if it would be convenient to visit them, but he had said, 'I really need to talk to someone who understands about horses and who is outside my own family.'

He and William had disappeared into the business room leaving Elizabeth and Charles, and Walter and Mary in the Great Hall. Walter and Mary had drifted over to a corner of the Great Hall and were obviously deeply engrossed in each other's company. Charles and Elizabeth exchanged looks and Charles said, 'Excuse me, I must go over to the dairy and talk to the cheese master,' and went out. Elizabeth muttered something about telling the housekeeper to prepare bedrooms for guests and she also left the room.

When everybody gathered in the Great Hall later that day, William had told them, 'Matthew came to me with a problem. It is not an insurmountable problem. In fact, I think we have resolved it.'

He explained that Matthew had told him that for the most part he had now given up daily responsibility for his horse breeding and training business and his elder son had taken over.

Then Matthew had taken up the story, 'It has become obvious to me that there is really no place for Walter, despite the fact that he has always been so interested in the horses and everything connected with them. I had hoped that after he came home from university, he and his older brother would work together. Unfortunately, I can see already that the two of them have such completely different personalities and want to conduct business in such different ways, that they will never be able to work together satisfactorily. Therefore, I came here to talk to my friend William and ask him the greatest possible favour. That favour was to ask if Walter could come here as an employee, working with the Snowy horses.'

William had said, 'As Walter has such a thorough knowledge of horse breeding, I thought that he would be an asset to Fortune but I did not want to make such a decision without asking Charles, who will be the next owner of Fortune, for his opinion. So I sent for him and asked him to join us in the business room. When I told him of Matthew's request, I am very happy to say that Charles immediately agreed that it would be an excellent idea for Walter to come and live and work here, concerning himself solely with the Snowy horses.'

Charles had said, 'As you all know, I have great affection for these beautiful horses that we have been breeding here for many years but they do not hold my interest as does the rest of Fortune's business. I am happy for Walter to take over all responsibilities for that part of Fortune thus freeing me to concentrate on the crops, the cheese business, and the breeding and sale of cattle and sheep.'

A long evening of talking had followed, and it was very late when everyone finally went to bed that night. When they were alone in their bedchamber, William had said to Elizabeth, 'It is amazing, isn't it, the way everything seems to fall into place. James has gone off to follow his dreams in Virginia, Charles is taking on many of the daily responsibilities from me so that I do not need to work so hard, and Walter wants to work here on the very thing that interests Charles least.'

Later, as they were both drifting off to sleep, William had said, 'And another thing. As we both know, Mary has always had a keen interest in those horses, and I am sure that she and Walter will work well together.'

'Yes, I'm sure you're right, dear,' Elizabeth had said, thinking to herself, 'and I guarantee that there will be more than work that brings those two close together.'

She had been proved right two years later, when Walter asked William's permission to marry Mary. Now they had been married almost seven years and had two small children who were already happiest when they were around the horses. Charles had married the same year as Mary, and he had a daughter and a son and his wife was pregnant again, with the new baby expected in three months. And now, thought Elizabeth, still holding James's letter, very soon I expect we shall have grandchildren growing up on the other side of the world.

She turned to talk to William and saw that he had drifted

off to sleep again. She stood, thinking that she would slip quietly out of the room and tell Charles that his father was still resting, when suddenly William's eyes opened.

'Elizabeth, Elizabeth ... don't leave me, please don't go.' His voice was hoarse and his breathing even more laboured. 'Please stay.' He was gasping for breath now.

'I won't go. Of course, I will stay,' but Elizabeth ran the few paces to the door, shouting into the hall, 'Jackie, Ben, anybody ...' Jackie, a manservant, and Annie, the housekeeper, appeared together both asking, 'Yes, Madam, what is it?'

'Quickly,' said Elizabeth. 'Annie, go and tell Charles to come at once. Jackie, run as fast as you can to the stables and tell Mr Walter and my daughter to hurry here.'

As they both ran to do her bidding, she went back to William's bedside. 'I'm here, my dear, I'm here,' and she slid her arm around his shoulders, lifting him slightly. 'Now, let's see if you can breathe more easily if I raise you just a little.'

Charles came into the room at a run. Elizabeth flapped a hand at him to warn him to approach quietly. He came over and stood on the other side of the bed. They exchanged looks but said nothing. Within minutes, Mary and Walter arrived, having ridden up from the stables together on one horse. William appeared now to be unconscious, then suddenly his eyes opened. He looked around and said in a clear voice, 'Ah, Fortune's family. All gathered together ...' Then he let out one long sighing breath and slumped against Elizabeth's arm.

Footnote: A year after William's death, Charles sold all the Snowy horses and the business of breeding them to Walter and Mary. Over the next years, the silvery white horses became famous throughout England and some were bought by the Royal Family and used for pulling carriages at Windsor.

The original Elizabeth House was capably managed by Susan and almost always had the full complement of ten young women living there. Whenever someone left, another was waiting to take up the place that had become available. Eventually two more such houses were built in other cities, and all three were called Elizabeth House in honour of their founder.

Part IV
1848

Chapter 1

The sun beat down on the men working on the terrace at the back of Fortune House. Although it was only mid-April, the sun was strong and the men were sweating as they moved the heavy bronze urns into place.

'Right, lads,' said the head gardener, 'One more big effort and this last one's in place. Ready … now … all together, heave …'

The men bent to their task again, muscles straining, veins standing out on their forearms.

'Heave! That's it! Well done.' The head gardener stood back and looked at the four urns, each standing about four feet high, that had been placed along the outer edge of the terrace. The men were mopping their brows and wiping the sweat from their necks.

Just then Sir Henry Snow stepped out of the house and surveyed the scene.

One of the men muttered, 'If he wants any of them moved, even if it's only one of them, I'll …'

'Ssshh, he's coming this way,' whispered one of the others.

Adam, the head gardener, doffed his cap. 'Good morning, Sir Henry. Not three minutes ago the men finished putting the last of the urns into place.'

'Don't they look marvellous!' exclaimed Sir Henry. 'Just where my son intended they should go when he bought them in Italy while he was on the grand tour.' He turned to the men and added, 'There's just one more thing for you to do.' A very low, but nonetheless audible, groan came from a couple of the men.

He went on, 'You've done a great job and I know it has been hard work, so I suggest we all go to the inn and drink a few pints of ale together. I imagine you've worked up quite a thirst?' He smiled at all of them, and was rewarded with smiles all round in return.

The group of men, headed by Sir Henry and Adam (everyone always said that with a name like Adam, how could he have become anything but a gardener?) strode down the long drive towards the gatehouse and the inn that lay just outside the Fortune estate.

A face appeared at an upstairs window. It was Henry's mother, the Dowager Lady Snow. She scowled at the backs of the group of men.

'Look at them, all going off with my son, no doubt to quench their thirst at the ale house. Not one of them cares for the headache they've given me, thumping and banging all morning, putting those urns into position, and all of them shouting and making such a noise while they did it!'

Her personal maid, Myrtle, said, 'Lady Snow, here is a fresh cloth for your head, wrung out in lavender water. It will help soothe the pain, I'm sure.'

'I don't think anything will soothe the pain.' Old Lady Snow was not going to be diverted from her complaints. 'And why that grandson of mine had to buy the wretched things and have them sent all the way from Italy, I do not know. The terrace looked perfectly fine without them.'

'Oh dear,' thought Myrtle, 'she's in a very bad mood indeed. She's never thought the terrace looked nice before.' She'd always complained and said how much she disliked the façade and terrace that had been built on to the back of the house some 50 years earlier.

In the last decade of the 18th century, Emma, now the Dowager Lady Snow, had married the elder son of the Snow family. At that time her father-in-law had decided that the front of the house was outdated and old fashioned. It had been built in the 16th century in the shape of an 'E' to compliment Queen Elizabeth I who was on the throne at the time. Her father-in-law had been very taken with the newer styles of architecture that he had seen on visits to London, and he wanted to have what he called 'this new classical style' at Fortune House.

He had originally intended to have the front of the house torn down, and rebuilt in the new style, but his wife managed to persuade him otherwise, saying that the old 16th century 'E' shaped frontage should be kept as part of Fortune House's history. He finally gave in to her arguments, and instead he had a completely new section built on to the back of the house in the style that he admired so much. Cream coloured rendering was applied to all the newly built area, a large triangular pediment over the main entrance was supported by columns on each side, and a terrace was built that ran right across the width of the house. He had liked this new addition so much that on his instructions the drive was extended so that it did not stop at the old front entrance, but swept around the house to the new entrance.

During the years since his death, however, gradually the new entrance had been used less and less, and nowadays the old, original door leading into the Great Hall, was the one that was always used.

Edgar, the eldest son and the heir to Fortune, had been out with the farm manager all morning, and now came riding home across the fields. As he looked towards the house, he saw that the bronze urns had been put in place and he reined in his horse. He sat for a few minutes looking at them, imagining them filled with plants such as he had seen and admired in Italy, and he couldn't help a smile spreading across his face.

'I'm so glad I bought them,' he thought. The art dealer from whom he bought them, along with some marble statues, had arranged to have everything packed and transported to England. During the months it had taken for the urns and statues to arrive, Edgar had worried in case the ship they were on sank, or that they might have been damaged in some way. But he need not have worried, he thought now. They had arrived safely, and the gardener's men had placed them exactly where he had envisaged them.

Suddenly, his eye was caught by a movement at one of the upper windows of the house. It was his grandmother's room and he knew she would have been watching the urns put in place, so he waved to her and spurred his horse on. As he turned from the drive towards the stables, a groom came out and took his horse, and Edgar went into the house and straight up to his grandmother's room.

He tapped on the door and went in. Her maid, Myrtle, said, 'Your grandmother has a bad headache, so please don't keep her talking too long.'

'That's all right, Myrtle. I don't mind how long my grandson stays,' said Emma. Edgar went over and kissed her on the cheek.

'What's this about a headache, Grandmother?' he asked.

'It was all the banging and thumping and the men shouting as they put those urns in place this morning! I still don't understand why you bought them and had them sent all the way from Italy,' she grumbled.

'Grandmother, wait till you see them later in the summer.

I am going to have the gardeners fill them with bright, colour-ful flowering plants, the way I saw them planted in Italy, and some flowers will be trailing out, and …'

'Well, I suppose they will at least be patches of colour on that dreary Georgian terrace,' said his grandmother. As Edgar and everyone knew, she always liked to have the last word but Edgar couldn't resist adding one more thing.

'And now that the building of Father's orangery is almost complete, the statues that I also bought in Italy will soon be put in place.'

'Some of them are beautiful, I will admit that,' the old lady conceded. 'But why you had to buy that one in black marble, I can't think! Black marble indeed!'

'You'll see, Grandmother, it will look outstanding amid all the greenery that will be growing in the orangery. And now, will you allow me to escort you downstairs? It must be about time for us to eat, and I'm really hungry.'

Emma smiled, her headache apparently forgotten, as she took Edgar's arm. Although she could be critical and complaining about many things, Emma did not have a bad thought in her head about her eldest grandson. Edgar was 24 and his parents and his grandmother all secretly hoped that he would marry his cousin, Amy. Henry's younger brother, George, was a doctor in a nearby town and had three daughters of whom Amy was the eldest. Emma's second grandson, Thomas, was two years younger than Edgar, and at the age of 22 he was, in his turn, doing the grand tour of Europe. He should be home soon, thought his grandmother, and she hoped that while he had been travelling he would have decided what he planned to do with his life. So far, his only interest seemed to be enjoyment, whether it was visiting London and its theatres, or going to the horse races in Newmarket and York.

'What a good thing,' the old lady had often said to her son

and daughter-in-law, 'that Edgar is the son who will inherit Fortune one day. I don't think Thomas has the right temperament to manage all of Fortune's affairs.'

Her elder granddaughter, Arabella, was 20. She was a clever girl, never happier than when reading a new book, and she taught for some hours every day at the Lady Eleanor School. But her grandmother used to say that she should change her ways or she'd never find a husband.

'Men don't like clever women,' she sometimes admonished Arabella, who had once replied rather tartly that she couldn't imagine wishing to marry any man who wanted a stupid woman for a wife. Arabella had been made to apologise for answering back to her grandmother.

Emma's other granddaughter, Harriet, was only 18, very pretty and already an accomplished flirt, which caused Emma to worry. 'She leads all the men a merry dance,' she often said.

Emma remembered that many years ago her son George, the doctor, had remarked that Henry and his wife Adelaide were producing a baby with indecent precision every two years. Both Emma and Adelaide had said that the only indecent thing was that a gentleman would make such a comment! Adelaide continued to have a baby every second year, but the next two died within an hour of birth, and the birth of their third son, Benjamin, had been so difficult and protracted that some damage had been done to his brain. Benjamin was now 12 and although simple-minded, he had such an affable nature that he was loved by everybody. What he lacked in intelligence was made up for by his good nature. He loved all animals and they in turn responded to him, and he was happiest on days when he was taken over to see the Snowy horses that were bred by a distant cousin, another branch of the Snow family.

Chapter 2

All the family, including Benjamin and his nurse, gathered around the large table for their midday meal. They all ate together again in the evening, except Benjamin who had his evening meal upstairs in the nursery. Today all the talk around the table was of the bronze urns and how they would look when they were filled with flowers.

'I talked to Adam about plants for the urns,' said Henry, 'and he said that someone told him that several years ago similar urns were placed in the gardens of one of the grand houses not too far from here. They have been filled with flowering plants, which make a very good show in summer. Adam suggested that he should ride over and talk to the head gardener there and take a look at the plants that they used. I think this is a good idea, and I am happy to leave the choice of plants and colours to him.'

'As I rode back to the house today, I thought that the orangery looks almost complete,' said Edgar. 'Will the builders finish there soon? I am so anxious to see how the statues look when they are placed there.'

'Why don't they make statues of animals?' asked Benjamin.

'Ah but they do make statues of animals,' said Edgar. 'It just happens that I did not purchase any.'

Benjamin looked downcast. 'I think a statue of a dog would be very beautiful.'

'You are right, Benjamin,' Henry said. 'And do you know

what I shall do? I shall order not just one but two statues of dogs from the same man in Italy who sold Edgar the other statues and the urns.'

Everybody around the table smiled. They were all pleased to indulge Benjamin when they could. He seldom asked for anything and he took so much happiness from small pleasures.

'In fact,' Henry went on, 'I have a surprise for all of you. I wrote to the dealer in Italy some time ago and asked if he could acquire for me a bronze fountain to be placed in the lawns beyond the terrace where the urns are now standing. He sent me some sketches of what he could supply, and said that if I purchase a fountain he will send over workmen with the shipment, and they will erect it here for me. I have arranged for a water engineer in York to come here and advise on the way the pipes should be laid in order to carry water from our wells to the fountain.'

'A fountain! How delightful! And you never said a word to me!' Adelaide was beaming. 'Oh, that will be such an elegant addition to our gardens.'

Arabella and Harriet were beaming too, and Harriet clapped her hands with pleasure. Henry said, 'I don't remember when I've ever done anything that has pleased everybody so much. After we have finished eating, I will show you the sketches that were sent to me so that you can see what this fountain will look like.'

The sketches were laid on a table in front of a large window in the Great Hall and they all gathered round to look.

'Now, what do you think? As you can see, the water jets up in the centre and then falls back into a large shallow bowl, which is supported by four figures. Those figures are said to represent four goddesses,' explained Henry.

'It looks very large,' said Adelaide. 'How high will it be?'

'Ah well, you can't tell from the sketches, of course,' said

Henry, 'but the accompanying notes say that it is just over 8 feet tall. And, especially to please you, Benjamin, I will write to the dealer today and tell him to add two marble statues of dogs to my order.'

For several years there had been a good postal service all over England, so Henry knew that his letter would reach London quickly, and from there be sent on to Italy. With the spread of railways, even mail sent across Europe moved swiftly compared to a few years ago. And now, mused Henry, as he addressed the envelope, since the railway had come all the way to York, travel all over England was easier and quicker than it had ever been. 'And certainly safer, too,' thought Henry. 'There's no danger of a train being held up by highwaymen!' For his own part, as a businessman as well as a farmer, he welcomed these changes because it meant that goods could be sent all over England and on to countries all over Europe easily and quickly.

Emma returned to her rooms to rest in the afternoon, and Adelaide went up to the solar to work on her needlework as she did most afternoons. When Emma had come to Fortune House as a young bride, she had seen the piece of embroidery that had been framed and placed in the Great Hall and she'd been told that when it was first made it had formed part of bed-hangings. And she was touched to hear the story that lay behind the other framed piece of embroidery that also hung in the Great Hall, which was the sampler with the unfinished name at the bottom. She was a skilled needlewoman herself, so she was interested to see work that had been done by women of the Snow family in years gone by.

She told her new husband, 'I should like to make something myself that will become a part of this house,' and soon decided that she, too, would make hangings for the bed she and her husband shared. She went into York to buy supplies and chose a crewelwork design to be worked in shades of blue, her favourite colour.

Many years later, when Adelaide married into the Snow family and came to live at Fortune, she had at first been intimidated by her mother-in-law. Then one day, casting around for a topic to make polite conversation, her eyes fell upon the framed embroideries hanging in the Great Hall. She said, 'This morning I was looking closely at the needlework hanging there and admiring the workmanship.'

'Do you enjoy needlework, Adelaide?' Emma asked her.

'Yes, very much,' said Adelaide. 'My mother taught me to use a needle when I was very young, and I have enjoyed working all kinds of embroidery ever since. I should so much like to make something that would take its place in this house.' She stopped speaking and blushed. 'Oh, does that seem impertinent when I have so recently come into the family?'

'Not impertinent at all, my dear.' It was the first time Emma had used any term of endearment to her new daughter-in-law. 'Why don't we talk about the sort of thing you could make that would be a useful and long-lasting addition to the house?'

And so the beginning of their friendship was founded on a mutual interest. Emma suggested that Adelaide too might like to make bed-hangings for the room she shared with Henry, and Adelaide said that she thought it was a delightful idea.

The two women went into York together to get the supplies that Adelaide would need, and in the carriage on the way home Emma said, 'This day has put me in mind of the time when I was a young bride, just like you. I, too, went into York to choose fabrics and wools for the pieces I intended to embroider.' Turning to Adelaide she went on, 'When we reach Fortune House, I should like you to come up to my bedchamber and see the hangings that I made all those years ago.'

'I should enjoy doing that,' said Adelaide, amazed that her mother-in-law would invite her into her bedchamber.

Now, almost 25 years later, Adelaide was working a design of acanthus leaves and roses in cross stitch on canvas. She was stitching eight pieces and when finished they would be used to make new covers for the seats of the chairs that stood around the large table where the family ate their meals.

Chapter 3

That evening Henry mentioned to Adelaide that he intended to go over to their woollen mill the next day. Fortune had been selling the wool from its sheep to spinners and weavers in many parts of Yorkshire for centuries, but a few years ago, Henry had gone into partnership with two other men and they had built a mill to produce woollen textiles. The machines for carding, combing, spinning and weaving were now steam powered; local pits supplied the coal to fuel the machines, and the huge quantity of soft water that textile-making needed was available from the nearby moorland streams and rivers. The cloth making business was booming in Yorkshire, and the mill used all the wool that the Fortune sheep produced as well as large quantities bought from many other local sheep farmers.

A year ago, Henry's two partners had decided that they were no longer interested in the mill and they had sold their shares of the business to Henry. Although there was an excellent mill manager, Amos Burton, the business demanded a lot of Henry's time and he visited the mill at least once a week. In some ways, Henry was happier now that he was in sole charge. His partners had been interested only in the profits of the mill and had no care for the well being of the workers. While Henry could not afford to be philanthropic, he insisted that his mill workers were treated with the same care and concern that was shown to all the workers at the Fortune estate, and he refused to have any child under the age of ten working in the mill. After he became the sole owner, it was with great pride that he had re-named the mill and it was now called Fortune Textile Mill.

Recently, Henry had talked to Adelaide about the mill.

'When Thomas returns to England,' he said, 'it is my hope and wish that he will learn the textile business and will gradually take over responsibility from me. Amos is very experienced in all aspects of the business and he would guide Thomas and teach him all he needs to know about running the mill. Of course, as the eldest son, Edgar will inherit the whole Fortune estate – the main house, the farms and all the buildings on them, and the cheese business. But as the textile mill is a completely separate entity, it is my intention that in due course I shall make it over to Thomas.'

Now, as Henry set off to ride over to the mill, Adelaide wished that she could shake off the feelings of foreboding that she always had about Henry's intentions that Thomas should take over the textile business. Something in her mind, some instinct, told her that Thomas was not yet ready to settle down to the regularity of a daily job, working with the mill manager, and having responsibility for so many employees. In fact, she wondered if he would ever want to take on such a routine. As his mother, she loved Thomas dearly, but she recognised that so far his interests revolved around pleasure and enjoyment. 'But,' she thought to herself, 'I must try to be more optimistic. He has been travelling for almost a year. When he comes home, perhaps he will have had his fill of pleasure and frivolity. I can but hope so.'

As she watched Henry's horse disappear through the gatehouse, she turned away from the window just as Dorothy, the housekeeper, came into the Great Hall.

'Good morning, Dorothy, and a very fine morning it is too,' said Adelaide.

'Yes, indeed, Madam. Let us hope that this good weather

stays for another two weeks so that we have sunshine for the Mayfair. But we are making preparations in case there is rain that day. All the things that are to be entered in competitions by both the men and the women will be laid out on tables in the old dairy buildings. In fact, my husband Joseph told me that he is going to set two men the task of clearing and cleaning those buildings this morning.'

'Dorothy, I swear that you have read my mind! This very morning I was going to talk to you about preparations for the Mayfair! I do declare, you know the business of Fortune House as well as I do,' said Adelaide. 'Even if I did not say a word to you, I am sure that you would see to it that everything was in hand to make things run smoothly!'

'Thank you, Madam. Of course, I've had a lot of practice. I've been here at Fortune almost as many years as you.'

The two women smiled at each other, comfortable in the familiarity of their roles.

'And will Doctor George and his family be coming to stay here for the Mayfair as usual?' asked Dorothy.

'Yes, that is something else I was going to tell you. I received a letter from his wife yesterday, and they and their three daughters will arrive two days before fair day.'

'I will have their usual rooms prepared, Madam, and I will also have two maids available to take care of all of them and any needs they might have.'

Every year, Henry's brother George, his wife Selina, and their three daughters, came to stay at Fortune House for a few days at the time of the Mayfair. The four adults had become very close friends over the years, and always enjoyed time spent in each other's company. Both families were hoping that Edgar and Amy would marry, though so far neither of them had ever exhibited any signs that they were attracted to each other. When Selina and Adelaide talked about this, they both said that the two of them had been brought up so much together that romantic thoughts probably never entered their minds.

'Now,' said Adelaide, 'tell me all that is happening about the women's competitions at the fair. Are many of the women exhibiting all their usual skills? Are they as enthusiastic as usual?'

'More enthusiastic than ever, I'd say, Madam. We shall have to set up extra tables for all the things they've made to exhibit! And some of the very young girls who have never entered the competitions in the past are doing so this year.'

'Oh, I'm so glad. That is good news,' said Adelaide. 'The competition every year is such a good way of keeping all the old crafts and handiwork alive. There are so many things made on machines nowadays. When I was last in York I was even shown lace that had been made on a machine! I don't think it is nearly as beautiful as the handmade lace but of course it costs a great deal less so it's popularity is growing, I'm told.

'Dorothy,' Adelaide continued, 'it is a lovely spring morning. Let us walk down together to see the space that is available for all the exhibits and how everything will be laid out.'

Both women put on bonnets and capes and set off for the old dairy buildings. On the way, they passed several cottages where farm workers and their families were housed. Three of the women who lived there were standing outside in the sunshine, chatting together.

Adelaide paused as they reached the group. 'Good morning to all of you.'

A chorus of 'Good mornings' came back to her and two of them bobbed a curtsey. The third tried to curtsey but was hampered by a very large baby in her arms. Adelaide paused to speak to her.

'Isn't that your little son Harry who was so sickly in his first months?' she asked. When the woman said yes, Adelaide went on, 'Well there is nothing sickly about him now, is there! He must be quite a weight for you to lift and carry. No doubt you are looking forward to him standing and walking on his own soon!'

She turned to one of the other women, 'Becky, I hope you have made your excellent honey and lavender soaps again this year. You know that my sister-in-law always likes to buy your soap when they come here for the Mayfair.'

'Oh yes, Milady. I have a good supply and this year I have also made a new variety. It is a soap scented with rose petals.'

As Adelaide and Dorothy continued towards the old dairy buildings, Adelaide said, 'I have known all the women who live and work at Fortune for so many years now. I've shared both their joys and their sadnesses, and I've seen so many of them born, grow up and marry, and now they have children of their own.'

'I think everybody who works and lives here feels very much part of what we call the Fortune family,' said Dorothy. 'Oh, Madam, I hope you don't take it that I am forgetting my place when I say that we feel part of the family. It is because we appreciate so much everything that you and Sir Henry do for all of us. There are not many places where all the people who work on the estate feel themselves to be valued and cared for, the way we feel here at Fortune.'

Chapter 4

After George and Selina and their three daughters arrived, it seemed that Fortune House rang with laughter from morning till night. The two families got along together very well, and it had long been established that in the evenings they played games together. When the children were younger it was games such as 'Hunt the Thimble' or 'I Spy', then as they grew older they liked to play games that involved one of them hiding somewhere in the house and the others having to search through many rooms to find them. In this game of 'Hide and Seek' the hiding places became ever more inventive, until one year when it was Thomas's turn to hide, he had gone into his parents' bedroom and climbed on top of the canopy over their four-poster bed. While the other children were hunting for him, they heard a sudden noise and a yell and, following the sound, they found him fallen on to the bed with all the fabric of the canopy ripped and hanging down.

Adult wrath descended on Thomas quickly.

'You damned young fool, you could have broken your neck,' said his Uncle George. Then, being a doctor, he added, 'Let me check you over ... have you turned an ankle? Twisted an elbow or wrist?' When he was assured that Thomas was fine, his anger returned. 'Well count yourself lucky, lad, and don't do such a stupid thing again.'

Meanwhile Thomas's mother and grandmother were in tears over the torn fabric.

'Thomas! How could you! Oh I'm too upset and angry to speak to you!' exclaimed his mother.

'Oh, dear, that canopy has been there, in place, since before

I came here as a bride,' said Emma, his grandmother, snuffling and dabbing at her eyes.

'Well, then, it's obviously very old fabric and probably would have needed replacing anyway!' Thomas retorted, climbing off the bed.

His father reached out and slapped him hard across the side of his head.

'Don't ever, ever, speak to your grandmother like that again! Do you hear me? Now you apologise to her at once. At once!'

Nowadays those youthful games had been replaced by adult games in which everybody took part. Some were games of cards and some were riddles that had to be solved. The evenings always ended in so much laughter that the women and girls would have tears running down their cheeks. Emma would hold her sides and say she had laughed so much that her ribs ached, and Benjamin's nurse would say that she would have difficulty getting him to sleep after so much excitement.

This year, at the end of the second evening that the two families had spent together, Adelaide and Henry were in their bedchamber and Adelaide said, 'We are so fortunate that you and your brother and his wife and I, as well as all our children, enjoy so much our time spent together. One hears so often of families who do not like each other's company, or a father and son who have had such arguments that they barely speak.'

'We are indeed lucky to have such a close, happy family. The only thing that would have made this evening even happier for me would have been to have had Thomas home from his grand tour, and ready to take his place in the family business.'

As soon as he said this, Adelaide had the familiar feelings of doubt that Thomas would do what his father hoped. 'But,' she thought, 'time enough to worry about that when it happens, indeed, *if* it happens,' and, as usual, she said nothing of her anxieties to Henry.

The next day, Mayfair day, was such a beautiful day that all over the Fortune estate, everyone was saying to each other, 'Isn't this a perfect May Day?' and 'Couldn't be better!' and 'We are always so lucky for the fair ... I don't remember it ever raining on May Day!'

Everyone who was exhibiting plants, flowers or their crafts, put everything on display early. Adam, the head gardener, gave pride of place in the centre of the table to a new rose he had bred. It was almost pure white, with just the faintest blush of pink at the edge of the petals, and as he put it on display he muttered a prayer of thanks that this bloom was at the perfect stage, between bud and full blown.

Everybody – family, workers, visitors – walked around admiring everything that was on show, until Henry called for their attention as he was ready to crown the girl who had been chosen Queen of the May. As Henry placed the crown on her head, everybody cheered and clapped, and the girl blushed prettily. Henry turned to the crowd and said, 'I do declare, the girl chosen to be May Queen is prettier each year,' and she blushed even more.

Then Henry watched all the men's competitions, and later he and Adelaide walked around the displays of fruits, flowers, vegetables, and the jams, sauces, cordials, herbal oils and ointments, soaps, baskets, and lace made by the women. As usual, Selina spoke to Becky, the woman who made the soap she liked, and arranged for her to bring a basket full of soaps to Fortune House later, when Selina would pay her for them. All three of her daughters talked to the lace makers and bought pretty lace from them.

As Adelaide and Henry approached the tables that held

the flower exhibits, Adam stepped forward and gestured to the beautiful rose in the centre of the exhibits.

'I have bred this new rose myself,' he said proudly. 'As you will see, it is almost completely snow-white. I would like to give this rose a name and, with respect, I ask your permission to call it "Lady Snow".'

A small cheer went up from the people standing around who could hear what Adam had said. Adelaide blushed as much as the May Queen had done, and Henry said, 'I think that is a charming compliment to which I have no objection and I am sure my dear wife will be delighted by your kind gesture.' He turned and asked, 'Isn't that so, my dear?'

Adelaide took a small step towards Adam, and said, 'It is not usual for women to speak in public but on this occasion I wish to do so. Thank you, Adam, I am flattered by your kindness in naming the rose for me. This is another event to be written in the chronicles of the Snow family and Fortune estate.'

Then everyone was asked to gather around the maypole, as Sir Henry was about to present the prizes to the winners of each category of competition. Before he could do so, the Reverend Dr Bagshaw, who was the headmaster at the large school for boys in neighbouring Middleby, approached, doffed his hat and bowed.

'Sir Henry, Lady Snow, what a splendid day it is for the fair.'

'How nice to see you again, Dr Bagshaw,' said Henry, and the others all inclined their heads towards him.

'May I present Mr Andrew Corfield, who has newly joined our school as assistant headmaster. Andrew, this is Sir Henry and Lady Snow, their son Edgar, and their two daughters, Miss Arabella Snow and Miss Harriet.'

All the ladies bobbed slightly to Andrew Corfield, and Henry said, 'I hope you will enjoy living and working in this part of Yorkshire.'

Mr Corfield bowed, 'Sir Henry, Lady Snow,' and then turned and bowed to Edgar, Arabella and Harriet.

There was no more time for conversation because Henry said, 'You will excuse me please, I must present prizes to the winners of the competitions held here today.'

As usual, he had a few words with each of the winners, and then he announced the name of the man who had won the most prizes, and was this year's recipient of the Fortune pewter platter. After he had presented it, Henry turned to the assembled crowd and spoke again.

'I have one more announcement to make. This year, I am going to start another Fortune tradition. Until now, nothing has been awarded to the woman who has won the most prizes. From this year on, however, that situation will be remedied and there will also be a special prize for her. I have had a silversmith in York make up a brooch in the form of a large letter "F" and a similar silver brooch will be presented to the winner each year. It is my pleasure to tell you that this year's winner is Bessie Budge.'

He turned to the woman who had the large baby called Harry that had been a sickly infant. She stepped forward and bobbed a curtsey as he gave her the brooch.

'Oh Sir. Oh Sir.' She could say no more. Dorothy the housekeeper stepped over to her and gave her a hug. 'Well done, Bessie,' she said and the crowd all applauded.

After Henry had presented the prizes, Andrew Corfield chatted to Arabella and Harriet. For once Harriet's prettiness and flirtatious manner was lost on a man. Andrew was paying attention only to Arabella.

'I have heard that you teach in the village school, so we have something in common. I would enjoy hearing about your work at the Lady Eleanor School,' he said. 'I wonder if you will permit me to call upon you one afternoon?'

'I am always free in the afternoons, as I only work in the mornings. I shall look forward to your visit,' said Arabella.

As the two families started to make their way back to the house, and all the stalls were being cleared and dismantled, and the things that had been entered in competition were being taken away by their owners, there was a loud clap of thunder. The day that had been so gloriously sunny suddenly changed and became overcast as huge black clouds rolled across the sky. The first large drops of rain fell and everyone hurried to collect their belongings and make their way home. The rain quickly became heavier, and as Edgar looked around to make sure that all his family were on their way back to the house, he found that Amy was hurrying along just behind him. Lightning streaked across the sky, followed immediately by another clap of thunder and the rain started to come down even more heavily.

'Quick … in here.' Edgar grabbed Amy's arm and they went through an archway at the end of one of the old dairy buildings. 'We'll stay here until the heaviest rain has passed.'

'Thank goodness we were just beside this place,' said Amy. 'It is still some distance to walk to the house from here.' She gave a sudden yelp as there was another clap of thunder, so loud that it seemed to shake the building.

Edgar put his arm around her. 'Don't be afraid. We're safe here, and we will stay until the rain has passed.'

'I'm not afraid. It was just that the thunder startled me,' Amy said, and started to pull away. Then she realised how much she liked having his arm around her shoulder. Instinctively, she turned towards him, and as she did so, his other arm went around her and she leaned in closer to him.

Edgar looked down at her. 'Amy, I know this is going to

sound silly but as I look at you, I feel as if I've never really seen you before. We've known each other for so many years, since we were children, and I have not noticed that you have grown up and become a truly beautiful young woman. In fact, Amy, I think you are the most beautiful woman I've ever seen!'

'It doesn't sound in the slightest bit silly,' Amy assured him. 'Because I have only just realised that you are a very handsome young man. How can it be that I haven't noticed until now?'

Chapter 5

Nobody noticed that Edgar and Amy reached Fortune House long after the rest of the family had arrived there. All the talk was of the storm and its intensity, and everybody said how lucky it was that the heavy rain hadn't come down earlier in the day when all the competitions were taking place.

George and Selina talked about their plans to leave in the morning. 'We don't have to rush away too early,' said George. 'I do not have any patients coming to see me till the day after tomorrow, and I've arranged for the other doctor to see any of my patients who might need urgent attention.'

He turned to his mother and added, 'Mother, in the morning we will all come to your bedchamber to see you before we leave, so you do not have to rise early.'

'I do feel rather tired, I must admit,' said Emma. 'I've been on my feet for several hours, walking all around the fair and I think I managed to speak with everybody I know. Very enjoyable, but rather tiring at my age.'

'Mother, it is tiring for anybody at any age!' interjected Henry. 'I for one am looking forward to us having a quiet supper together, followed by a leisurely evening.'

Not surprisingly, all the talk that evening was of the fair, and they all agreed that it had been the biggest and best ever.

'It really has become a major event for all the village and also for people who live in the surrounding area,' said Adelaide. 'I saw people who told me that they had walked all the way from Little Denton and from Middleby. They are both at least four miles away!'

Amy and Edgar talked quietly together the whole evening but nobody seemed to notice. They were discreet and stayed close to the others so that it was not very obvious that they were engrossed in talking only with each other and were not taking part in the general conversation.

Next morning, George and his family were assembled near the great front door after breakfast. The maids had packed their belongings and brought them down so that they were ready to be placed in their coach.

Selina carried the basket full of soaps herself. 'Doesn't this soap smell delightful! I am so pleased to buy it each year. As you know, all my daughters and I use only this soap and no other. If ever Becky wants to set up in business, I would think of putting up the money to start her in a little shop!'

'Come along,' said George, 'let's go up and say goodbye to Mother. Amy ... come along with us.' Amy had been standing to one side of the hall, talking to Edgar, but now she dutifully followed her father up the stairs, with her mother and sisters.

When they came down George looked concerned.

'Henry, Adelaide, I am a little worried about mother. She is still in bed and says she is very tired and intends to stay there resting until the midday meal.'

'As soon as you have left, we will both go up and see her,' Adelaide assured him. 'And if we think she should rest all day, I will insist that she takes her meals in her room.'

'But you know what she's like. She never wants to be fussed over!' said Selina. 'It's difficult to make her rest sometimes.'

Adelaide and Henry assured George and his family that

they would keep a close watch on Emma, and Henry said that if he felt it warranted it, he would send a messenger and ask George to come back. Meanwhile, Edgar and Amy were saying their goodbyes privately in a corner near the door. Selina looked around, 'Now where is Amy? Ah, there you are, come along, we're about to leave.'

Edgar spoke up quite loudly, 'Well, goodbye Amy. As I have told you, I have some business that will take me to Moortown in just two days so I will call at your house and see you again then.'

Henry started to say, 'I didn't know you had to go to Moortown' but Adelaide silenced him with a look. Amy had gone quite pink and hurried out to the waiting coach. Then everybody was waving, shouting their goodbyes. 'Thank you for a most enjoyable stay at Fortune House,' and the coachmen started up the horses, and Doctor George, Selina and their three daughters had gone.

Henry turned to Edgar. 'You are going to Moortown in a couple of days? What's that about, then?'

'Oh, er ... it's something Jack Henson, the farm manager, asked me to check on. A man who bought some of our cattle ...' Edgar's explanation drifted off into nothing.

Adelaide said briskly, 'Henry, come with me, there is something I need to show you.' She turned away and Henry followed. She went into the business room, and shut the door behind them.

'Henry. When Edgar made that remark about going to Moortown, I happened to be looking in Amy's direction and I noticed that she was flushed very pink. And did you see the way she hurried out to the coach?'

'Yes, now that I think of it ...' Henry started to say, but Adelaide went on, 'And then my mind started to put together things to which I'd paid no attention. Yesterday, they arrived back at the house a long while after everybody else had come back, and then last night, while we were all conversing generally, the two of them sat slightly off to one side, talking only to each other. And now, suddenly, Edgar says he is going to see her again in just two days when he goes to Moortown, and he is going there, as we have both noticed, on business that we knew nothing about!'

'Do you think ... is it possible, after all this time, that they have suddenly noticed each other? I mean noticed each other as grown up young people, not as childhood friends?' Henry wondered.

'That is what I am thinking. And that is what I am hoping, as I know you are too,' said Adelaide.

For the next two days, Edgar talked of anything and everything but his forthcoming visit to Moortown. On the morning he was leaving he said in a very casual manner, 'I shall be off to Moortown straight after breakfast. I will take care of my business there as quickly as possible, and then I shall call in to see Aunt Selina before I start home.'

'Yes, dear. That will be nice. We shall expect to see you for supper this evening,' said Adelaide, fixing Henry with a look that said 'don't say another word!'

As they both went up to see Emma, Henry asked, 'Do you think we should tell Mother of our suspicions about Edgar and Amy? She would be delighted to think they might marry, as we've all always hoped.'

'I don't know,' said Adelaide. 'She still seems so tired. She has not been downstairs since the day of the fair. I think perhaps we should just let her rest and not excite her. After all, Edgar has said nothing to us, and we presume that he has not yet spoken to George, as Amy's father, about any intentions he may have. No, better to leave things as they are for a while, I think. If we told her, she would be pleased and excited, and it would be such a pity if our hopes came to nought.'

Adelaide, Henry and their two daughters were halfway through eating supper when Edgar arrived. He apologised profusely for his lateness, then tucked into his supper saying, 'Mmmm … oh this is good … delicious,' and Adelaide thought, 'Well, he's certainly not lovesick enough to be losing his appetite!'

As the family sat talking after their meal, Edgar said, 'I must talk to Jack Henson tomorrow morning. He may need me to go over to Moortown again in a few days.'

'Why should you have to go again so soon?' Henry asked. 'You usually go there only twice a year, when the livestock sales are on.'

'It's just that we think – that is, I talked to Jack and he agrees – that we could sell more of our beasts at the livestock markets there. And it is very convenient – not so far for the drovers to take the animals to market.'

'Yes, I see. Yes, it is much closer than Beverley or any of the other cattle and sheep markets.' Then Henry added in a casual tone, 'Will you call in to see your aunt and cousins again while you are there?'

'Yes, I had thought that I might. I find their company very congenial,' said Edgar.

His answer was said so smoothly and casually that Henry and Adelaide exchanged looks, both thinking that their son had grown up quite suddenly. Adelaide pretended to stifle a yawn in order to hide the fact that she was smiling broadly.

'I know that you see your grandmother at least once each day, Edgar,' said Henry, 'but do make sure that, when you go to Moortown again, you go in to see her before you leave. I want you to be able to give your Uncle George a fresh report on her health. She still seems to have so little energy and your mother and I both think she is becoming frail.'

On the afternoon of the day that Edgar was away in Moortown, Emma's personal maid, Myrtle, sent word to Adelaide asking her to come up to Emma's room. When Adelaide went in, Myrtle said, 'I am not one to worry unnecessarily, as you know, but I am quite anxious about Lady Emma's condition. She seems not to respond when I speak to her, and …'

Adelaide went straight over to Emma's bed and stood beside it. 'Mother-in-law, how are you feeling now? Not as good as this morning?' Emma's eyelids fluttered open and though she looked at Adelaide, her gaze did not seem to focus properly.

Adelaide bent over the bed and took one of Emma's hands in both of hers, 'Are you feeling worse? Would you like me to get that nice young doctor to come in to take a look at you?'

Emma took a deep breath and tried to say something but what she said was indistinct.

'Tell me again, if you can,' said Adelaide.

This time Emma clearly said one word: 'George.'

'Yes, yes. We'll get George to come here at once. A man will ride over there on the fastest horse we have.'

Adelaide turned to leave the room, saying to Myrtle, 'Stay with her. Assure her that I will be back within minutes and that I will bring Henry with me. And also tell her that George will be on his way very soon.'

Chapter 6

At the same time that the rider was making his way from Fortune to Moortown, Edgar was standing in George's rooms.

'Well, Edgar, you asked to see me. What is it about? And do sit down lad, you look very uncomfortable standing there.'

'It's about ...' Suddenly Edgar's voice deserted him. He took a deep breath, cleared his throat and started again.

'I have come to ask your permission to marry Amy,' the words tumbled out in a rush. 'Oh, I'm sorry, Uncle George. I should have put that in a less direct way, but ...'

'No, no, my boy. I prefer people who are direct. Wastes less time, don't you know! Now, do sit down. I don't like to sit here talking up to you, it makes my neck ache!' Edgar sat down, but he perched nervously on the edge of his seat.

'Well, I said that I prefer people who are direct and don't waste time, so I will be equally direct with you. I am delighted to give my consent to you marrying my daughter Amy. And I know that your Aunt Selina will be just as happy as I am.' George came round his desk, and held out his hand to shake Edgar's. 'It's what we've always hoped for, my boy, and I will tell you outright that I know your parents have always hoped for such a marriage too. And now,' he said with a twinkle in his eye and a broad smile on his face, 'shall we go and find the young lady and tell her that she will soon be a bride?'

George came out of his rooms shouting for Selina. 'Come here, Selina, Amy. Both of you come here.'

They both came into the central hall of the house at a run.

'What's happening? What's all this shouting, George?'
asked Selina.

Amy took one look at Edgar's beaming face and said,
'You've talked to him?'

Edgar nodded.

George turned to his wife and said, 'Selina, you and Amy
had better start making plans for a marriage. I know how
long women take to attend to all the details of a wedding!'

Selina turned to Edgar, held out her arms and hugged him,
tears of joy running down her cheeks.

'Oh I'm so pleased. I'm so happy. Do your parents know
that you were going to speak to George today?'

Edgar started to say no but got no further, because as he
started to speak there was a loud insistent knocking at the
front door.

'What on earth?' George was at the door in two long
strides and wrenched it open. The rider from Fortune stood
there.

'Sir, please come at once. Your mother, old Lady Snow ...'
George did not need to be told any more. He turned to go to
the back of the house, shouting, 'Get my horse. At once.
Edgar, come with me, we will ride together.'

Selina realised what was happening and said, 'Amy and I
will follow in the carriage. We will be there as soon as
possible.'

George and Edgar set off at a gallop, and kept their horses
going as fast as possible all the way to Fortune. Dorothy, the
housekeeper, had been watching for them, and as they came
up the drive, she threw the door wide open. She bobbed a
quick curtsey, and they flung their coats and hats to her as
they rushed towards the foot of the stairs.

'How is my mother? What is the latest news of her

condition?' George called over his shoulder as he and Edgar went up the stairs at a run.

'There's no change, I'm afraid, Sir.' Dorothy's answer was scarcely heard by the two men as they reached the top of the stairs. They paused, looked at each other briefly, and then went to the door to Emma's room.

'We will go in quietly,' admonished George, and Edgar nodded. He felt stunned. He almost felt that he could not take in the situation fully and had to keep saying over and over to himself, 'This is my grandmother. My grandmother is dying.'

As they entered the room they saw that Henry stood on one side of the bed, and Adelaide stood on the side nearest to them. She was holding one of Emma's hands, and saying something softly and gently. She turned and moved towards the head of the bed, without letting go of Emma's hand, so that George could take her place nearest to his mother. Edgar went to the far side of the bed and stood next to his father. He bent over and took his grandmother's other hand and kissed it gently.

'Mother, it's George. I'm here. And Selina and Amy are on their way.' There was no response from Emma. Her breathing was very shallow, almost imperceptible. George nodded across the bed towards Edgar. 'Speak to her,' he whispered.

'Grandmother, it's Edgar. I'm here too.' The faintest smile seemed to touch Emma's lips. Without taking his eyes off his grandmother's face, Edgar whispered to George, 'Did she hear me, do you think?'

George whispered back, 'She is deeply unconscious, but it is possible she heard and knows it is you. Many people in the medical profession believe that even when a patient is unconscious, the hearing remains. Speak to her again.'

Edgar bent closer to his grandmother. 'Grandmother, dearest. I've come to tell you some wonderful news.' Again there was the smallest movement at the corners of Emma's mouth.

Edgar took a deep breath, looked at his mother and father and very quietly murmured, 'I'm sorry. I have not had time to tell you first.' Then he turned away from them.

'Grandmother, my wonderful news is that Amy and I are to be married. Amy will be my wife!'

Now there was no mistaking it. A smile, just a faint smile, pulled at Emma's mouth.

'She's trying to speak,' said George and they all bent closer.

Very faintly, Emma said, 'Good' or was it 'Glad'? Afterwards, none of the people present were sure which word she had said.

With the smile still on her lips she let out a long sighing breath. George slipped his fingers around her wrist and felt for her pulse. Then he bent and put his ear to her chest and placed his fingers on the side of her neck, feeling again for the pulse.

He straightened up, tears in his eyes, and said in an almost inaudible voice, 'She's gone.'

He bent and gently kissed her cheek. As he straightened up, Henry, standing on the other side of the bed, did the same. Edgar, beside him, also kissed her cheek, and then his mother Adelaide, standing beside George, leaned forward and kissed Emma on the forehead. From the foot of the bed came a muffled sob. Everybody had forgotten that Emma's maid Myrtle was also in the room.

Adelaide went to her, put an arm around her and said gently, 'Come, Myrtle, come and say your goodbyes. You and Emma have been together a very long time.'

Myrtle wiped her eyes, came to the side of the bed where

Adelaide had been standing, and dropping to her knees, took Emma's hand in hers and whispered a short prayer.

George cleared his throat and said, 'Er, Adelaide … what is the name of the woman who attends to …'

There was no need for him to finish. Adelaide said, 'Nellie Gentry. She is both midwife and … I will send for her to come at once.'

When Adelaide stepped out of Emma's room she found that several of the household staff had gathered there, along with Dorothy and her husband.

'Joseph,' said Adelaide, 'please go to Nellie Gentry and tell her to come.' As soon as the group of servants heard the message sending for Nellie Gentry, they knew that what they had been expecting had happened. Two or three of them bent their heads in silent prayer, and one of the men went down on one knee.

Adelaide went back into Emma's room and took Myrtle by the elbow and said, 'Come, Myrtle, come and sit outside her room for a while.'

Henry, George and Edgar all now came out to the large upper hall. Henry immediately went to Myrtle and said, 'You were more than a personal maid to my mother. You and she have been together for many years but there is nothing you can do for her now, so please go home and rest. Of course, you may come back and see her again after Nellie Gentry has completed her tasks.'

Henry's mind now turned to practical matters. 'I will send for the vicar to come here tomorrow morning so that we can arrange mother's funeral. I shall suggest to the vicar that it might be suitable for the bishop to conduct the funeral service. And I will have word passed around that every worker at Fortune shall have time free that day to attend the funeral in the church.'

Just then they heard the main door being opened. Selina

and Amy had arrived. George said he would go down and tell them the news, and Adelaide, Henry and Edgar said, 'We will come down too.'

While they were all still in the Great Hall, and tears were being shed, Nellie Gentry came from the back of the house into the hall. She bobbed a curtsey to the family group, and turned towards the stairs. Henry went over and said, 'Nellie, thank you for coming so quickly. As soon as you have completed your tasks with my mother, please let us know so that we can come up and see her.'

'Now,' he continued, turning back to the family, 'I think we all need some refreshment. Adelaide please have tea brought to us.'

While they waited for tea, Edgar said, 'Mother and Father, I know that it was a gross breach of normal good manners that I did not acquaint both of you first with the news that Amy and I are to be married. But I wanted grandmother to know. I thought the news would please her.'

'And it did please her, I'm sure,' said Adelaide. 'We all saw her smile and we heard her say … what was it? Was it "good" or "glad"? Whichever it was, we know that she was pleased to hear the news, as indeed are your father and I. And of course you were right to break the news when you did. Neither of us would expect you to hold back in such circumstances.'

She turned to Amy. 'And now, dear Amy, come and let me embrace you. I cannot say that I welcome you to the Snow family, as you are already a Snow, but I say most sincerely that I welcome you as a daughter-in-law.' She kissed Amy's cheek.

'And I welcome you too,' said Henry. 'Come, let me kiss the bride-to-be!'

Selina said, 'I think Emma would have been very glad that

the sadness of her death was eased by this joyous news. She would have been happy that the two events occurred on the very same day.'

Chapter 7

As soon as the vicar arrived at the house, he was shown into the business room where Henry and George were awaiting him.

'May I express my condolences and extend my sympathy to both of you and your families,' said the vicar. 'The Dowager Lady Snow was well known to so many people, and liked and respected by all. I could scarce believe the news when I was told. I spoke to her just a few days ago at the Mayfair and she seemed so well, walking around and wanting to see everything.'

Henry said, 'It has come as a surprise to all of us. But we can be thankful that she did not suffer a long illness. And now,' Henry cleared his throat and continued briskly, 'let us discuss the arrangements for her funeral.'

'May I suggest, Sir Henry, that it would be appropriate if I contact the bishop and ask him to come here to conduct the service?'

'Yes, I think that would be a very good idea.' Henry was relieved that the vicar had suggested it himself, as he had been concerned that the vicar might feel slighted that he was not conducting the service. 'Of course, we – the family that is – would want you to play a part in the service, as the vicar of my mother's local church.'

To allow for the time it would take to send a messenger to the bishop, and for him to travel to Fortune, it was decided that the funeral would be held in five days' time. Henry and

George both agreed that their mother would prefer a simple service, and they would ask the organist to play her favourite hymn as the coffin was carried out of the church for interment in the family vault in the churchyard.

'I wonder if anybody has ever counted up the number of Snow family members who lie there,' commented George.

'Oh, the names are all in the parish records,' said the vicar. 'It would be quite a simple matter for me to draw up a list for you.'

'I would be grateful if you would do that,' said Henry. 'Lady Snow notes everything of importance that happens to the Snow family and the Fortune estate in documents that she has been writing since we were first married.'

The vicar said that he would now go back to the church to start attending to all the details of the funeral.

'I will have the bell tolled once for every year of the late Lady Snow's life, and I will instruct the organist and the gravediggers to make preparations.'

As the great door opened and the vicar stepped out, the sunshine seemed brighter than usual because the house, being in mourning, had the heavy curtains pulled halfway across the windows, making the inside gloomy.

As soon as the vicar had left Henry said to George, 'I have it in mind to give mother's engagement ring to Edgar, so that he in turn can give it to Amy to mark their betrothal. It is an old fashioned setting but the stones are good and he can have it re-set. What do you think? Do you agree?'

George immediately said that he thought it was an excellent idea.

'Have you mentioned it to Edgar yet?' he asked. 'I am sure both he and Amy will be touched by your thought and most happy to have mother's ring.'

When the family were all sitting together after their midday meal, Henry said, 'Edgar, I have your grandmother's engagement ring here. I have thought to give it to you so that Amy can wear it to mark your intention to marry. I think it is appropriate, since she was grandmother to both of you.' Henry held out the ring to Edgar. It was quite a heavy gold ring, set with a diamond in the centre and a ruby on each side. 'It is, of course, rather old fashioned but the jeweller in York could design a new setting.'

Edgar was holding the ring, and he turned to Amy, saying, 'I think it is beautiful and I feel honoured, Father, that you are giving it to me. I hope you like it too, Amy?'

Amy blinked back tears and said, 'I am very touched by this gesture. I think the ring is beautiful, and it is a very kind thought, Father-in-law.' She turned to Edgar and said, 'I do not think I would want it re-designed. I would like to preserve the memory of our grandmother by keeping it just as it is.'

Adelaide could contain herself no longer. 'Oh Edgar, as Amy likes it, do put it on her finger now!'

Edgar raised the ring to his lips, kissed it, and said, 'I am so happy that you have agreed to be my wife, Amy,' and he put the ring on her finger.

They both immediately broke into laughter.

'Well,' said Edgar, 'we do not want to have the ring reset, but we will have to have it made smaller. What tiny hands you have, Amy!'

The whole family laughed, glad to have something to relieve the sombre mood of the house. Just then Harriet, who was sitting facing the window, said, 'Somebody is coming up the drive. I do not recognise the rider.'

Adelaide said, 'I will speak to Dorothy. She will explain to whoever it is that we are in mourning and cannot receive visitors.'

'Oh,' burst out Arabella, looking out of the window, 'I know who it is. It is that young Mr Corfield, the new assistant headmaster. Dr Bagshaw introduced him to us at the Mayfair.'

'Oh dear,' said Adelaide. 'He has obviously not heard about your grandmother's death. The news would not yet have reached Middleby. Perhaps I should speak to him myself and explain the circumstances.' Adelaide left the room and went towards the door.

As a servant opened the door, Adelaide looked out and saw a groom taking the horse's bridle. The rider had dismounted and started towards the steps. He looked up, saw her standing there, and taking off his hat, bowed.

'Lady Snow, I thought it was such a beautiful day that I would ride over to Fortune House and pay a call upon you.' He had now reached her, as she stood at the open door.

'Mr Corfield,' she inclined her head to him and, gesturing to her black gown, she said, 'As you can see I am in mourning. It is my sad duty to tell you that Sir Henry's mother has died.'

'Lady Snow, you have no need to say more. Please allow me to express my sympathy and also my apologies for coming at such a time. Of course, we have not heard this sad news at Middleby.' He bowed to her again. 'I will leave at once.'

'Mr Corfield, it seems churlish to turn you away, even in these circumstances. Won't you please come in and join us for tea? The whole family are here; my daughters, my son Edgar, and my husband's brother and his family. You met all of us at the Mayfair.'

'Lady Snow, I will be pleased to join you, if you are sure that you would welcome a visitor at such a time? I will not stay long.'

Chapter 8

Andrew Corfield stayed longer than he had expected on that first visit. All the members of the Snow family were pleased to see him again and after he had left they all told Adelaide that she had made the right decision, to waive the formalities of family mourning, and invite him to join them.

'I am so pleased that you asked him to come in,' said Henry, 'but also very surprised because in so many ways, you are a most conventional woman and abide by the rules of society quite firmly.'

'You are right, my dear,' replied Adelaide, 'but I also believe that good manners mainly consist of making other people feel comfortable and at ease in one's company. Mr Corfield obviously had no way of knowing that your mother had died and was embarrassed to have arrived at such a time. I felt that it was considerate to make him feel welcome.'

'And I'm glad, too,' said Selina. 'What a charming young man he is, and how easily he fitted in with our family group.'

Benjamin's nurse came in and said that it was time for her to take Benjamin for his afternoon walk, and after they had left, Arabella said, 'I think Mr Corfield must be an excellent teacher. Did you notice how easily he talked with Benjamin? I think he has the gift of being able to engage children in conversation. I've seldom seen Benjamin so animated when talking with an adult, especially someone he does not know. I know from teaching children in the school that they respond naturally to someone who is genuinely interested in them.'

'And young Mr Corfield seems to be genuinely interested

in you, too, Arabella!' Henry teased her. 'You certainly talked together for quite some time.'

'Oh Father! Mr Corfield was asking me about the Lady Eleanor School. He wanted to know how many children attend the school, and what subjects I teach. I enjoyed talking to someone who shares my interest in the schooling of young children.'

'Well, you will be able to continue that conversation, I'm sure,' said Adelaide, 'because as your father and I walked Mr Corfield to the door when he left, he asked if he might call on us again, after the funeral formalities are over. We both said that we would be delighted to see him again.'

Henry said, 'I'm sorry to change the subject, my dear, but while the family are all together, I would like to tell you about some thoughts I have had and I would like to know how each of you feel.' He looked around; everybody was watching him, waiting for his next words. 'You just mentioned the Lady Eleanor School, Arabella, and as everybody here knows that was founded by a Lady Snow long ago. And there are the Elizabeth Houses, which were also founded by a former Lady Snow. I have been thinking that I would like to endow something bearing my mother's name. It should be something that would benefit the people who work for the Snow family and the Fortune estate.'

'I like the sound of your thoughts so far,' said George. 'Please continue.'

'When I was talking to Myrtle the other day, I realised that having been my mother's personal maid for a very long time, she is now elderly herself. I am thinking that I would like to endow almshouses in my mother's name. We could build a few small cottages, perhaps ten, for the use of people, such as Myrtle, who have worked most of their lives here.'

'It's a good idea, Henry,' said George, 'but when any of

our people stop working they stay on in the homes we have provided for them during their working lives. So they already have somewhere to live. What would be the purpose of additional accommodation?'

'It's true, they do normally stay on in the cottage that they are living in when they stop working. But I think that it would be pleasant for them to live the rest of their lives in a comfortable cottage surrounded by a group of people of similar age, all retired from many years in our employ. Also there would be a benefit to the Fortune estate in that the cottage that they had been living in would become available to whoever took over their work. So really, I suppose, what it comes down to is that instead of building more cottages to house employees, we would have a small group of cottages to house the retired people.'

'Yes, that makes good sense, Father,' Edgar spoke up for the first time. 'It has always been a Fortune tradition that we take care of our employees when they are too old to work, and I think that almshouses would be a very good idea. Also, you said that you thought of endowing them in grandmother's name, so would they be known as the Lady Emma Almshouses? I think that would be an excellent way of perpetuating her name.'

'I'm glad you approve, Edgar,' said Henry. 'I want all of us to agree on this use of money from the Fortune estate, but it is especially important that you, as the heir to Fortune, think it is a good idea. Can I take it that everybody is in agreement?'

They all nodded. 'Good. I will give more thought to these ideas after the funeral, then I will get an architect to come and discuss plans for such buildings.'

When Emma left Fortune House for the last time, her coffin was borne on the shoulders of her sons Henry and George, her grandson Edgar, Adam the head gardener, the housekeeper's husband, Joseph, and the farm manager, Jack Henson. When the plans were being made for the funeral procession from the house to the church Henry had taken Benjamin to one side and explained that all the men carrying the coffin had to be about the same height. 'But you are her grandson, too, Ben, and will have an important place in the cortege. I want you to walk immediately behind the coffin.'

All the way to the gatehouse the drive was lined with workers employed in the house and the gardens and the farm. All stood silently, the men bareheaded, as the small funeral procession passed. Inside the church, the family members took their places in the front pews, and everybody else filed in, completely filling the small, ancient church. The bishop conducted the traditional funeral service, with the vicar reading two of the prayers. After both Henry and George had spoken about their mother, Edgar made his way forward and mounted the two steps to the pulpit.

He stood facing everybody and said, 'I want to say just a few words to all of you. In the past week or so, I have learned what I think is an important lesson that I shall remember for the rest of my life. Just a few days before my grandmother died, we had the opportunity to tell her some good news, but because she was so frail it was decided that we would wait until she was stronger to tell her this news. She never became stronger and it was when she was unconscious, just minutes before she died, that I finally told her my good news. Although all of us who were with her saw her smile and we believe that she heard and understood, it has taught me that if you have some good news to impart, do not wait. Say it as soon as you can. I shall never again hold back on expressing good news and good thoughts, and I commend this thought to everybody here.'

As Edgar stepped down from the pulpit, his mother, his

sisters, his Aunt Selina, and Amy and her sisters, wiped a tear from the corners of their eyes, as did many of the women in the congregation who had all been moved by Edgar's words. The organ started to play Emma's favourite hymn and everybody joined in singing the familiar words, as the same six men who had carried the coffin into the church stepped forward and lifted it again on to their shoulders. The music of the hymn and the singing accompanied Emma as she was borne out of the church, towards the family vault which lay already opened to receive her.

Chapter 9

A few days after the funeral, Henry was in his business room with Matthew Danson, the architect who had come over from York. Henry told him his ideas for building a group of cottages as almshouses for the people who had retired from active work on the Fortune estate, and they walked to the area that Henry thought would be a suitable place for these buildings. It was on the edge of the estate, to one side of the gatehouse at the entrance to the drive, and overlooked the common green area.

'This area of land is not used for farming or grazing, so it would be convenient to use it for almshouses,' Henry explained to the Matthew. 'Also, the people who live here would still be close to all the people they've known and worked with for many years, and their friends can visit them easily. As you see, this site overlooks the common green space and is close to the inn, so the almshouses would be very much at the heart of the village's activities.'

The architect agreed that the site was a good one for all the reasons Henry had mentioned, and he added that because there was woodland on two sides, it would be a good, sheltered spot for the houses. Henry had made some rough drawings of what he envisaged the almshouses would look like and Matthew said he would take them away with him to use in his designs.

'A well to provide water will have to be added, so I will

walk around the site and look for a suitable place for it,' said the architect, 'and include it in the plans.'

'I think it is best if I leave you here to look around on your own,' said Henry. 'I will go back to the house and when you have finished here, Lady Snow and I would be pleased if you would join us for a meal before you travel back to York.'

The architect thanked him, and said it would take him about an hour to walk over the site, and make sketches and notes of ideas, and then he would come to Fortune House.

Adelaide and Henry were sitting on the terrace when the architect came up the drive. Henry waved and called to him. 'Come and join us here.'

As the architect came on to the terrace, Henry said, 'Adelaide, let me present our architect, Matthew Danson,' and turning to the architect, he said, 'Mr Danson, my wife, Lady Snow.' Matthew bowed to Adelaide and she inclined her head and held out her hand to him. 'Mr Danson, please come and sit in the shade and we will have a cool drink before the meal is served.'

Adelaide asked him about buildings he was working on or had completed, and he mentioned several buildings that she had seen on recent visits to York.

'It must be exciting to see your ideas and drawings translated into a finished building,' she said. 'I very much admire your design of the houses near the Minster. If we ever decide to make changes or additions to Fortune House we shall consult you.'

'Do you have some thoughts of making additions to Fortune House?' Matthew asked.

'Well, I have been thinking that I would like to provide better sleeping rooms for the servants who live in the house,' said Henry. 'We have increased the number of household staff over the years and there are now about 20. At present their rooms are mostly in the basements, and as the number of people working and living in the house has grown, so has the need for more bedrooms for them. I have wondered how best to provide these extra rooms. Perhaps we should add another wing?'

'Have you thought about using the attic space to provide such rooms?' asked Matthew. 'That would avoid the need for any additional building, and extra rooms could quite easily be made simply by putting up walls and dividing the large attic spaces into several small rooms.'

'That sounds like an excellent idea. Such a sensible and simple solution to our needs. Now why didn't I think of that for myself?' said Henry.

'Because you are not an architect, my dear, and Mr Danson is!' said Adelaide. Turning to Matthew she added, 'And I am sure that to do such work in the attics would be much less costly than building on another wing?'

Before Matthew could answer, Dorothy, the housekeeper, came out on to the terrace.

'I am sorry to disturb you, Sir, may I speak to you?' Dorothy stepped back into the house.

Henry got up, saying, 'Please excuse me for a moment,' to Matthew, and went into the house.

'Sir, I beg your pardon for the interruption but a messenger has arrived, bringing this letter. He said it was urgent and that I should hand it to you straight away.' Dorothy held out the letter, and added, 'The messenger also said that he had been instructed to wait so that he could take your reply back to France.'

'To France? What the devil?' Henry broke the seal on the envelope and started to read the letter. 'Dorothy, take the messenger to the kitchens and give him some refreshment. Tell him that I will see him after I have read this.'

Henry went back to the terrace, where Adelaide and Matthew Danson were still talking. 'I have to ask you to excuse me, please, Mr Danson. Some urgent family business has come up that I must deal with immediately and I need to talk to my wife on the matter. I will tell the housekeeper to serve you a meal in the small room off the Great Hall. Again, I ask your pardon for leaving you so abruptly but I do assure you that I must deal with this matter straight away.' Henry held out his hand to the architect. 'We will meet again when you have your plans and drawings ready to show me, and I thank you for the time you have spent here today.'

Adelaide waited until she and Henry were in the business room with the door closed behind them and then she asked, 'What on earth has happened, Henry? Is it bad news? Please tell me straight away. What is it? What is it?'

Henry guided her to a chair, and then pulled up another chair so that he was sitting close beside her.

'I have not yet finished reading this letter which has just been brought by a messenger. The letter is from Thomas.'

'From Thomas! What has happened? Where is he? Is he back in England?' The words burst from Adelaide's mouth.

'It is bad news, I'm afraid, Adelaide, though not as bad as I feared at first. Let me tell you. Thomas is still in France, and the letter says that he was making preparations for his travel back to England when he was set upon and robbed.'

Adelaide gasped, her hand flew to her mouth, 'Oh, Henry! Set upon! Is he all right?'

'Let me finish, Adelaide dear. He says that the robbers – a group of men – seized him as he left the inn where he is staying, and some of them held him down while the others went through his pockets and the small travel bag that he had

251

with him. All his money and valuables have been taken, and he has sent this letter with a request that I send him money immediately so that he can pay for his passage home.'

'Oh Henry! How awful! Poor Thomas! He has spent all this time, almost a year, travelling around Europe perfectly safely; and now, just as he is preparing to come home, this dreadful thing has happened. Of course, you will send him money so that he can pay for his passage back to England but how will you get the money to him quickly?'

'The messenger who brought the letter was instructed to take my reply straight back to Thomas. I will have a draft made available by my bank, and the messenger will take it with him so that Thomas will be able to obtain money from a bank in France. The messenger is in the kitchens, being given a meal at the moment. He will rest here while I go into Beverley and arrange for a draft to be drawn on our bank that can be converted into cash in France. I will bring it back with me, and the messenger can then leave straight away and be on his way.'

As Henry spoke, he was already going out into the hall and said to the servant there, 'Go to the stables, and tell them to saddle my horse and bring it round to the front immediately.' As the servant sped off, Henry said, 'I will get my coat and hat and be ready to leave as soon as my horse is here.'

'And I will go to the kitchen and speak to this messenger. I want to ask if he can tell me any more, give me more information about Thomas.' Adelaide was already hurrying towards the kitchens.

Chapter 10

Adelaide sat in the solar, her needlework dropped in her lap, her gaze concentrated on the drive. She did not hear Henry come in, and when he stood behind her and put his hand on her shoulder she jumped.

'Oh Henry! You startled me. I did not hear you approach!'

'I'm not surprised that you didn't hear my footsteps. You were watching the drive so intently, as you have done for days,' Henry said. 'You will probably have to be patient for a little longer, my dear. Remember, the messenger only left here two weeks ago. It would probably take him at least a week to get back to Thomas in France, then Thomas would have to arrange for the money transfer at the bank, and make arrangements for his travel home, and that journey would take another week.'

'I know you're right,' Adelaide gave a little shrug, 'and I know I should occupy my mind with other things, but somehow I just can't stop looking out at the drive, watching and waiting for Thomas to come home. Sometimes when I've been sitting here I have wondered how many other women have sat in this house, looking down the drive, watching for their husband or son to return. And I keep thinking that Thomas should be able to make a speedy journey; it is now the middle of June, so the seas should be calm, and there should not be any storms between France and England.'

She turned to Henry, 'I was thinking this morning that we have so much to look forward to that will bring us happiness.

When the period of family mourning for Emma is over, Edgar and Amy will marry. And soon Thomas will be home with us, and the whole family will be together again. In the past few years we have spent so much time with one of our family away. Firstly Edgar went off on the grand tour and was gone for over a year, and no sooner was he home than Thomas went off for his year of travelling.'

'Yes, you're right. We have some good times to look forward to. And, if I am not mistaken, it is possible that we may have another family wedding in the near future.' Henry smiled at the thought. 'Young Mr Corfield has been visiting us twice every week. I think whenever he has an afternoon free, he comes here, to call on Arabella, and it appears that they enjoy each other's company very much. I have noticed them walking in the gardens together, and they never seem to run out of conversation.'

'You have put into words exactly what I had been thinking but I did not dare hope too much. After all, it is early days yet,' said Adelaide. 'It is only a few weeks since Arabella and Mr Corfield first met. But I must say, although we have only known him such a short time, I feel completely at ease with him and find his personality charming. It is easy to see why Arabella finds him very attractive.'

Adelaide had to wait another two weeks before Thomas finally reached home. He arrived late one evening at the end of June, as the sun was setting over the woods to the west, having ridden all day. Although Adelaide had been watching for his arrival so intently, she was not the first to see him.

After the family had eaten their evening meal, they were sitting together in the Great Hall when Benjamin came in with his nurse to say goodnight to them before going to bed. As he went from one to the other, saying goodnight, and kissing each of them on the cheek, it happened that he was facing the window and leaning towards his mother to kiss her when his eye caught a movement.

'Look! Someone is coming up the drive!'

They all turned to look. 'Benjamin!' his mother cried, 'I do believe it is Thomas. It is Thomas come home at last!'

There was so much excitement over Thomas's return that everybody went to bed very late that night. Despite that, next morning, Adelaide got up earlier than usual. As she moved around the bedroom, Henry woke up too.

'Adelaide? What's the matter? You are up very early,' he said.

'Oh I just could not sleep for another minute. I want to go downstairs and be ready and waiting for Thomas, whenever he gets up. I have so many questions to ask him,' Adelaide explained, as she turned away from him and continued to pin up her hair.

'Well, give him a little time to get used to being at home,' Henry cautioned. 'He has been gone a long time, and no doubt has so much to tell us that it will take quite a time to hear everything. I confess that I, too, am anxious to hear about the places he has visited and the people he has met.'

In fact, Thomas did not appear in the Great Hall until it was almost time to serve the midday meal. He started to apologise for his lateness but Adelaide cut him short.

'You must be exhausted, dear, from your long journey. Of course, we want to hear everything about your travels but we will try to be patient. Though that will not be easy!'

Over the meal, Thomas started to talk about some of the places he had visited and the sights he had seen.

'I have so much to tell you, I fear I will bore you,' he said.

'No, no, of course you won't bore us,' Arabella started to

255

say, and Harriet interrupted with, 'I shall never be bored hearing about your travels. Oh, it is so unfair that only young men go off travelling! How I wish that girls could do the grand tour too!'

Adelaide's interest was not in the places Thomas had visited, or the people he had met, but she wanted to be reassured that he had not been injured when he had been robbed just before coming home.

'No, Mother, I was not hurt at all,' Thomas insisted.

'You have not mentioned any purchases that you made, Thomas. Did you buy any large items that are being sent to England?' asked Henry. 'Paintings? Pieces of marble? It takes such a long time for shipments to reach here. The very large urns that Edgar bought took almost a year to reach here and have only recently been put into position on the terrace. Some statuary that he purchased has also arrived and been placed in the orangery. Of course, you haven't seen the orangery which we had built since you went away. Also, I have ordered a fountain for the lawns, and more statues, including two little marble dogs to please young Benjamin!'

'No, Father,' said Thomas. 'Somehow, while I was in Italy the time seemed to go by so fast that I did not make any purchases. Perhaps you should be glad that I did not buy such things. After all, Edgar had already bought those large pieces. I have saved you money by not buying more!'

'And you did not buy any paintings in France?' Adelaide asked.

'Again, the time seemed to go so fast that although I saw many paintings that I very much liked, I did not actually buy any.'

Henry looked somewhat disappointed. 'Well, after all your travelling around, what have you brought back, Thomas? Nothing it seems!'

'Oh Father, don't be displeased. I have broadened my

mind and expanded my knowledge of people and life,' said Thomas. 'Isn't that something worthwhile to bring back? And something that will last my whole life.'

Thomas sensed that Henry was disgruntled with him, so he lightened the tone by saying, 'Now that we are all together again as a family, I have a wonderful idea. Instead of having a painting of our family, we should have one of the portraits made that are now becoming the fashion in France. A Monsieur Daguerre has invented a process where he uses a small machine, and somehow reproduces a likeness of anything or anybody. They have named the process after him and they call the likenesses "Daguerrotypes". We should have one made of our family. They are the latest fashion and quite the rage in France.' Thomas hoped that by changing the subject and showing such enthusiasm, he could change his father's mood.

Both Arabella and Harriet clapped their hands. 'Oh that sounds like fun. Can someone come here to the house to make this dagger thing?'

'Daguerrotype, Harriet, not dagger!' Thomas laughed. 'Yes, I'm sure Father could find out more and arrange for such a portrait to be made here.'

Henry cleared his throat. 'If everyone has finished eating, I would like Edgar and Thomas to come into my business room.'

'Sounds very serious!' said Thomas.

'It is,' said Henry. 'I think it is time we had a serious discussion about your future.' He turned and led the way into the business room.

Once the three of them were settled comfortably in the business room, Henry said, 'I won't waste time, I will come straight to the point. As I said, Thomas, I want to talk to you about your future. Now that you are home permanently, it is

257

time to think about what you will do with your life. You know that just before you went off on your travels, I took over sole ownership of the textile mill. Amos Burton is an excellent manager there, and we have good staff and it is a thriving business. In fact, the textile business has expanded considerably in the past year and I would like you to start to learn from Amos so that gradually you will be able to take over full responsibility from me. In time, I will make over the whole business to you and it will be an excellent source of income for you.'

There was silence. Henry spoke again, 'Well, Thomas, haven't you anything to say?'

'Er, Father, er, I'm quite overcome. Quite surprised. I have given no thought to my future in terms of work and an income.' Thomas looked stunned.

'Did you think that I would continue to provide for you for the rest of your life, without you making any contribution to Fortune or working in any way?' Henry did not look pleased at the way this conversation was going.

'I didn't think of anything at all. I mean, I have only just arrived home, and not had time to think.'

'You have had plenty of time to think of your future while you have been travelling. You say that you didn't think of anything at all, and that seems to be the truth. Thomas, to say that I am disappointed is putting it very mildly. I had hoped that you might have had some thoughts about your future, and I had hoped even more that you would feel some enthusiasm for taking over the flourishing business of the Fortune textile mill. Just what had you thought you would do now that you are home?'

'Well, I hadn't thought very far ahead, Father. There is the big race meeting at York in three weeks' time, and I had planned to go there for that, and then the following month I thought I would go to Newmarket for the horse racing there. After that I thought that I would go to London to visit some friends. There will be a lot of parties and balls …' Thomas got no further.

Henry said, 'I am trying very hard not to lose my temper with you, Thomas. So far you have had all the benefits that I can offer you – a comfortable home with servants to wait on you, an excellent education, and then your year of travelling. Now the time has come for you to apply yourself to more serious matters.'

'Apply myself? To serious matters? Oh Father, you are so amusing!' Thomas's remarks and the insolent smile on his face proved too much for Henry. Finally he could not control his temper any longer.

'Thomas, get out! Leave this room at once. I am too angry to talk to you now. We will continue this discussion when I have calmed down and when you, I hope, will have given some serious thought to your future. Now get out!'

Chapter 11

'Dorothy! Dorothy!' Henry's shout echoed through the Great Hall.

'Yes, Sir … I'm here.' Dorothy appeared around a side screen.

'Where is my wife?' Henry shouted at her.

'She is in her small sitting room, Sir. Shall I ask her to come down?'

'No. I will go up to her.' Henry started up the stairs and turned. 'Dorothy, I'm sorry, I was not shouting at you or about anything you have done.'

Dorothy smiled her acknowledgment of his apology and disappeared again behind the serving screen.

When Henry reached Adelaide's sitting room (he always refused to call this room her boudoir. 'Damned new-fangled French word,' he would say) he found her sitting at her desk, writing.

'Are you writing something that you must finish now, Adelaide?' he asked. 'If it is not something important, please come with me and let us walk in the rose garden.'

Adelaide turned to face him, 'No, I am just catching up on writing my record of family happenings. Henry! My dear, what is the matter? Your face is so red!'

'Come, let us walk, and I will tell you.' Henry held out his hand to her. 'Here is your shawl,' he draped it around her shoulders, and they went downstairs.

Adelaide did not say anything as they went through the

Great Hall, crossed the terrace, and went down the steps and walked towards the rose garden. She kept stealing a look at Henry but his gaze was fixed firmly ahead. When they reached the rose garden, he still did not speak but guided her to one of the seats.

Sitting down, he took a deep breath and exhaled slowly.

'I will tell you why I am so angry. I just talked to Thomas about his future and I hoped and expected to discuss plans for his life. I had asked Edgar to join us, because after I am gone he will have to administer all the business of Fortune so I wanted him to know exactly what I was suggesting to Thomas. Both you and Edgar were already aware that I have been thinking that Thomas should take over complete control of the Fortune textile mill. And, further, as the mill does not form part of the estate that is entailed upon the eldest son, I could in time give it completely and in its entirety to Thomas.'

'Yes, you had told me that you would suggest this to Thomas after his return. So, when he heard your thought, what did he have to say?' asked Adelaide.

'He said very little, except to be downright insolent to me! That is what has made me so angry! Thomas seems not to have thought of doing anything with his life. He has no plans except to go to race courses and to attend parties with his friends in London!' Henry's face turned red again, his anger bubbling up once more as he thought of the scene in his business room.

'Henry, calm down, my dear.' Adelaide patted his hand. 'Just tell me what Thomas said in response to your suggestions.' Adelaide thought she had never seen Henry so close to losing his temper with one of their children.

'That's what is making me so angry. He said very little. In fact, he laughed in my face and ridiculed the thought that he should do some serious work. He seems to have thought that he would have no need to work and that I would continue to supply him with money for his carefree lifestyle!' Henry took Adelaide's hand in his. 'Thank God I have you to talk to. You always understand.' Henry raised her hand and kissed it.

'I don't wish to anger you further, Henry, but I will confess that I have had some misgivings about Thomas taking over the mill. Whenever you have mentioned it, I have had the feeling that he would not want to do it, but I hoped that I was wrong and that perhaps he would have grown up, matured, during his travels.'

'Well, Adelaide, it seems that your feelings were right – a mother's instinct, perhaps. But it isn't just that Thomas seems unwilling to consider his future seriously. I was angered because he treated the whole matter so flippantly and he laughed at me.' He sighed. 'Let us walk on a little more now. Your company and the scent of the roses are doing wonders for me.'

'Well, let us all try to keep cool heads and have a pleasant evening together with no ugly conversation. Oh look …' As Adelaide stood up she pointed down one of the pathways between the roses. 'There is Arabella with Mr Corfield. Come, dear, let us join them.' Adelaide stood up and held out her hand to Henry. 'Come, dear, please.'

'I am not sure they will want us to join them? They look very happy and content with just each other's company,' Henry said, but Arabella had seen them and waved, and she and Andrew started to come towards them. Henry got up and together he and Adelaide walked towards the young couple.

Andrew raised his hat and bowed slightly, 'Lady Snow,' and he turned, 'Sir Henry. Your rose garden is one of the most delightful places imaginable. The colour of all the roses and the scent are so beautiful.'

'Thank you, Mr Corfield. I'm glad you enjoy it as much as

we do. It's always been one of my favourite places,' said Henry.

'Mr Corfield, we are about to return to the house to take tea. Will you join us?' Adelaide asked.

'Thank you, that is most kind. I shall be delighted.' Andrew extended his arm to Arabella and the four walked back to the house together.

While they were sitting on the terrace waiting for the tea to be served, Andrew Corfield stood up and said, 'Sir Henry, may I speak to you privately, please?'

'Of course. Come with me.' Henry and Andrew went towards the door to go into the house. 'Excuse us for just a few minutes, please,' Henry said over his shoulder to Adelaide and Arabella.

Once they were inside the house, in the Great Hall, Henry said, 'Now what was it you wished to talk to me about, Mr Corfield?'

'Sir Henry. It cannot have escaped your notice that I have been visiting Fortune regularly, and have been spending time with your daughter Arabella.' Andrew stopped speaking.

'Yes, go on.'

'Sir Henry, although I have not known Arabella very long, I have come to admire her greatly and we both enjoy the time we spend together. We have many common interests.' He took a great gulping breath and his words came out in a rush: 'Sir Henry, I wish to ask your permission to propose marriage to Arabella!'

'You'd better come into my business room, young man,' said Henry, leading the way.

When Henry and Andrew Corfield emerged from the business room, they walked back to the terrace.

'Tea has been served for several minutes, Henry,' said Adelaide reprovingly.

'Well, I will take my tea now, but I think Mr Corfield and

Arabella will want to walk in the gardens again, eh, Mr Corfield?'

'Oh yes, Sir. Yes, thank you. Arabella, will you come with me?' Andrew held out his hand to her.

As they went down the steps towards the gardens, Henry took his tea from Adelaide and said, 'Well, there's another instance where your feelings and instincts were accurate. Mr Corfield just asked my permission to propose to Arabella. We had a discussion about his income and future prospects, and I gave him my approval. I imagine that he is asking her to marry him at this very moment.'

'Oh, Henry! How delightful! I am so pleased that you gave your consent. I am so happy! And just think, what an amazing turn around of events in just an hour or two. Firstly, you were so angry after your unpleasant discussion with Thomas and now ... now ... such happiness!' Adelaide was beaming widely. 'I can't wait for them to come back from their walk! Oh Henry! As soon as our official mourning time for your mother is over, we shall have two weddings to celebrate!'

As Arabella and Andrew emerged from the rose garden and started to cross the lawn, Arabella saw that her parents were still sitting on the terrace. She waved to them and broke into a run. Coming up the steps she held out her arms and rushed to embrace Henry.

'Father! Thank you so much for giving your consent. Oh, I am presuming that you have already told Mother?' Arabella turned to Adelaide who was now standing up, holding out her arms.

'Yes, he has told me, and my darling girl, I am delighted!' Turning to Andrew Corfield, Adelaide said, 'Andrew – I need

no longer stand upon formality and call you Mr Corfield –
Andrew, come here and let me embrace you too.'

Andrew Corfield kissed her cheek, and then her hand.

'Lady Snow, may I say that as well as the joy of having
Arabella for my wife, it will be a pleasure to have you for my
mother-in-law.'

'What a delightful compliment,' said Adelaide. 'Andrew,
do you have to hurry back to Middleby? Do you have some
duties at the school this evening? If not, won't you please stay
and dine with us? It is just past midsummer's day and it is
light until quite late at this time of year, so your ride back
would not be in darkness.'

'That is most kind of you, Lady Snow. I should be delighted
to dine with your family.'

'Andrew!' Adelaide could not stop smiling widely. 'It is
now your family too … or it will be quite soon.'

That night, as Henry and Adelaide were getting ready for bed,
Adelaide said, 'Oh what a lot I shall have to write in the family
chronicle tomorrow. And I shall write to Selina and George
too, and let them know that there will be two family weddings
late this year.'

'This family chronicle that you write, Adelaide, you have
been adding to it since soon after we married. It must be very
long by now,' said Henry.

'It is long, but it is not only *my* writings that make it so,'
said Adelaide. 'Many Snow wives have written of events in
the family for a very long time. In fact, sometimes when I am
writing, I think of all the women who have recorded family
happenings over the centuries. For example, there was a Lady
Snow back in the late 1670s who discovered that all the earliest
documents were scattered around the house and she organised
them into chronological order. I often think of her and feel

grateful that she started to bring order to all the family papers. And now I consider it partly a duty and partly a privilege to contribute to and continue the family story.'

Chapter 12

The summer that year was a particularly good one and the days went by in a haze of golden sunshine resulting in an excellent harvest. All the crops were gathered early, and by September, when the apple-pickers were in the orchards, the beauty of autumn started to spread across the countryside around Fortune. Leaves on the trees turned from green to golden and bronze, and the hedgerows were full of red berries.

One morning Henry looked up from reading his newspaper and said, 'Adelaide, there is an interesting article here about a man whose name is Robert Fenton. He has brought back plants from all parts of the world and they can now be grown successfully in England. I think I will contact this Mr Fenton, and ask if he can send one of his assistants here, with details of the new plants that are available and advise us as to which plants would be suitable for our soil. There are some called azaleas that, from the descriptions, sound beautiful. They talk about having them planted along each side of a path so that they form "an azalea walk". Doesn't that sound charming?'

Henry wrote to Robert Fenton that day and was delighted when he received a reply in only two weeks.

'He says that if it is convenient, he can immediately send two of his assistants who will assess our soil and the climate here, and advise us on plantings. I will write to Mr Fenton today and ask him to send his assistants as soon as possible. I shall also talk to Adam and tell him to hire more men to work in the gardens. Perhaps some of the young lads growing up here on the estate might be interested in training to work in the gardens.'

Adelaide liked the idea of an azalea walk because, she said, apart from being pretty, it would be something that would be a lasting part of Fortune. She explained to Henry, 'Over the centuries, different generations of Snows have contributed something special to the House and estate. There is the Armada Tower, the Lady Eleanor School, the rose garden, the alterations to the front of the house to form an "E" shape, and the addition to the back that your mother disliked so much. You are adding almshouses, and now we might also add this delightful sounding azalea walk.'

Although the six months of family mourning for Emma would not be complete until the end of November, both Adelaide and Arabella were anxious to start making wedding plans. A letter arrived from Selina in which she said that she and Amy, too, wanted to start to make plans for Amy's marriage. The letter went on:

'Although the wedding cannot take place until the mourning period is over, surely it would not be unseemly to start making arrangements? I don't think that Emma herself would mind; she always wanted Amy and Edgar to marry.'

It was decided that Amy and Edgar would marry at the parish church in Moortown a few days before Christmas, and Arabella and Andrew would marry in the church that stood just outside the gates of Fortune House in the week between Christmas and New Year's Day. Both brides said that they wished to follow the new fashion set by Queen Victoria when she had married a few years earlier, and have their bridal gowns in white. Harriet would be bridesmaid to Arabella, and

Amy would have her two sisters, Prudence and Polly, as her attendants.

One day when both families were spending the day together, discussing details of the two weddings, Henry looked at Edgar and Andrew and said, 'Just you wait, you two young men. One day you will probably have daughters of your own and then you will know what problems can beset a man when his daughter is to be a bride!' His tone was serious but his eyes twinkled. He was clearly delighted with the prospect of Edgar marrying Amy, and Arabella marrying Andrew.

Thomas came home in November, having stayed in London for some months. Every week Henry had grumbled that Thomas had been gone a long time, and wondered just what he could be doing that kept him so long in London. Adelaide tried to soothe him by saying, 'We know he has several good friends who live in London, and I am sure he is caught up in the whirl of social life there.' But she, too, wondered when he was coming home, and above all, when he would decide what he was going to do with the rest of his life.

After Thomas had been home about two weeks, two letters arrived addressed to Henry. He took them into his business room to read them, and after a few minutes, he wrenched the door open so violently that it almost came off its hinges.

'Thomas! Thomas!' His voice was a bellow that echoed through the house. Adelaide hurried through the hall towards him, and several servants came running into the area outside his business room.

'Where the devil is Thomas? Somebody find him, and send him in here immediately!' he shouted, and then he went back into his room slamming the door behind him. As the servants scuttled in several different directions, Adelaide took a deep breath, squared her shoulders and, knocking briefly on the door, went into the business room. Henry's face was bright red, and veins on his forehead stood out.

'Henry. What on earth has happened to make you so angry? Please sit down and try to calm yourself or I fear you will have an apoplexy!'

'Apoplexy? Apoplexy? I'd like to horsewhip that young bounder!'

Adelaide asked again, 'What has happened?'

Henry was pacing up and down the room and suddenly he whirled on his heel, and said, 'I will tell you what has happened, Adelaide, and I don't doubt that you will be as angry as I am.'

He indicated the two letters lying on his desk. 'Normally, I would try to shield you from something as distasteful, as disgraceful, as this, but you will have to know some time, so I will tell you now. In fact, better than telling you, I will simply read these two letters to you.'

The first letter came from Paris, the second from London. Both were similar in words and in tone, saying that Thomas had run up considerable gambling debts, that he had been given as much time as possible to settle those debts, but that now the money must be paid. The writers of both letters said that unless the money owed was paid in full within 30 days, they would have no alternative but to take legal action.

Henry had calmed down a little while he was reading the letters to Adelaide, but now it was her turn to suffer the shock of hearing the news contained in them. When he had finished reading, Henry looked across his desk at her and seeing her face so white, he came around and put his arms around her immediately.

'Now you know the cause of my anger. Oh my dear, what have we done wrong, why has our son turned out this way?'

Adelaide said, 'I am as angry as you, Henry. I feel as if a blow, a physical blow, has been struck at my body. My mind feels almost numb. I can scarcely comprehend this situation.'

There was a brief tap at the door and Thomas came in.

'You wanted to see me, I believe, Father?'

'Come in and sit down.' Henry sat down, looked again at the two letters, then across at Thomas. When he spoke it was obvious that he was using all his might to keep his temper under control.

'I have received two letters. One from Paris, and one from London. Both are from gaming establishments that say that you gambled heavily at their tables, and that you owe them a very great amount of money. Can you deny the truth of these accusations?'

'Which clubs are they, Father? I have gambled in many different clubs, so I cannot vouch for the truth of their charges. I daresay they are true, I've not had much luck at cards or any other game.'

'Don't be so damned insolent, young sir! You sit there, lounging in the chair, seemingly without a care in the world, when I confront you with the fact that you have debts amounting to several thousands of pounds! You seem completely unconcerned that if these debts are not paid, legal proceedings will be started and you could end up in debtors' prison.'

'Oh, I think not, Father,' drawled Thomas. 'You are being overly dramatic! You would pay my debts before you let things reach that stage. After all, you would not want the name of the Snow family dragged through a court of law.'

Henry bounded round his desk so fast that Adelaide thought that he was going to hit Thomas. She gasped, 'Henry, please …'

Henry seized Thomas by his lapels and shook him as if he were a doll.

'You are right on that point! No, I will not have this family's good name and reputation besmirched by you. You apparently care nothing for your own good name. But the Snows have always been an honourable family and I will not have our reputation destroyed by one young fool. I will indeed pay these debts but there will be conditions attached which I doubt you will like but you either abide by the conditions or I will let the law take its course.'

Thomas looked disbelieving as Henry continued speaking.

'The first thing for me to do is to settle these debts. The second thing is to decide your future. Now get out. I will talk to you again later after I have had time to give the matter some serious thought.'

Chapter 13

The next afternoon Henry sent for Thomas to come to the business room.

'Come in and sit down, Thomas. Yesterday I was so shocked and angered by the news contained in those two letters that I could not trust myself to think rationally. Now, I have had some time for calm reflection, and so have you, and I think we should talk again.'

Thomas had lost his arrogant swagger and his demeanour was more that of a supplicant.

'Father, I too have had time to think. I know how much I have disappointed you and Mother, but I think I have reasons for my behaviour.'

'Reasons? What reasons could you possibly have for such irresponsible behaviour?' Henry asked.

'Well, Father, think of things from my point of view. I am the second son. Edgar as the first-born will inherit everything. He will have the house, the land, and all the businesses set up in the family name. And he will succeed to the title. I will have nothing. I have always been "the one who comes second". So I have had none of Edgar's reasons to be responsible or to live up to the family name.'

'By God, I preferred you when you were arrogant and insolent rather than snivelling and whining as you are now!' Henry's voice shook and it was obvious he was working hard to control his temper.

'You are right when you say you will not inherit the house

and the land and the businesses,' he went on, 'but along with that inheritance comes the work and the worry of keeping everything successful. In time, your brother Edgar will have to shoulder that burden and he will also be responsible for the well-being of all the people who work for us. He has no choice. It seems to me that you, as the second son, have all the advantages and none of the disadvantages and responsibilities. You have had all the benefits that Edgar has had – a comfortable home, servants to look after you, an excellent education, and the opportunity to travel – and all without the need to take on any responsibility. As the second son, you are free to choose your path in life. When I grew up, as the elder son, I had no choice but to take on the Fortune estate. My brother George, your uncle, was the second son and he became a doctor. You, too, could have chosen a worthwhile profession for yourself. So please let's hear no more whining about the miserable lot that falls to the second son.'

For three days a gloom hung over the house. Henry came and went several times but said nothing to Adelaide. The servants crept around the house whenever Henry was at home, not wishing to provoke further anger. Thomas stayed mostly in his room, coming down only for meals and even then speaking very little.

On the afternoon of the fourth day, Henry summoned Adelaide, Edgar and Thomas to his business room.

'I have brought you all here together so that I can tell you what decisions I have made regarding Thomas's future. Firstly, Thomas, your debts have been paid. Luckily, I was able to raise sufficient capital quickly. Secondly, as to your future, you will go to Australia.'

There was a gasp from everyone in the room, but nobody spoke. Henry continued, 'I will not have you living in this country where you may run up debts again or in other ways sully the family's good name. In the past few days, I have paid for your passage to Sydney, Australia. Your ship, "The English Rose", sails from Tilbury one week from tomorrow. I will entrust a sum of money to the captain and he will hand that money to you when you disembark in Sydney. To ensure that you actually board the ship and leave England, you will be escorted to London by Adam, and Dorothy's husband, Joseph, and two strong young men who work on the estate. They will have instructions not to let you out of their sight until after you are on board, and they are to watch the ship until it has sailed away. Do you have any questions?'

'Father, this is the most terrible shock. Will you not reconsider and allow me to stay in England? Couldn't I perhaps take on the management of the textile mill as you once suggested?'

Henry's face looked as if it had been cast in stone.

'After the way you have behaved do you think I would ever be able to trust you with our textile business? No, young man. It will grieve your mother and it will grieve me too, but you will leave England. You will have enough money to settle yourself comfortably in Australia. Everything has been arranged for you and your escorts to leave here at eight o'clock tomorrow morning. Before you leave, the whole family will have breakfast together. After your coach leaves here, I do not wish to see you ever again.'

As Henry left the room there was a sob from Adelaide, which she stifled behind a hand clenched to her mouth. She kissed Thomas, then she too left the room.

Edgar walked over to his brother and, putting a hand on his shoulder, said, 'I shall see you at breakfast in the morning.'

Thomas sat alone in the business room for quite a long

275

time. Finally he roused himself, went over to the desk and pulling out writing materials, sat in his father's chair and started to write a letter to his parents.

When he had finished the letter, he read through it and, satisfied, he folded it, and wrote 'Mother and Father' on the outside, and left it lying on Henry's desk.

Breakfast next morning was a silent affair. There was no conversation, until Harriet tried to lighten the gloom by saying brightly, 'This morning, I am to have another fitting for the dress I shall wear as bridesmaid. Oh, all thoughts of the wedding are so exciting …' Her voice tapered away. Nobody said so, but they were all thinking that Thomas would not be with them for the two forthcoming weddings. After Harriet's failed attempt, nobody else tried to make any conversation.

Henry looked at his pocket watch. 'Time to go.' His voice was gruff. Clearing his throat, he went to Thomas, extended his hand to shake Thomas's and said, 'I wish you luck, my son.' Thomas clasped his father's hand, then suddenly let it go and put his arms around his father, embracing him.

Adelaide came to Thomas, kissed him quickly on the cheek and left the room, dabbing at her eyes. Both of his sisters kissed Thomas, as did Benjamin.

Edgar shook his hand and said, 'I wish you God speed and good luck,' and then they too embraced.

When Thomas walked out of the room, he found his four escorts waiting for him. He was taken out of the front door, down the terrace steps and into the waiting carriage.

All the family came out on to the terrace to watch the carriage roll down the long drive and they all gave a final wave as it went out through the gates.

Henry went into his business room and, sitting down at his desk, he saw the letter addressed 'Mother and Father'. He read it, then refolded it, and went to find Adelaide. She was sitting alone in the solar in one of the window seats.

When she looked up at him, he could see that she had been crying.

'This letter, addressed to both of us, was left on my desk,' said Henry, handing her the letter.

Adelaide took it, glanced at the signature, and whispered, 'From Thomas,' and then she started to read:

'My dearest Mother and Father, I know how much I have disappointed you and I want to say how very sorry I am for the hurt I have caused you. I can see that I have wasted many years on foolishness but I have now resolved to put all that behind me.

'My first thoughts and feelings on being told that you were sending me to Australia were of shock. But I have decided to view this as a new beginning, a second chance in life. Australia is a young country, a land full of opportunities, and I intend to seize those opportunities. I will make a success of my life there and I will make you proud of me.

'Wherever I go and whatever I do, my dearest thoughts and love will always be with you. Thomas.'

Footnote:
In letters received from Thomas, the family heard that upon arrival in Sydney he had bought a house with some of the money Henry had made available to him. It was larger than he needed just for himself, so he let out some rooms to boarders. Soon the house was too small for the number of boarders wanting to live there, and Thomas bought a small hotel. Business boomed and as Sydney grew, so did Thomas's hotel. By 1860 Snow's Hotel was the largest in the city.

Part V
2006

Chapter 1

Richard's footsteps crunched on the gravel of the path leading to the church. The handle on the church door was a huge iron ring and as Richard tried to turn it, he found that it was stiff but then there was a satisfactory 'clunk' as the latch on the inside of the door opened.

Going into the church, and turning to close the door behind him, Richard paused for a moment. He knew, from the sign outside, that the church dated from the 12th century, and he looked at the door and wondered if that dated from the time the church was built. Could an oak door last for more than eight centuries? He ran his fingertips over the wood, savouring the thought that he was touching something so old. Where he came from, although there were some very old buildings that had been built by the original settlers, it was also the case that people pointed out 'old' houses that had been built just a hundred years ago. On a small table inside the door, there were some leaflets with information about the church. Picking one up, he read that there had been a church on this site since approximately 1120 AD, and it was thought that even before that, in pre-Christian times, this spot had been a place of worship. He looked around him, taking in the stained glass windows, the pews that were so old that their oak was blackened with age, and the candle holders on the end of the pews all along the aisle. The sunlight streaming through the coloured glass of the windows showed that there were several gleaming brass plaques placed on the walls of the church.

As he started to read the leaflet, he found that it referred to various parts of the church's architecture, such as 'the lancet window in the north wall' and 'the arched doorway in the southwest corner' and he paused for a moment trying to locate them. Which way was north? Ah, he remembered, in the Church of England, the altar is always in the east, so standing at the foot of the aisle and facing the altar, he could identify the north and south walls. As he started to walk around, his eyes adjusted to the dimness of the light inside the church. There was just enough light to read what was written on the brasses. Many of them were memorials to members of the Snow family and this was just what he had hoped to find. As he read them, he noticed that several men of the Snow family had been killed in battle in different parts of the world over the centuries.

'But here,' he thought, pausing in front of one of them, 'here's a man from the Snow family who was in a major battle but survived. And he has the same name as me,' he realised as he read about a Richard Snow who was described on the plaque as 'a hero of the Battle of Agincourt' and who had died at Fortune House in 1463. Richard read the words again, and thought, '1463 ... that's almost 550 years ago!'

As he walked around the small church, Richard found that the brass memorials were in no particular order. He passed from the one commemorating the hero of Agincourt, to one for Arthur Snow who had served with the Royal Flying Corps in the First World War and had been killed flying over the battlefields of the Somme in 1916.

Then, a few yards further along the wall, there was a memorial to Jonathan Snow who had been 'killed on D-Day in 1944, and whose body has no known grave'.

'Hello. Are you finding your way around all right, or can I be of any help?'

The sudden sound of a woman's voice made Richard jump.

She went on, 'Oh I'm so sorry, I didn't mean to startle you.'
A middle-aged woman came forward holding out her hand.

'I'm Viv Hudson. My husband is the vicar of this church, and it's my turn to do the flowers on the altar this week. I'm just arranging them now.'

'Good morning. I was so totally absorbed in reading some of these memorials that I didn't notice anybody else was in the church.'

He shook her hand and went on, 'My name is Richard Snow.'

'Oh, your name is Snow! Well, then you'll find plenty to interest you in this church and in the surrounding area. The big house, just up the long drive near the church, is Fortune House and it has been the family home of the Snows for, oh, more than 600 years.'

'That's why I'm visiting this part of England. I've read that Fortune House is open to the public, and I intend to visit there later today. I'm staying at the inn in the village, and I'll have lunch there, as the house isn't open till two o'clock this afternoon.'

'What a very pleasant young man, and what a coincidence that his name is Snow,' thought Viv. 'I must telephone Katherine at the House and tell her to look out for him among the visitors.'

Viv looked carefully at his face and hair, and noted the colour of his jacket, so that she could describe him to Katherine.

'I think, from your accent, that I detect that you are American?' Viv asked.

'That's right, Ma'am.'

'Aren't American young men charming,' thought Viv, 'the way they address a woman as Ma'am.'

He went on, 'I was born in Virginia, and the company I work for recently transferred me to their London office. So

I've come here, hoping to check up on the family stories that say that one of my ancestors left this very place and went to Virginia, to grow tobacco, back in the 17th Century.'

'Will you be staying long?' asked Viv.

'I'm staying for the whole of the Easter weekend. In America we don't have four days off from work at Easter, so I thought this was a good time to come and make a first visit to Fortune. I drove here yesterday, Friday, and I'll drive back to London on Monday.'

Viv excused herself, saying that she really must finish the flowers, and adding that she was sure he would find plenty to interest him in the small church.

'And,' she added, 'I'm sure you will enjoy your visit to Fortune House.'

Richard continued looking around the church, reading the leaflet as he went. He read that the font had been given by the Snow family in the late 1500s, and that the bells now in the bell tower replaced much older ones, and had been given by the Snow family to mark the accession of the young Queen Victoria in 1837. Soon after the bells were hung, the Archbishop of York had visited the parish especially to bless them.

A panel of embroidery around a portion of the altar had been worked, he read in the leaflet, by Adelaide Snow in the 1860s, and it had taken her almost two years to complete.

As he was letting himself out of the church, Viv Hudson suddenly appeared near the door.

'Did you find your visit interesting?' she asked.

'I certainly did, and I'm wondering if it would be possible to meet your husband some time when it is convenient for him? I'd like to find out more about the Snow family and I'm sure the parish records have a great deal of information about them.'

'Well,' Viv paused. 'This weekend, being Easter, is a very

busy time for my husband as you can imagine, but I'm sure he'd be interested to meet you. Perhaps you will come down from London again some time?'

'Oh, I certainly intend to come back again,' said Richard. 'There's so much that I want to find out about the Snow family and I can see already that there is more than I can do in just this long weekend. And after I've visited Fortune House, I expect I shall have even more questions.'

'Well, goodbye, Mr Snow. I hope you enjoy your lunch and your visit to the house.'

As Richard walked down the path through the church's graveyard, heading towards the inn for his lunch, Viv pulled out her mobile phone.

At Fortune House, Katherine was doing a check of the rooms that would be open to visitors this afternoon when her mobile phone rang.

'Katherine ... it's Viv Hudson. Yes, it is a lovely day and I'm sure that a lot of people have taken advantage of the good weather and the long Easter weekend to get away to the countryside. I know that there are a lot of visitors in this area, all the hotels are full, so you will probably have quite a crowd of visitors to Fortune House this afternoon.'

'I do hope so,' said Katherine. 'We're working so hard to try to attract more visitors.'

Viv went on, 'I wanted to let you know that one of your visitors today will be a young American called Richard Snow. Yes, Snow. Yes, it is a remarkable coincidence. I had a short chat with him when he was looking around the church, and he says that there have always been stories in his family about one of his ancestors who lived here, at Fortune House, and went off to Virginia to grow tobacco.'

'Viv, that's fascinating. There certainly was a son of the

285

house who did just that. I've read about him in the family records and papers. Oh, I'd love to meet this young man and talk to him when he is at the house,' said Katherine. 'Viv, did you notice what he is wearing so that I can look for him?'

Viv described Richard's looks and told Katherine that he was wearing grey flannel trousers and a dark blue blazer.

'Thanks, Viv. I'll certainly look out for him.'

Chapter 2

As Richard ate his meal at the inn, he looked again through the leaflet he'd picked up in the church. 'Aha, those are the plaques that I noticed,' he said to himself, as he read a short paragraph that referred to the number of brass memorials in the church dedicated to members of the Snow family. The leaflet also said that in the cemetery around the church there were several headstones marking the graves of members of the Snow family. The church's records, he read, showed christenings, marriages, and funerals of members of the Snow family that had taken place in the church over several centuries. 'That's exactly why I really want to talk to the vicar some time,' he thought, 'and see if it would be possible for me to look at those records.'

'I hope you have you enjoyed your lunch, Sir? Can I get you anything else?' The landlord's questions pierced his thoughts about the Snow family.

'Yes, I did enjoy my lunch very much, thank you. Would it be possible to have a cup of coffee?'

'Of course. I'll get the waitress to bring it over to you.' As the landlord cleared away the plates Richard glanced at his watch. It was 1.45 p.m. 'Perfect timing,' he thought.

A few minutes after two o'clock, Richard started walking up the long drive to Fortune House. He paused and took a photograph of the house, and then swung around and photographed the views on both sides. 'It looks just like a picture in a book about the beauty of rural England,' he thought. 'A painter could have arranged the landscape, with gentle slopes of green meadows, clusters of trees in exactly the right places, hedgerows dividing the fields, and some cattle in one area, and sheep grazing in another. I can't wait to send these photographs to my parents – they'll be so interested to see the original Snow family home.'

Just inside the main door of the house he bought a ticket from a woman sitting at the desk, and noticed that there was a small book called *A Guide to Snow House*.

'I'd like to buy a copy of that book, too,' he said, pulling money out of his wallet.

Opening the guide book, he read that the main door with its gabled portico through which he'd just entered had been added to the house in the days of the first Queen Elizabeth, when additions to the front of the house had given it the fashionable 'E' shape. Walking with the guide book open in his hand, Richard went into the Great Hall. He was delighted to find that the guide book told him about the beautiful old panelling that covered the walls, the huge fireplace that was decorated with a stone called Derbyshire Bluejohn, and about the paintings on the walls. As he walked around checking back and forth between reading from the book and looking at the paintings, he thought, 'Already I feel completely absorbed by this house and the family.'

In each of the main rooms of the house a guide stood to one side, ready to answer any questions posed by visitors. Richard paused each time he heard the guide describing some particular feature of the house, and occasionally asked a question himself. As he mounted the great oak staircase, a young woman appeared at the top.

'Hello, are you Richard Snow?' she asked.

Richard was startled. 'I am ... but how could you possibly know my name?' He had stopped halfway up the stairs.

The young woman laughed. 'Well, I could tell you I'm psychic, or I could say that you bear a marked resemblance to some of the young men in old family portraits, but neither would be true! To be honest, I had a telephone call from the vicar's wife. She said she had spoken to you in the church and that, as you believe you might have some distant family connection to this house, I should look out for you.'

'Oh, the vicar's wife. Viv Hudson ... I think that was her name?'

'Yes, that's right.'

As Richard mounted the last few stairs, the young woman held out her hand. 'I'm Katherine Snow, and Fortune House is my family home.'

'How wonderful to meet a member of the family. I'm so pleased and I'm sure I shall have a thousand questions to ask you! I hope you won't mind?'

'Well ... a thousand might be a few too many, but come and sit over here,' she indicated a large tapestry covered sofa that stood on the landing, 'and we can start by having a chat.'

Richard told her what he had told Viv Hudson; that he came from America and his family's history, as he had heard it, was that a son of the Snow family of England had gone to America in the late 17th century and had started growing tobacco in Virginia.

'He made a success of growing tobacco, and in fact to this day that is the main business of our branch of the Snow family and we still own the same land that he bought. From our family records, we knew that this young man came from a place called Fortune House in Yorkshire in England. Recently the company I work for transferred me to their London office, and so I've come here at the first opportunity to visit Fortune House.'

'Well, as far as I know, the stories you've heard are true and your family records are correct. The eldest son has always inherited the whole Fortune estate, which includes the house, the land and some businesses, and younger sons have always had to make their own way in life. In the case of the young man who went to America, his name was James and he was a second son, and I believe it was actually 1703 when he left here. In our family archives, we have some letters that he sent to his family back here after his arrival in Virginia.'

'How fascinating! I wonder, would it be possible to see those letters, and anything else you have that relates to this James Snow?'

'Well, there is a huge quantity of documents, letters, all sorts of family information chronicling events through several centuries. Normally, we don't allow visitors access to all those documents. We have opened the archives to one or two local historians and to the person who wrote the guide book about Fortune House, so that he had all necessary information, but ...'

'Oh, I'm sorry. I do understand. Much as I would love to see some of the letters and other papers, of course, as I've said, I do understand.'

'If it is any compensation, Mr Snow, may I show you around the rest of the house myself? We can read from the guide book as we go, and I can add more details about each room.'

'If you can spare the time, I'd be delighted, but may I ask one thing first? Would you please call me Richard and not Mr Snow?'

'Of course. And you must call me Katherine.'

It took them over an hour to walk through the rooms upstairs and then they came down the back staircase to the old kitchen. From there a corridor led into a gift shop.

Richard looked around at the items displayed on the shop's shelves and his eyes brightened.

'Oh, I see that some of the things you sell here have Fortune House shown on them. Look, placemats and coasters with a delightful watercolour painting of the house. I must buy some of those and send them to my parents. Oh, and I see lots of other lovely things.'

'Richard, why don't I leave you here in the shop and when you have made your purchases, come through the exit and you will see a small café on your right. I will wait for you in there and we can have a cup of tea together.'

'Wonderful! Great idea. Yes, I'll see you in a few minutes.'

When Richard joined Katherine in the café, she asked if he would like tea or would he prefer coffee?

'Contrary to what most Americans think, we *can* make a decent cup of coffee!' Katherine smiled at him.

'No, no, I'd like to be very English and have tea, and whatever small cakes you have that are normally served with tea.'

They ordered tea and toasted teacakes, and Katherine said, 'Oh, I've remembered something most important. When we were talking about James Snow, the one who went off to America, I told you that we had some letters that he wrote after his arrival there, but I forgot completely to tell you that you've already walked past his portrait! He is in the family group painting by Michael Ahmson, that hangs in the Great Hall.'

'Oh, I wish I'd known that,' Richard said.

'Never mind, after we've had our tea, we will walk back through the main entrance and go into the Great Hall again and I can point him out to you.'

As they stood in front of the large painting of the family group, Richard said, 'I saw the notice that says you don't allow photography in the house, but do you have any photograph or copy of that painting that I could send to my parents? They would be absolutely fascinated to see it.'

'I don't think we do ...' Katherine paused to think. 'No, we don't have anything that shows that painting. But I'll tell you what, Richard. The house has just closed and no more visitors will be allowed to come through today. So we will let these last few people go through the Hall and continue their tour of the house, and as I see that you have a camera, you can take a photograph yourself.'

'But photography isn't allowed ...' Richard started to say.

'Richard!' Katherine smiled at him mischievously. 'I am the owner of the house. I make the rules, so I can break them, and I say you can take a photograph!'

Chapter 3

The next morning was bright and sunny. 'A perfect morning for walking,' thought Richard as he ate his breakfast at the inn. He planned to walk all around the small village and take photographs that he would send to his parents. He would also attend the morning service in the village church and he thought that, as the congregation left the church at the end of the service, he would be able to introduce himself to the vicar.

Last night, before he went to sleep, he had looked again at the guide book to Fortune House. The last few pages were devoted to the gardens surrounding the house and he had decided that after lunch he would go again to Fortune House, but today, instead of going into the house, he would walk around the gardens.

As he had hoped, at the end of the morning service, the vicar stood outside the church door greeting and shaking hands with members of the congregation as they left. As Richard shook his hand he said, 'You must be Reverend Hudson? I met your wife briefly yesterday when I was looking around the church.'

'Ah yes, you are our young American visitor who shares the name Snow with our local family. My wife told me you were most interested to read the memorials to various members of the Snow family that are placed in the church. And I believe you visited Fortune House yesterday afternoon?'

'That's right, and I was lucky enough to meet Miss Snow who took some time to show me around and tell me some interesting details about the young man who went to America and is one of my ancestors.'

There was a crowd of people behind Richard as the last of the congregation left the church, so he said goodbye to the vicar and moved on down the path through the cemetery. Viv Hudson appeared at his side.

'Hello again! Remember me? Viv Hudson ...'

'Yes, of course I remember you, Mrs Hudson. And thank you for telephoning Miss Snow and suggesting that she should look out for me when I toured Fortune House. That was very kind of you, and Miss Snow was able to take the time to show me around and fill me in on some details about my ancestor.'

'One thing that may interest you, now that you've been round the house. Do you remember seeing the huge fireplace in the Great Hall? It is decorated with Derbyshire Bluejohn, a stone that was brought from land in Derbyshire that was owned by the Snow family at the time the fireplace was built.'

'Oh yes, I remember that massive fireplace, and I remember thinking that the stone is very unusual.'

'Well, I can show you another piece of that unusual stone. Come over here with me.' Viv led the way between the gravestones close to the church. 'Look,' she pointed to a small headstone. 'In the church yesterday you saw a memorial to a man with the same name as you, Richard Snow, the man who fought in the Battle of Agincourt. This marks the grave of his small son, also called Richard, and a piece of polished Derbyshire Bluejohn has been set into the headstone.'

Richard pulled up his camera. 'Mrs Hudson, would it be all right to take a photograph of the headstone? I mean, it wouldn't be thought to be disrespectful? It wouldn't offend anybody?'

'Oh, nobody would mind. By all means, take a photograph, and now that everyone has left the church, if you wish to go back and take photographs inside, please do so.'

Richard said goodbye to Viv Hudson then he went back into the church and took several photographs of the church interior, and close-ups of each of the Snow memorials. When he had prints of the photographs of the brass memorials, he would put them in chronological order and, he thought, if and when he could arrange a meeting with the vicar, he would ask if the church records could give him more details about each of these people.

As he walked out of the church, Richard glanced at his watch.

'Once again, perfect timing!' he thought, and went over to the inn to have lunch.

When Richard walked up the long drive to Fortune House that afternoon, instead of heading to the house's main entrance, he followed a path that led off around the right-hand end of the house. This led him to what the guide book described as 'the walled rose garden, originally laid out in the late 1500s'. At this time of year, no roses were in bloom but all the rose bushes and the climbing roses were covered in buds, showing the promise of many flowers to come in the summer.

Richard glanced again at the guide book; ah yes, it noted that the roses were at their best in June and July, though many continued blooming into the autumn.

'Well, I shall have to come back again in midsummer to see them all,' he thought. 'I can just imagine what it will look like when all these roses are in full bloom.'

He also noticed that many of the beds were edged with lavender hedges that had been clipped low, and he thought that the combination of the scent of roses and lavender must be quite heady.

Leaving the rose garden through an archway in one of the

walls, he found himself at the back of the house and he stopped in amazement. The back was so completely different from the front! He looked back at the guide book and found that this was the Georgian style façade that had been added to the house in the late 1700s. And there, on the terrace, were the large bronze urns that the guide book said had been brought back to England from Italy, when one of the young men of the family had been on the grand tour. And, as he turned away from the house, he saw the fountain that was bought from Italy at about the same time. On the back cover of the guide book there was a small map to the gardens and Richard saw that by continuing across the back of the house, he would come to the tulip garden.

As he headed in that direction, a voice called out, 'Richard! Mr Snow!' and turning, he saw that Katherine was hurrying out of the back of the house, coming across the terrace towards him.

'I thought it was you! I looked out of an upstairs windows and saw you coming through the wall of the rose garden.'

'Miss Snow ... I mean, Katherine. How very nice to see you again! It is such a lovely day that I really wanted to walk around the gardens after reading about them in the guide book.'

'It is a perfect day, but unfortunately, in mid-April there isn't a lot to be seen. Actually you are only two or three weeks too early to see the tulips in full bloom. Come through this way, and take a look at them. You will see they are just beginning to get colour on the buds.'

Richard looked over the beds full of tulip plants.

'My goodness ... how many tulips do you have?'

'I'm not sure of the exact number, but I know there are several thousand.. Oliver, our wonderful head gardener could tell you exactly how many there are. I say he is the "head gardener" but really he works with just a couple of assistants and also some students from the local agricultural college come to help here most weekends and during the college's breaks. A hundred years ago there were 20 gardeners employed full time.'

Katherine looked around at the gardens and then said, 'Richard, as there isn't a lot to see in the gardens right now, why don't we go through to the small café and have tea – that is if you can spare the time?'

'I certainly have the time to do that, if you can stand it if I bombard you with more questions!' said Richard.

Chapter 4

Once they were settled in the café, with their tea in front of them, Katherine said, 'When you bought some things in the gift shop yesterday, it was my mother who served you. I'd like to introduce the two of you properly. If you don't mind, I'll go through to the gift shop now and see if she can spare the time to join us.'

'I'd be delighted to meet her,' said Richard.

Within minutes Katherine was back with a woman who looked surprisingly young to be her mother. Richard stood up as they approached the table.

'Mummy, this is the young American I told you about, whose name is Richard Snow. Richard, this is my mother, Lady Snow.'

'Mr Snow, how interesting to meet you. Katherine has told me about the probable family connection. Do please sit down, and Katherine, see if you can catch the eye of the waitress and get her to bring more tea and cakes.'

'Lady Snow, it is interesting for me, too, to be here and to meet you and your daughter. I never imagined that when I came to visit Fortune House that I'd be so lucky … or should I say that I'd have such good "fortune"!'

'Oh! A man with a sense of humour as well as being handsome!' said Lady Snow.

'Mummy! What a flirt you are. I'm sure you'll embarrass Richard,' said Katherine.

As they drank their tea, Richard told them that he had

been back to the church that morning and had taken photographs of the Snow family memorials, as well as the gravestone with the Derbyshire Bluejohn set into it.

'Oh yes, that is so unusual,' said Lady Snow. 'And I've always thought how ironic that the little boy died here, at home, while his father was fighting at Agincourt in France and came through that battle without a scratch.'

'These are just the sort of small family details that I am so keen to hear. Katherine tells me that the family's story is well chronicled in documents and papers, and stories like that really bring the family alive, even though the actual events took place several hundred years ago.'

'Richard was walking around the gardens this afternoon, and when I saw him through a window I came down and explained to him that there is very little to see in the gardens right now,' Katherine said to her mother.

'Yes, Katherine showed me the tulip gardens and I am amazed to see how many you have there.' He turned to Katherine, 'And you say that they will be in full bloom in just two or three weeks? I can surely drive up from London again to see them,' said Richard.

'Oh, I've just had a thought,' said Katherine. 'There will be a three-day weekend at the beginning of May. As you haven't been in England very long you probably don't know that we have what are called "bank holiday Mondays", and one of them falls right at the beginning of May this year, so everybody will have a three-day weekend.'

'Couldn't be better!' exclaimed Richard. 'I shall most certainly come back then. These tulips are a "must see" I'm sure.'

'Actually, that would be a particularly good weekend to come again,' said Katherine, 'because the village fair will be held then. Centuries ago it used to be called the Mayfair and it was always held on the first day of May. But the name was gradually changed to the village fair, and now it is held on the first weekend in May. I think you'd find that quite interesting too … a bit of old England, if you like.'

'Oh yes, I think you'd enjoy being here for the village fair, Mr Snow,' said Lady Snow.

'Please, Lady Snow. I've asked Katherine to call me Richard. Would you do the same? And when you say a fair, do you mean it is like a fairground, with all sorts of rides and swings?' asked Richard.

'I'll be happy to call you Richard, but please will you call me Caroline? Lady Snow is so formal. And no, we don't have rides and swings at the fair. It is really an exhibition of all the things that are produced by people in the village. There are horticultural exhibits – vegetables and flowers – and there are handicrafts, and home-made jams, chutneys, cakes and so on. They are all put on display, and we have judges who come and award prizes in each category,' explained Caroline.

'I shall definitely come that weekend,' said Richard. 'All those tulips in bloom, and a village fair! I really can't miss out on all that.'

'Although we don't have swings and rides, we do have a maypole with coloured ribbons hanging from it, and the children from the village school dance around the maypole, weaving and twining the ribbons into a pattern,' Katherine said. 'It is a very old English tradition that we are proud to have continued here. And you will see another Snow family tradition that goes back hundreds of years. After the judges have awarded the first, second and third prizes to the exhibitors, the points are added up and the man and the woman with the most points are each given a special prize. The man receives a pewter platter, and the woman receives a silver brooch made in the shape of a letter "F". The "F" stands for Fortune, to mark the connection between the village and Fortune House.'

'This year, Katherine will be presenting those two awards,' said Lady Snow. 'Traditionally, the special prizes have been presented by the owner of the Fortune estate. Over the centuries, this has always been a man, because the whole estate was entailed upon the eldest son. However, a series of most unusual events happened during the 20th century and because of this my husband worked with lawyers to have the provisions of the entail altered so that Katherine could inherit.'

'Unusual events? What happened?' Richard asked, then immediately said, 'Oh do forgive me, I don't wish to pry. I probably should not have asked.'

'Not at all, Richard, you aren't prying,' said Lady Snow. 'I raised the subject, and if it were something I wished to be kept private, I would not have mentioned it. The unusual events really started with the First World War. When you were in the church, and you read the brass memorials commemorating various members of the Snow family, you must have seen one referring to Arthur Snow who was a pilot in The Royal Flying Corps and was killed in 1916.'

'Yes, I do remember seeing that. I think, if I remember correctly, he was flying over the Somme battlefields when he was killed?'

'That's correct. Well, his death started the series of events that I've mentioned. He had just one child, a son, Jonathan, who had been born earlier that year. So Jonathan inherited Fortune when he was only a few months old. And then,' went on Lady Snow, 'you could say that history repeated itself in the Second World War. In the church there is also a memorial to Jonathan. He was killed on D-Day in June, 1944. His body was never found and, as the plaque in the church says, he has no known grave. I said that history repeated itself, because when he was killed, his only child, his son Roderick, was just one year old and he inherited Fortune.'

'And,' Katherine took up the story, 'Roderick was my father, who died almost two years ago. After I was born, the doctors told my parents that my mother could never have another child. So my father, knowing that there would never be a male heir to Fortune, worked with lawyers who specialise in inheritance law and eventually, it was arranged so that I could inherit the Fortune estate. Actually, I hold it in trust for any male heir that I might have.'

'The story of the Snow family gets more and more fascinating,' said Richard. 'It certainly was most unusual for it to happen that in two consecutive generations a child of a year or less inherited this whole estate. Thank you both for telling me about it.'

Lady Snow looked at her watch. 'Oh dear, I'm afraid I must go back to the gift shop. We have two wonderful young girls who help in the shop but I shouldn't leave them alone too long, especially as we are quite busy today. Goodbye, Mr Snow ... I mean Richard. I've enjoyed talking with you so much, and I'm looking forward to meeting you again when you come back at the beginning of May.'

Chapter 5

After her mother had left, Katherine asked, 'More tea, Richard?'

'I'd love some more, but I'm afraid I'm taking up too much of your time. You probably have a lot to do, with so many visitors to the house today.'

'No, I have the full complement of guides on duty today, and I'm quite free to have more tea with you, Richard,' said Katherine.

'I am still thinking about you inheriting the house and the estate, and all that you had to take on so suddenly. A monumental task! Didn't you feel almost overwhelmed at first?' he asked.

'Well, from the time I was about 16 my father had included me in all meetings and discussions about the estate's business. And we have an excellent estate manager, Nicholas Robb, who has been here for years, and he and I work very closely together. When there are major decisions concerning the estate or the house's maintenance, we make those decisions together. His sister, Sally, is the housekeeper and she is in charge of all the cleaning staff who look after all the rooms that are open to the public, and also the private areas. Sally does most of the cooking for my mother and I, and when we have guests, she gets in some extra help in the kitchens. My mother, as you know, manages the gift shop, and I am in charge of the house's day-to-day running. I decide the dates and hours Fortune House will be open to the public, and I train all the guides who help in the house. I'm also in charge of the café and the staff there. But I want to hear more about you. What kind of work do you do, and what sort of company do you work for?'

'I work for a company that develops new products of all kinds and brings them to the market. Usually, it will be something that someone has invented and has been selling in a fairly narrow market or a small area. If we think the product warrants it, we devise ways of advertising and promoting it and, hopefully, selling it nationally, and possibly worldwide,' Richard explained.

'That sounds fascinating. It must be intriguing to find a new product that you think has the potential to become a household name, and then help it to become so. I presume that you have some special training in marketing?' Katherine asked.

'Yes, I have an MBA.' Katherine looked questioningly at him, so he added, 'That's a Master's degree in Business Administration, and I specialised in Marketing. I find the subject fascinating and one always hopes that a product will become a really major seller though, of course, there are some failures – products that just don't take off, no matter what we do.'

'Mmmm,' Katherine was thoughtful. 'You are probably just the sort of person we need to advise us and give us some ideas of additional things we can sell in the gift shop. Although the shop is successful, we really need to expand that business. I'm sure that we could be doing so much more.'

'Well, would it be presumptuous of me to suggest that I take another look around the gift shop now, and then make notes of ideas and let you have them when I come back in two or three weeks' time?' asked Richard.

'No, of course it wouldn't be presumptuous. It would be

very helpful. Quite honestly, Richard, sometimes I really worry about how we can raise enough money to keep everything going here. The sales in the gift shop and ticket sales to visitors are only a very small percentage of the money we need to earn. I don't want to bore you with details, but for example just keeping the roof of Fortune House in good repair is a huge expense. The roof covers such a large area!' Katherine sighed. 'Oh, I know how lucky I am to have inherited the house and the estate and believe me, I truly love this place, but at the same time, the responsibility is enormous.'

'Well let me ask you another question,' Richard paused because he was trying to phrase the question correctly. 'How would you feel about it if I thought up some other ideas, some other ways that you might consider as additional income-raising projects? In other words, I'd like to think of the Fortune estate as "a product", as I would think of one of the products that we promote and market.'

'Oh Richard, that would be so helpful. Of course, I'd be delighted to hear any ideas that you might have. Thank you very much for thinking of it.' Katherine was genuinely grateful for his offer of help.

'Well, I'll tell you what I will do. I will give the whole matter some thought, and come up with some preliminary ideas. I may need to telephone you to ask questions, to clarify some points, if that will be all right?'

Katherine nodded and Richard went on, 'By the time I come back, I will have some ideas prepared, so that I can go over them with you and leave you to think about them. Then later we can go into more detail about any of the ideas that you think appropriate. And now,' Richard stood up, 'if you'll excuse me, as I'm driving back to London tomorrow, I'd like to make the best use of my time here today. I shall walk around the estate, and take a look at all the outbuildings, and generally get a better idea of what potential there is for making the estate earn its keep.'

Katherine stood up too, and held out her hand. 'Thank you so much, Richard. I do hope that you don't feel it is an imposition to spend time and effort thinking about Fortune and what we can do to increase the income?'

'It certainly isn't an imposition and in any case, I suggested it myself! And, I find the whole place completely fascinating.'

As they shook hands they both said in unison, 'Look forward to seeing you again soon!' and both burst out laughing.

'Is that what you'd call great minds thinking alike?' asked Katherine.

Richard said, 'What I must do is go back to the gift shop and buy a notebook. I'm sure they sell them. I didn't come prepared to make notes of ideas.'

'Oh, the gift shop doesn't sell any notebook large enough for that purpose. Come with me, we can go through the door over there, the back way into the house, and I will take you into my office.'

Katherine led the way through the door into the house, and along a corridor. Richard could see the Great Hall ahead of them at the end of the corridor, but just before they reached it, Katherine opened the door to her office.

'What a delightful room!' exclaimed Richard. 'What a wonderful room to have as your office! This old panelling is exquisite!'

'This room has been used for a very long time to conduct the business of the estate. In fact, for many years it was called "the business room" but I always call it my office,' said Katherine. 'Now, a writing pad … here, one of these should be just what you need.' She held out a large pad of lined writing paper.

'That's perfect. Thank you so much. And now, armed

with this and my camera, I'll make a start. If it's all right with you, I'll walk through the house again, and then go outside to the gardens, and then take a look around the outbuildings. I read in the guide book that some of those buildings used to be used for cheese making, but that nowadays the cheese is made off the premises. I'd like to look at all the buildings, find out which are not used or not put to full use now, and see if I can come up with some ideas of ways they could best be used.'

'There is one thing you should know, Richard. You may have seen the almshouses that are right on the edge of the estate? They cannot be used for any other purpose. They were built to house people who had retired from working on the Fortune estate, and they are restricted to that use. I think there is some sort of covenant that protects the use of those buildings.'

As Richard set off, clutching the pad and his camera, he turned and looked back.

'Thank you for spending so much time with me today, and please tell your mother what a pleasure it was to meet her.'

'I'm sure my mother enjoyed meeting you too, Richard. And thank you again for your offer of help. I shall really look forward to hearing your ideas.'

Chapter 6

During the next two weeks, Richard telephoned Katherine twice to ask some questions about the Fortune estate. In the second conversation he said that he had had some ideas about promoting the gardens more, and he had thought of some ways that income could be generated from them.

'You mentioned that there is a head gardener, and I think it would be a good idea if he could be present at meetings when you and I are discussing my ideas about the gardens,' Richard suggested.

'Yes, of course,' said Katherine. 'His name is Oliver and I will ask him to join us for the parts of the meetings that have anything to do with the gardens. I will also ask Nicholas, the estate manager, to be at all the meetings.'

Richard agreed. 'Yes, good idea to have Nicholas there. I already have a number of ideas but of course I realise that you might not like some of my ideas, or you might turn them down for some practical reasons that haven't occurred to me. However, as there is such a lot to discuss, I've decided that I'll drive up to Yorkshire on Friday, straight after work, and then we shall have the whole of Saturday and Sunday to get together. On Monday I know you will be busy with events at the village fair and, of course, I want to see everything there too before I drive back to London on Monday evening.'

'Richard, it's so good of you to spend so much time on ideas for, what shall we call it, marketing Fortune? Promoting Fortune?'

'Call it whatever you like, Katherine, but let me assure

you, I am thoroughly enjoying what I am doing. There is something about Fortune House and estate that is really triggering my creative streak. By the way, I have already telephoned the inn and made my reservation for the Friday night as well as the Saturday and Sunday nights, and as I shall be arriving very late they've assured me that they will hold my room till whatever time I arrive. And when I spoke to Dennis, the owner of the inn, to make sure he'd hold the room till late, he immediately said that as the kitchens would be closed by the time I arrived, they would have a light supper waiting for me in my room. Now that's what I call service!'

'That's one reason the inn is so successful. Both Dennis and his wife Betsy are the perfect hosts for such a place, always willing to do that little bit extra to ensure that their guests, whether they are staying at the inn, or just going in for a drink or a meal, enjoy their visit. Richard,' Katherine went on, 'shall we plan that you will come to Fortune House straight after breakfast on the Saturday morning? If you are here by 9.30 that morning I will get Oliver and Nicholas to be here then and we can start by discussing your ideas about the gardens, so that Oliver can get back to the gardens as soon as possible. Then the rest of us can spend as long as necessary, going over all your other ideas.'

'I'll be there at 9.30, Katherine. And when we take a break from our discussions, I really want to walk over and see all the tulips in full bloom.'

'Of course,' said Katherine. 'The tulips are one of "the" sights of Fortune's gardens. In fact, I'd go further and say that they are one of "the" sights of this part of the country.'

'And that's exactly why I think we should really promote them. They are an unusual, possibly a unique feature, and I'm thinking along the lines of calling it an "annual tulip festival".'

'Richard! That's a wonderful idea. I really like that.'

Katherine was obviously pleased. 'If your other ideas are as exciting, I can hardly wait to hear them! Oh, I'm so much looking forward to our meeting!'

After Katherine finished talking to Richard she went over to the wing of the house where her mother lived.

'I've just been talking to Richard, and I think he is going to come up with some wonderful ideas for encouraging more visitors to Fortune and increasing our income,' she said. 'For instance, he said that he particularly wants to see all the tulips which will be in full bloom when he is here at the beginning of May. He said that he thinks that the thousands of tulips we have here must be a unique garden feature, and we could advertise it and encourage many more visitors by calling it an annual tulip festival.'

'Mmmm,' her mother looked thoughtful. 'Yes, that does sound an interesting idea, but ...' she hesitated, 'Katherine, I don't want to appear to be negative about Richard's ideas before we've even heard them, but I do hope he doesn't think that this place should be turned into a sort of amusement park. You know what I mean, a "theme park" with Fortune House as its centrepiece.'

'Oh Mummy, I'm sure he wouldn't have any such ideas,' Katherine said, but she added, 'however, I think it would be a good idea for you to be present at our meetings. After all, you have been here at Fortune House ever since you and Daddy married nearly 30 years ago, and you and Daddy first opened the house to the public soon after I was born. Your experience over the years will be a valuable contribution to any discussions, I'm sure.'

'Well, I will certainly consider all his ideas and, Heaven knows, we do need to increase the income of the estate. I've always wondered if it was worry over the constantly rising costs of keeping the house in good repair, and trying to keep the farm business profitable, that contributed to your father's early death. He'd always been so healthy, never any hint that anything was wrong with him ...' Caroline's voice dwindled away.

'I know what you mean, Mummy, but when Daddy died so suddenly, the doctors told us that there are often no symptoms or forewarning of an aneurism.' Katherine paused for a moment or two, then went on, 'Anyhow, let's go out for supper together tonight. It will be nice to walk down to the inn, even though it's a bit chilly, we'll just wrap up warmly.'

When they reached the inn, they found seats near a huge log fire roaring in the inglenook fireplace. Betsy greeted them and asked, 'Can I get you something to drink? And are you here for supper? I'll bring the menu so that you can look at it while you're having your drinks.'

When she came back with their drinks and the menu, Betsy said, 'That American, Mr Snow, is coming back in a couple of weeks. He's phoned to say that he wants a room here for three nights, not just the two he had originally booked. I think he is really fascinated by the English Snow family!'

'Yes, he wants to be here for both the village fair and to see all the tulips which will be in bloom then,' Katherine said.

As mother and daughter walked back to Fortune House after supper, the full moon lit their way up the drive.

'Doesn't the house look beautiful in the moonlight,' said Caroline. 'I remember the very first time your father brought me here. We went out to walk in the grounds after dinner and there was a full moon that night too. I think I fell in love with the house as well as your father! And I've loved this place ever since.'

Katherine took her mother's arm. 'I know how much you

miss Daddy, but it's rather wonderful, isn't it, to know that he and you and I, and any children I might have, are all links in the chain that makes up the continuing story of Fortune.'

Chapter 7

Katherine was looking out of her office window, down the drive, and she saw Richard as he came through the gatehouse carrying a brief case and rolls of papers. She glanced at her watch, it was 9.25 a.m. At the same time, she saw Oliver and Nicholas coming along the path that led from the side of the house, and her mother tapped on her office door, 'Am I too early, or is it all right to come in?'

'Hello, Mummy. My goodness, we are all very prompt and businesslike! I see both Oliver and Nicholas heading this way, and Richard's walking up the drive. I'll go and let them all in through the side door,' said Katherine.

Katherine introduced Richard and Oliver and Nicholas to each other, and Richard said, 'I am so much looking forward to seeing the tulips in bloom. I've brought my camera and I hope to get lots of good photographs.'

As they all went into the office, Oliver and Nicholas said good morning to Lady Snow. Richard said, 'I'm so glad to see you again,' and Katherine waved everyone to seats at a large table to one side of the room.

'I have put out notepads and pencils for each of us, and if we all sit at one end of the table we can spread out any larger paperwork or sketches at the other end of the table.'

Richard started by saying, 'I've written up my thoughts and ideas, and I've made copies so that we each have our own set. Also, I have made some preliminary sketches, to show some plans that I thought we could consider. The sketches are quite large so I will lay those out at the end of the table. Oliver, Katherine has told me that you want to get back to the gardens as soon as possible, so I think if everyone is agreed, we should discuss ideas about the gardens first.'

'Sounds good,' said Katherine, as Richard distributed a set of papers to each person.

As everyone took the set of notes that Richard handed to them, he said, 'If you go to page 8, that is where my ideas about the gardens start. Now, as Katherine knows from a telephone conversation we had, I think that the thousands of tulips here are an outstanding and most unusual feature. In fact, so unusual that I think we can draw in visitors from a wide area, not just the local area, to see them. We must give this feature a name and my suggestions are that we can call it "tulip time" or "the tulip festival" or "the tulip festival at Fortune". How do you feel about those names?' Richard looked around the table.

'I very much prefer "tulip festival" to "tulip time",' said Katherine promptly. 'The word "festival" has a good sound to it.'

'I agree,' said Oliver, a man of few words.

'My preference would be to call it "the tulip festival at Fortune",' said Caroline. 'I agree with my daughter that the word "festival" has a good sound to it, and I think that we should mention the name of Fortune whenever possible.'

'I agree,' said Richard. 'As we all know, the main objective for all our plans is to encourage visitors to Fortune, and to increase the revenue from such visits. Therefore, it is better to establish the link between the tulip festival and Fortune right from the beginning. In fact, I think we should include the name of Fortune in any of the plans that I am going to suggest to you.'

Everybody around the table nodded in agreement.

'Well, let's start with the tulip festival. While I am here this weekend, I will take photographs and we will use some of them in a small colour leaflet that we will have printed. During next autumn and winter, we will write to travel agents and companies that offer day trips and tours by coach, sending each of them one of those leaflets, and suggesting that they make bookings for visits to Fortune to see the tulips.'

'Oh,' said Caroline, 'Richard, if you are suggesting coach trips, we would have to have a limit of not more than three coach parties booked at the same time, because the car park here is not large and could only accommodate about three coaches.'

'And also,' Katherine said, 'I think a coach holds something just over 50 people? We would hope that they would all have lunch in our café – perhaps the price of their coach tour would include lunch here? So again we would have to have a limit of not more than three coaches at any one time, as the café can only accommodate about 160 people.' She looked around the table, 'And there is another important point. When my parents first opened Fortune House to visitors, my father talked to owners of some houses that had been open to the public for some time and asked their advice. I remember he always said that the experienced owners all told him that the first thing everybody asks when they get off a coach is "where are the lavatories?" So we would probably have to build more lavatories, if we are going to have all those additional visitors here at the same time.'

'The points you have raised about the car park, the capacity of the café, and the numbers of lavatories are all good, valid points,' said Richard, 'and I have covered them in my general plans. In order not to hold up Oliver too long on non-garden matters, let me say briefly that we should look around and see if the car park can be expanded, or if a second park just for coaches should be made. As far as the café is concerned, all our plans are geared towards increasing the numbers of visitors and also getting them to spend money while they are here, so we will have to accommodate more people who may wish to eat here. My first thought on that point is that we could convert the orangery into a coffee shop, which would serve an abbreviated version of the full menu offered in the café. Not main meals, only drinks and snacks and light meals. This would be a good location, because as I have shown on one of my sketches, the back of the orangery is just the other side of the wall from the café's kitchens. That wall could be opened up to give the orangery access to the kitchens and also that would allow for the kitchens to be expanded. We will need to enlarge the kitchens in order to handle the greater numbers of visitors who we hope will be eating while they are visiting Fortune.

'As to additional lavatories, another of my large sketches on the table shows that I have noted an area at the end of one of the outbuildings that could be used to construct about ten lavatories. I have chosen that location primarily because it is close to the car park, and also because that building is well placed to hook up with plumbing and sewer lines.'

Caroline leaned back in her chair. 'Richard, I can only say that I feel almost stunned!'

'Oh Lady Snow, I hope I haven't said something that offends you?' Richard asked quickly.

'No, no, not at all,' Caroline said immediately. 'I say that I am stunned because in just a few minutes and a few words, you have shown us how thoroughly you have considered so many things that must be included in our hopes and plans to encourage more visitors. No, no, Richard, far from being offended, I congratulate you!'

Richard smiled. 'Well, perhaps the congratulations should go to the professors who took me through the marketing classes!'

Chapter 8

Before Oliver headed back to the gardens, Richard brought up a few more thoughts he had had about encouraging visitors to other parts of the gardens.

'Let me ask you about the rose garden and the azalea walk,' Richard started. 'Do you have photographs of both of them in full bloom?'

'Yes, I have a lot of photographs taken over the years by my father,' said Katherine.

'Good,' said Richard, 'because I would like to include small photographs of other parts of the gardens on the back of the leaflet we distribute to promote the tulip festival. That might encourage people to come back again at other times of the year.'

'I can certainly look out all the photographs we have and I'm sure that some would be perfect to use for that,' said Katherine.

'And what about the herb garden?' asked Richard. 'When I was walking round last time I was here, I noticed that area. Has it been part of the gardens for a long time?'

'Oh yes! A herb garden was first laid out in the late 1500s, I think,' said Katherine. 'I can certainly look through the family records to check that. Oliver, do you know anything about it?'

'Yes, I have some newspaper articles among the garden records and I remember that they say that the herb garden has been here for about 400 years.'

Oliver paused to think. 'Of course, we have never devoted

much time or attention to the herb garden; we've more or less just kept it tidy, and taken out any herbs that died and replaced them.'

'Well, I'd like to see the herb garden re-established,' said Richard. 'People are very interested in herbs nowadays. As well as their culinary use, herbs are used a lot for health foods and cosmetics.'

'I'm not sure just how much work we can put into the herb garden …' Oliver started to say, but Richard interrupted him.

'Of course, you'd need extra help if we go ahead with the idea of making it a feature of the gardens. What do you think, Katherine?'

'I like the idea. I agree that people are really interested in herbs nowadays – look at all the cooking shows on TV that have made us familiar with herbs that were unusual just a few years ago, and lots of people like to grow herbs. Even people living in apartments quite often grow a few in pots or in a window box.'

'That's a good point and it leads me to another of my ideas,' said Richard. 'Providing, of course, that Oliver has the extra help he needs, we should also sell herb plants. It would be yet another attraction of a visit to Fortune. In fact, we should consider selling plants of all kinds.'

'Well, I cast my vote in favour of getting the herb garden flourishing again,' said Caroline. 'And you, Oliver? How do you feel? And you, Nicholas?'

'As far as I'm concerned, as long as I have enough manpower, I'd like to see all parts of the gardens improved,' said Oliver, 'and I agree that we should make a point of bringing all the different areas to the attention of visitors.'

'Everything you've said so far sounds good to me too,' said Nicholas

Oliver declined the offer of a cup of coffee, saying that he really had to get back to his work in the gardens. As he left he shook hands with Richard and said, 'I'm delighted to hear your plans. I have always thought that the gardens here at Fortune are very special. I believe that the family records can tell us just when the different sections were added, and about the members of the family who were living here at that time. I think this is something that would interest visitors.'

'You're right, Oliver,' said Richard. 'I will add to my notes that we should think about having more information about the history of the gardens either in the guide book to the house, or in a separate leaflet that could be given to each visitor.'

As Katherine, Caroline, Richard and Nicholas were drinking their coffee, Caroline said, 'Richard, when you offered to think up some ways that we could increase the number of visitors to Fortune, I had no idea that you would go into so much detail. I'm particularly glad that you thought about expanding our ability to serve meals and snacks, because that is a very profitable area.'

'I hope you will like my other ideas, too,' said Richard. 'I have several suggestions of ways that the gift shop could be made more profitable. As you manage the gift shop, Caroline, I hope you will not feel that the suggestions I make are in any way a criticism of the way you have been running it. It is simply that I am sure that the shop could generate more income.'

'Richard, you don't have to be tentative when making suggestions about the gift shop,' Caroline said. 'If I don't like or agree with any of your ideas, I shall say so. I think it is essential that both of us, in fact all of us, are absolutely honest, and open, and direct with each other.'

'You're a woman who likes to do business the way I do,' Richard smiled at Caroline. 'I'm a great believer in being absolutely frank in business discussions. It saves a lot of time.'

They finished their coffee and put the cups on a small side table so that Richard could spread out his sketches on the main table.

'This sketch,' he explained, 'shows the area of the orangery and the alterations that would be made to connect it to the back of the present kitchens, and it also shows how the kitchens can be enlarged.'

He turned to the next sketch. 'This drawing shows preliminary building plans for where we have talked about adding new lavatories.

'And here is another of my ideas,' Richard indicated a large sketch, 'that I think will bring in a very good income, incurring very little expenditure on our part, and also it is something that can really help to put Fortune "on the map" as you might say. I am sure we could expect to get a lot of press and TV coverage for this project.' Richard spread out the very large drawing.

'Those are the buildings that used to be used for cheese making, until that business grew so much that we had to build the new place over on the edge of the farm,' said Katherine.

'And now, I think, they are not used for anything in particular?' asked Richard.

Both Katherine and Caroline nodded, and Nicholas said, 'They haven't been used at all for, oh it must be 20 years or more.'

'A waste of really useful space that I think can be put to good use. Look,' Richard pointed to the heading on his drawings. It read "The Fortune Studios".

'Studios? Do you mean that we should have artists there?' Katherine looked puzzled.

'My idea is that these spaces should be rented out to various local crafts people. Several other great houses have created studio space for artists, sculptors, potters – many different

320

kinds of creative people. I am sure that such people would be attracted to this space, and this setting. Instead of these buildings standing empty, they would generate income from the rents and, in turn, the crafts people would attract people to come here because they would be showing and selling their products.'

Caroline said, 'The artist who painted the watercolour of Fortune House that is on the placemats that you bought told me not too long ago that she would like to set up a studio locally. She is quite well known in the area for her watercolours of local buildings and views. So that's one person who would probably be interested in becoming a tenant. Oh, and Katherine, do you remember the man who builds those exquisite dolls' houses? I ran into him a few weeks ago and he said that he wanted to have a place where he could make and show and sell the dolls' houses. I think this is just the sort of place he would like.'

'Those are exactly the sort of people I had in mind,' said Richard. 'I am certain that they would like this kind of setting for their businesses. Of course, the buildings would have to be cleaned up, decorated, and the power and water supplies and the drainage would have to be checked professionally.'

Katherine was still studying the drawings. 'I really like this idea. I see that your drawing shows that there should be space for about a dozen tenants with their businesses. I'm all for doing this, but – and I do hate to pour cold water on things – everything we have discussed is going to cost an awful lot of money. Nicholas, what do you think?'

'I think it's an excellent idea,' said Nicholas, 'but obviously, you would have to talk to the accountants about the financial side of all this. And I wonder if, as this is such a historic house, there might be any grants that would be available for such alterations and improvements.'

'What you've just said is quite a coincidence, because it

brings me to my next point,' said Richard. 'Take a look at this.' He held out a typed sheet. 'Here are details of grants that are available for such work to be done on historic houses and buildings. I'm sure your accountants could advise you about applying for such grants.'

'A grant! Fantastic! That would be absolutely wonderful!' Katherine and Caroline beamed at each other. 'Richard, I have to say it again, you have thought of everything!'

Chapter 9

The phone on Katherine's desk rang shrilly, making her jump. She answered it with her mind still on the sheets of financial information in front or her.

'Hello. Are you very busy? Is this a bad time to talk to you?' Richard's voice came down the line.

'No, it's not a bad time. In fact it's a very good time. I need a break from going over numbers and money calculations,' Katherine answered. 'And all this complicated financial stuff is your fault!'

'My fault? What have I done?' Richard sounded concerned.

'Oh, Richard, I'm joking. All I meant is that you came up with all sorts of plans – excellent plans, by the way – and since you were here I've talked to the accountants a couple of times. They sent over someone who knows about which grants we might be eligible to receive, and now I'm surrounded by pages and pages of numbers, calculations, estimates for building works …'

'Stop, stop,' Richard interrupted. 'Katherine, I hate to think I've heaped all this work and worry on you. And, of course, I realise that even though the accountants and this man who knows about grants can help and advise, you are the one who has to read and understand all the details, and you are the one whose signature has to go on contracts. Something like the old saying that the buck stops here!'

'I know,' Katherine's voice was almost a wail. 'My mother

has read through all the paperwork and she is trying to help, but honestly, Richard, financial affairs are not her strong suit, and …' Her voice tailed away.

'Katherine, you sound so dejected and so worried. Look, this coming weekend is another of your English bank holiday weekends, and I would like to come up and do whatever I can to help.'

'Oh, Richard, it would be wonderful if you could come this weekend. But are you sure you are free? I just hate to feel that I am taking up all your free time with Fortune House affairs. I don't want to impose on you. After all, you were here for the long weekend just a month ago.'

'You won't be imposing at all. Katherine, I've known for a couple of weeks or more about this three-day weekend coming up, but I hesitated to suggest coming again, because I thought it would seem that *I* was imposing on *you*, by coming to Fortune at every opportunity. I'm no financial expert, but I will happily go through all the paperwork with you and help in any way I can.'

'Help? Richard, it would be marvellous. Oh, I've just thought … the inn is probably already fully booked for this weekend. But I'll tell you what, stay here in Fortune House. We have several guest rooms.'

'I hate to put you to that trouble, Katherine. I'll telephone the inn now, and if they are full they can probably suggest some other place I could stay – perhaps over at Moortown?'

'Richard it won't be any trouble at all. I'll ask the housekeeper to get one of the guest rooms ready and we will expect you … when?'

'I'd like to get there late Friday night if that's convenient, then we can have two full days to look at all the paperwork, before I have to drive back to London on Monday.'

'Richard, I feel relieved already. It doesn't matter that

you aren't, as you say, a financial expert. It will be so much help if you go through everything with me. And as all of this is connected with your ideas and suggestions, it's probably good that you look over everything and make sure nothing has been omitted.'

'Fine, I'll see you late Friday night then; oh and Katherine, I'll bring the photographs I took at the village fair.'

When she hung up the telephone, Katherine was smiling to herself. Suddenly, the pile of papers and all the financial calculations didn't seem such a burden. She was humming to herself when her mother came into the office.

'My goodness, it's not often that a pile of quotations and estimates can make someone sing!'

'Oh Mummy, I've just had a telephone call from Richard, and he has suggested that he should come up this weekend and he will go over all this …' Katherine gestured to the stack of paperwork, 'with me.'

'Well that's a good idea but oh dear, I expect the inn will be fully booked …'

'Yes, I thought of that,' Katherine said, 'and I've suggested he should stay here. I must talk to Sally and ask her to prepare one of the guest rooms. I'll go and find her now.'

As Katherine left the office she was humming a tune again. Caroline looked after her, thinking, 'Well, well! Katherine certainly seems very happy at the prospect of Richard being here again this weekend … I wonder …' She stopped in mid-thought. 'Stop being silly. You're thinking like a romantic young girl!'

Richard arrived earlier than either Katherine or Caroline had expected on Friday evening.

'My goodness!' exclaimed Katherine, going to meet him at the main door. 'How on earth did you get here so quickly?

Even if you broke the speed limit all the way, I don't know how you managed to get here at this time.'

'I left the office at midday, and got a head start on all the weekend traffic leaving London,' explained Richard.

'Well, your timing is perfect. Mummy and I are just going to have a drink before dinner, so let me show you up to your room, then come down as soon as you can and join us in the small sitting room behind the Great Hall. Meanwhile, I'll let Sally know that we shall be three for dinner.'

While they were sipping their drinks, Richard gave them a packet of photographs to look at.

'Oh, the village fair photographs.' Caroline moved over to sit next to Katherine on the sofa so that they could look at them together.

'These are very good. They capture the atmosphere of the fair perfectly,' said Katherine. 'And I really like this – you've photographed me presenting the special brooch to the woman who won it this year, and then you have an excellent close-up photograph of the brooch. If I may keep this, I'd like to put it into the family records. We know that the brooch shaped as "F" for Fortune was first presented back in the middle 1800s, that much is well documented, but we have never had a sketch or picture of the brooch.'

'Of course you may keep it. I've had that set of photographs printed for you,' said Richard.

'Both Katherine and I are anxious to keep the Snow family records as complete as possible,' explained Caroline. 'When I first came to Fortune House as a new young bride, I discovered that succeeding generations of Fortune wives had done a marvellous job of keeping all the family documents in order, and adding information about events that happened during their lifetime. So, naturally, I have always felt that it was my duty as well as a pleasure to continue that tradition.'

'You've mentioned the family documents and archives before, Katherine. How far back do records go? And how complete are they?' Richard asked.

'They go all the way back to 1415 and they are fairly complete from the late 1600s. A woman called Elizabeth married into the family at that time, and she became fascinated by the family history. She found that all the documents were scattered in several different places in the house and so she gave herself the task of sorting them into chronological order, and keeping them all in one place. Then she started adding her own notes about events she considered important to the family, and she kept copies of bills for work done, letters from or about family members. In fact, Richard, she was the mother of your ancestor James. So Elizabeth herself is one of your forebears and in the archives there are letters sent by James from Virginia, which Elizabeth kept.'

Katherine paused and thought for a moment, then went on, 'Richard, when you first visited here you asked me about seeing the family archives and I said that we don't normally let visitors to the house see them, which is true. But you aren't just a visitor to the house. You are in a different, special category, and as there are documents relating to your own personal history, I think you should see them.'

'I'd certainly like to do that. Thank you. But one thought occurs to me ... well two thoughts. Firstly, the old documents must be very fragile and it is probably not a good idea to let people handle them. And secondly, I imagine that both the style of the writing and of the English language centuries ago, must make them difficult to read?'

'I can answer both your thoughts. In the 19th century, a woman called Adelaide, who was married to Henry Snow, realised that the oldest documents were deteriorating so she copied every single one of them! Her handwritten copy still exists, but then in the 1920s another Snow wife took Adelaide's handwritten pages and typed them so that now they are much easier to read. Of course, they have been faithfully copied both times and the oldest documents are, as you thought, written in a style of English that isn't always easy to follow. By the way, the woman who did all the typing was my great-grandmother, the widow of the man who was killed flying over the Somme battlefields.'

Chapter 10

After they had finished dinner, Katherine said to Richard, 'I'll show you where all the family records are kept. When you see them, you will realise what an enormous task it will be to read through them, and how long it will take. There are so many documents of all kinds.'

The three of them went up to the top floor of the house. At one end of the solar, there were several large wooden chests, and one wall had deep shelves from floor to ceiling.

'My father had these shelves built especially,' said Katherine, 'because ordinary bookshelves are not deep enough to hold this kind of paperwork. The oldest documents are all in these chests.' She bent over one and started to lift the lid.

Richard jumped forward. 'Here, let me help. That lid looks really heavy.'

'Thanks. It *is* heavy.' Together they pulled the lid fully open. Inside the chest, the documents and papers lay in rolls.

'There is special acid-free tissue paper wrapped around each roll, and placed between each of the documents,' explained Katherine. 'You can't imagine how long it took my parents and I to put all that tissue paper in place!'

Richard stood back. He looked around him, then asked, 'Are each of these chests as full as this one?'

'Oh yes,' said Katherine. 'We are careful not to pack things tightly, or to let them weigh heavily on each other. And all those shelves are pretty full, too, as you can see.'

'This is the most amazing collection. It is far, far more than I had imagined.'

'When the historian was here getting information for the

guide book, he said that he thought this collection of family documents and the detail they contain was probably unrivalled except for records kept by the Royal Family,' said Katherine.

'I can believe it,' said Richard. 'One thing I would suggest is that you have the oldest, most precious documents and letters photographed. In fact, photograph all of them. That will preserve perfect copies. Then the photographic copies could be put on view in the house.' He paused. 'Even better, you could mount a special exhibition showing many of the documents, especially some of the letters that survive. Those would really bring the Snow family to life.'

'And,' Katherine took up his thread of thought, 'such an exhibition could be put on at a time when there are normally very few visitors to the house. As you know, the house is not open to the public through the winter months because it would cost so much to heat it, but we could have the exhibition either very early or very late in the "open season". What do you think, Richard?'

'I think you are talking like a marketing man!' said Richard. 'It's a brilliant idea. What do you think, Caroline?'

'I agree, it's a great idea and apart from bringing visitors to the house, I think that such an exhibition is something that would attract media interest. We could get the local TV station to visit the exhibition. Oh! Am I talking like a marketing man, too?'

'You certainly are,' Richard was smiling broadly, 'and what's more, a really good marketing man!'

'Well, let me bring up a practical point.' Now Caroline was looking very serious. 'Such an exhibition would need a lot of space in order to show everything to best advantage. Katherine, where could we find enough space?'

Katherine looked serious, too, and shook her head. 'Obviously we couldn't use the Great Hall, or any of the other rooms that are open to the public because they all have a lot of furniture in them, as well as paintings and framed embroideries and so on. I suppose we could have the exhibition up here in the solar but we don't normally allow visitors to come up to this floor. Oh dear, an exhibition is such a good idea, but I just can't think where we could put it.'

'Then let me make a suggestion,' Caroline had their attention. 'Let's all go downstairs and get some more coffee and I will tell you what I'm thinking.'

While they were waiting for the fresh coffee to be ready, Katherine said, 'Don't keep us waiting, Mummy. Tell us what you have in mind.'

'Well, I've been thinking ...' Caroline started, then broke off. 'Oh, the coffee is ready.' She poured the coffee, handed cups to Katherine and Richard, took a cup herself and sat down.

'You could use part of what is now my wing for the exhibition. I've been thinking that I'd really like to have my own house again,' she said.

'What? Mummy, you don't mean that you want to leave Fortune?' Katherine was astounded.

'No, not leave Fortune, but leave this house and have a place of my own again.'

There was a stunned silence then Katherine found her voice.

'But why, Mummy? I thought you were comfortable in your wing. Aren't you happy here?'

Caroline glanced at Richard, as if seeking his support. He caught the look and said, 'Katherine, perhaps this house has too many memories for your mother. Good, happy memories, but nevertheless, perhaps she feels it is time to move on. I'm sorry, Caroline, it's not my business. I probably shouldn't say anything.'

'It's all right, Richard. If this was something that I didn't want to discuss in front of you, I would not have brought the subject up now. Katherine, I am very comfortable in my wing but just the other day after we'd been discussing plans to make good use of some of the empty buildings here, I thought about the dower house. Your grandmother was the last person to live there, and it's been empty ever since she died. I went and walked all around the outside of it, and then I got the key from Nicholas and went inside.'

'You didn't mention this. You didn't say anything about it.' Katherine was completely taken aback. 'And I still don't understand …'

'Well, when I thought about the dower house and especially after I'd walked around inside it, I suppose it was as if everything dropped into place,' said Caroline. 'Firstly, dower houses were built to be lived in by widows, and secondly, I realised that I would like to have my own house again. My own house and my own life.' She paused. 'Oh Katherine, don't look so worried.'

'Well, I *am* worried, Mummy,' said Katherine. 'I've been so busy running the house and the estate, and trying to understand all the finances, that I'm afraid I haven't given any thought to you and your life.'

'And that's how it should be,' said Caroline. 'Your first duty is to ensure that the house is kept in good order and that the estate is well run and is profitable. After more than 600 years, you can't be the one to let it all go.'

Katherine smiled gently. 'That's exactly what Daddy used to say. He always said that he only had this place for his lifetime, and that he held it in trust for future generations. But that's nothing to do with you moving to the dower house.

Anyhow,' Katherine waved her hand as if brushing aside the idea. 'After all these years of standing empty, it can't be in a fit condition for you to live in.'

'No, it isn't fit for me to live in as it is. But I have some money of my own and I want to spend it on bringing the dower house back to life. I know that it will cost quite a lot of money to make it the way I want it, but I don't want to travel the world, or buy jewels or expensive clothes. I want to spend my money on restoring the dower house and making it into my own comfortable home. Besides, you will marry one day and you should have this place for your own family, just as previous generations have done.'

Katherine looked at Richard. 'Can you think of anything I can say to change her mind?'

Richard held up his hands and said, 'Oh whoa there, Katherine. I'm not going to take sides. I don't want to come between mother and daughter!'

'Actually, Richard, I'd like to hear your opinion,' said Caroline. 'My mind is almost made up, but I'd like to hear if you can think of any real drawbacks to my plan?'

'This is very awkward for me,' said Richard. 'You've said that you don't mind discussing the subject in front of me, but frankly, I would rather not discuss your finances, and the only potential drawback that I can see is that it may cost too much money to put it back in good condition.'

'I understand, Richard. But other than any financial considerations, you don't see any good reason for me not to go ahead with these ideas?' Caroline asked.

Before he could answer, Katherine burst out, 'But what about how *I* feel? Richard, can't you understand that I like having my mother living right here, in the same house? Why should I want to change anything?'

'I've said that I don't want to take sides, but I must say

that I agree with your mother, Katherine. Some day you will marry and have your own family here. And the dower house is only a matter of a few minutes' walk away. I expect that grandchildren will be beating a path to Caroline's door every day!'

Chapter 11

Next morning, right after breakfast, Richard and Katherine went into the office so that Richard could take a look at all the paperwork relating to the proposed changes and additions to Fortune House.

'Let me take a quick look through all this, just scan through it quickly by myself, and then we can go through it page by page.'

Katherine left Richard sitting at her large desk with the pile of papers in front of him, and she moved to a small chair near the window. After about 20 minutes, Richard straightened up.

'Right, I've looked at everything and it all seems quite straightforward. The only thing I would suggest, Katherine, is that you talk to the builders about some of the prices they have quoted and see if you can get a reduction. After all, this is a job that will bring them a great deal of prestige locally. Anyhow, let's go through all this page by page and you tell me anything you don't understand and I will see if I can explain it.'

Richard broke off, as there was the sound of a car driving across the gravel of the drive and drawing up at the main door. He and Katherine both looked out of the window and saw a small van with the name 'Yorkshire Building Works' painted on the side, and Caroline going down the steps and greeting the man who got out of the van.

'Well! My mother isn't wasting any time! When she told

335

us last night about her plans to move to the dower house, she didn't mention that she had already arranged for the builders to come here this morning.'

As they both watched Caroline and the builder walk round the corner of Fortune House, going towards the dower house, Katherine turned away from the window and said briskly, 'Right, Richard. Let's go over the paperwork about applying for grants. The man that the accountants sent over to see me said that he would take care of all the formalities, but I need to be sure I understand everything before we actually make an application.'

They spent the next hour poring over the documents that explained all the requirements that had to be met in order to obtain grants for the sort of work that was planned for Fortune House. Finally Richard said, 'Well, it seems to me that Fortune meets the criteria required to obtain several different kinds of grants. I think you should get in touch with the man who came to see you and ask him to proceed with making applications. The sooner you know how much grant money can be awarded, and how much money you will have to spend yourself, the better.'

'Richard, I am so grateful to you for going through all this with me.'

'I didn't really do anything, except read through all the papers with you.'

'Yes, I know,' said Katherine, 'but just the fact of you being here and being able to go through the paperwork together made it easier somehow. Oh, how I wish that …' she broke off.

'What were you going to say?' asked Richard.

'Oh, nothing. Oh well, I was going to say that it would be wonderful if you could be here all the time, but I realised what a stupid thing that was to say. That's all,' replied Katherine.

'Believe me,' said Richard, 'I find myself wishing more

and more that I could be here all the time. There is something about this place. I don't know ... am I being foolish because of that family connection from way back? Foolish or not, I know that from the very first day I came here, I felt I'd come home.'

Katherine looked at him, and started to say something, then suddenly she felt very emotional and tears were coming to her eyes. 'Sorry,' she said brusquely. 'I'm being silly. Come on, let's go for a walk around the gardens. Some of the tulips are still looking good.'

As they went down the terrace steps and turned towards the gardens, Katherine led the way, setting a brisk pace. She felt embarrassed that she'd felt so emotional at the thought of Richard spending more time – all the time – at Fortune. The strength of her feelings for him had taken her by surprise. Mentally she told herself, 'Stop being foolish. You hardly know the man. How often have you met? How much time have you spent in each other's company? You're not some teenage girl who believes in love at first sight.'

They had reached the walled rose garden and Richard said, 'Let's go in here, Katherine. It's the end of May and some of the roses should be coming into bloom. I'd love to see them.'

As they went through the archway in the wall Richard paused and looked around.

'Magnificent! Absolutely magnificent!' he murmured.

'Well, in another couple of weeks, mid-June, they will be even more beautiful, and when they are in full bloom their scent is something that visitors always say is remarkable,' said Katherine.

Richard was walking ahead of her along the stone pathways between the beds, and he bent down.

'Oh good, there is a little metal stake in each bed, giving the name of the rose. That's really helpful. And what lovely names some of them have.' He looked around and said, 'Oh look, this one is called Lady Snow!'

'Yes, there is a story about that rose in the family papers. In 1848, it was produced by the man who was head gardener at that time, and he presented it to the then Lady Snow on the day of the village fair. For many years the gardeners here took cuttings and made grafts so that "Lady Snow" rose bushes were always available. However, they are available commercially nowadays, so we can buy new ones if they are needed.'

'The story about the origin of that rose is just the sort of thing that really illustrates the story of the Snow family and their life in this house for centuries. There cannot be many places that have been home to one family continuously for such a long time.'

'That's true,' said Katherine. 'In fact, it has been a great point of pride with succeeding generations of Snows that we have been here for so many centuries. I once told my father that I was worried that when I married and had children, they wouldn't be called Snow and I'd be the one to break all those centuries of tradition. But my father told me that in such circumstances, arrangements are sometimes made for the husband to take the wife's surname. So if I did that, and if my husband agreed to dropping his name and taking mine, any children I may have would be called Snow.'

Richard turned to face her. 'Katherine,' he said, taking one of her hands in his, 'you wouldn't have to make those special arrangements if you married a man whose name was already Snow.'

Katherine looked puzzled. 'What do you mean, Richard? A man whose ... oh!' She dropped his hand and turned away from him.

'Oh, Katherine, I'm so sorry,' said Richard. 'I'm a fool, a

stupid clumsy fool. I shouldn't have said anything, it's too soon. But now that I've said it, it's out and I will confess that I've fallen completely in love with you. Katherine, please turn around. Please look at me. I'm so very sorry. I didn't mean to upset you.'

Katherine turned to face him and her eyes were glistening with tears.

'Oh Katherine … I've really upset you …' Richard's face was miserable.

'No, no, I'm not really crying, Richard,' Katherine explained. 'I'm crying with happiness! Just this morning, when I said that I wished you could be here all the time, I realised how wonderful that would be, and at that moment, I knew that I'd fallen in love with you!'

At exactly the same moment they both moved towards each other, and standing in the rose garden, exchanged their first kiss.

As they separated, Richard said, 'Well, I only suggested that if you could find a man called Mr Snow, you should marry him, and look what has happened!'

They both laughed, then Richard said, 'Let me phrase it another way. Katherine, my darling Katherine, will you please marry me?'

'Richard! I don't think you need my answer in words, do you? But just in case you do … yes, yes, yes. Yes please, I will marry you!'

As they were kissing again, Katherine pulled away.

'But Richard, how can we marry? Your job is in London, and my place is here at Fortune.'

'Well, you did say that it would be wonderful if I could be here all the time,' said Richard, 'and for my part, I can't think of anything that I would like more. I will happily quit my job in London and after we are married, we will live here. My "job" will then be to help you in every way that I can. And then, just as your mother said, you will have your own family living here in this house. Another generation of Snows will be living at Fortune.'

'Speaking of my mother, do you think we should tell her right away? Or should we wait?' Katherine asked Richard.

'I think we should tell her straight away,' said Richard. 'because I don't think I can keep this news to myself. I know I won't be able to stop smiling all the time!'

Chapter 12

They found Caroline in her sitting room, and when they told her their news, she burst into tears. As she was dabbing at her eyes Richard said, 'Oh, I'm so sorry. We had hoped that you would be pleased about our news.'

Caroline interrupted him, 'Richard, Richard. I'm not crying because I'm upset. I'm crying because I am so happy!'

'I seem to make a habit of making the women in the Snow family cry,' said Richard. 'But as long as the tears are always from happiness, then I don't mind.'

'We must have some champagne,' said Caroline. 'I'll go down and get a bottle.' She turned to Richard and added, 'We always keep a couple of bottles ready chilled. It's something my husband insisted on.'

'Now that's a Snow family tradition that I think should be continued,' said Richard.

As they were drinking the champagne, Caroline said, 'Richard, what about telling your family? And we must tell all the Fortune staff, too.'

Richard said, 'I will telephone my parents in a couple of hours. It is still only about six o'clock in the morning in Virginia.'

'Oh, when you speak to your mother, would you mind if I talk to her and introduce myself?' asked Caroline.

When Richard spoke to his parents, his father immediately said, 'Your mother said that she thought you were getting very fond of this young lady, Katherine, from the way you've talked about her whenever we spoke on the telephone. I guess women pick up on such things!'

Richard's mother and Caroline talked for quite a long time, and when she finally put the telephone down, Caroline said, 'We seemed able to chat together as if we'd been friends for years. She asked when I thought the wedding would be held, and I said that I didn't think you'd had time to think about that yet. I said that I thought it would probably be late in the year, so that you have a few months to prepare for it, and you can hold the reception in the Great Hall, if it is at a time when the house isn't open to visitors.'

'You're absolutely right, Mummy. We haven't thought about a date for the wedding yet, but it would be lovely to have the reception right here in the Great Hall. Perhaps December, just before Christmas would be nice? What do you think, Richard?'

'Katherine, my love, I don't mind when the wedding is held. I leave that entirely to you as the bride.'

'The bride! The bride! Oh that does sound so nice! I just wish that your father could be here,' Caroline said. She paused for a moment, then went on briskly, 'Let me think ... how shall we announce the engagement to all the staff? I know, we'll have a small party. Do you think next weekend would be a good time? I'll ask Sally to invite all the household staff, and Nicholas as estate manager will invite all the farm and estate staff.'

'If we are to have a party to announce the engagement, I would like you to be able to wear your engagement ring, Katherine,' said Richard. 'Today is Saturday. No shops will be open tomorrow or Monday, as it is a holiday, and then I shall be back in London all next week. Shall we go into Beverley this afternoon and look around the jewellers' shops there? Or am I rushing you?'

'No, darling, you aren't rushing me. I'd love to be wearing

your ring as soon as possible. I want to feel "labelled" as your fiancée,' she answered.

Richard resigned from his job as soon as he went back to London and gave his company three months' notice. Then he moved to Yorkshire in the middle of September. At the back of the inn in the village, there were four furnished apartments that were used by holidaymakers in the summer, but one was vacant in September and as nobody else had booked it for the autumn and winter months, Richard rented it. He would live there until their wedding. He had also rented another apartment for the week before the wedding and a few days after, and his parents and brother and sister would stay there when they came to England for the wedding.

Katherine decided that she wanted a small wedding. 'I'm glad I don't have several sisters,' she told her mother, 'I've never wanted a whole posse of bridesmaids.'

'What about some of your old friends?' her mother asked. 'Wouldn't you like one or two of them to be bridesmaids?'

But Katherine was quite definite. 'No bridesmaids, and as Daddy is dead, I want you to give me away, Mummy.'

Caroline demurred but the vicar had assured her that quite often nowadays the bride's mother gave her away.

'People don't stick to rigid rules these days,' he had said. 'And as you probably know, many young couples even write their own wedding vows.'

'That's something I definitely do *not* want to do,' said Katherine. 'I want everything traditional. I want the old form of the marriage service, and I'd like the design of my wedding dress to be based on a gown worn in one of the family portraits hanging in the Great Hall.'

Soon after the engagement was announced, Katherine was contacted by two magazines who both offered a large sum of

343

money for the exclusive rights to photograph the wedding and the reception. Katherine had immediately declined, saying that she wanted to keep the wedding private. She told Richard about the offers and said, 'I hope you agree with my decision? I really don't want to use our wedding as part of the effort to publicise Fortune House. Although the amount of money they are talking about would go a long way towards paying for all the alterations and building work we are doing.'

Richard immediately said that he agreed with her decision. 'This is our wedding, just for us and our families and the staff of Fortune. I don't mind who takes photographs, and I don't mind if photographs appear in some newspapers and magazines, but I agree with you that we don't want to sell exclusive rights to anybody.'

From the time he moved to Yorkshire, Richard spent part of every day reading through the family stories contained in the records. Several times he had said, 'God bless your great-grandmother! Without her typed copy, it would take far longer to read everything. I'm glad my family will be here for a few days before the wedding, because I have so much to tell them about the Snow family. And I want to show them copies of the letters that James sent back from Virginia. They will be fascinated.'

One evening Katherine said, 'Richard, it's a lovely evening. Take your head out of those family chronicles and let's go for a walk before dinner.'

They walked through the rose garden, around the herb garden, and then turned back towards the house. The sun was going down quickly, turning the sky a bright salmon colour in the west.

'Just look at that!' exclaimed Richard. 'Fortune House is so beautiful with the setting sun glistening in all its windows.'

'Do you know, Richard, not too long ago my mother told me that she thought she had fallen in love with both Fortune House and my father, and I do believe that you've fallen in love with the house as well as me!'

Richard laughed. 'I can't deny it! I really do love this place! And I'm glad you told me that your mother said that because it makes me feel I'm following a family tradition. And,' he went on, 'there is another family tradition that I've been reading about that I'd like us to follow.'

'Oh, what's that?' asked Katherine.

'Apparently, sons in the Snow family are all given the name Crispin as one of their names. It goes back to the year 1415, when Richard Snow came home safely from the Battle of Agincourt. The battle was fought on St Crispin's Day and to honour the saint, Richard named his son Crispin. That is the Richard Snow whose memorial I noticed in the church the very first day I came here, because he has the same name as me.' He turned to Katherine and went on, 'As you know, the earliest family records are from that year – 1415 – and that Richard Snow was also married to a woman called Katherine, though he called her Kate. So the whole story, as far back as we know it, starts with another Katherine and Richard.'

'What a lovely coincidence,' said Katherine. 'And I will be very happy to give any sons we have the name Crispin. My father and grandfather had Crispin as a middle name, and I was told that it was a Snow family tradition.'

'There are so many good stories in those family records, Katherine,' said Richard. 'They would make a terrific book. You should think about writing it some day.'

Richard woke up and rolled over, stretching out an arm to touch Katherine. He came awake suddenly when he found that her side of their bed was empty.

Pulling himself upright, he saw that Katherine was sitting

at the small writing desk that stood in front of one of the large windows in their bedroom.

'Katherine, what are you doing?' he asked. 'Come back to bed, my darling. It is our third anniversary!'

'What do you mean? Our third anniversary?' Katherine walked back to their bed.

Richard held out his arms and said, 'It is three weeks today since we were married!'

Katherine laughed and climbed into bed beside him, snuggling into his arms. He kissed her and whispered 'happy anniversary' and they started to make love, very slowly and very gently.

Afterwards, Richard said, 'By the way, what were you so busily writing when I woke up this morning?'

'I was starting to write the book that you've been telling me I should write some day,' she said. 'The book based on all the Snow family stories that are in those old documents and papers.'

'Good. Those old records are full of such good stories, and such detail. Have you thought about a title for this book?' Richard asked.

'Oh yes,' answered Katherine. 'The title is the easy part. It will be called *The Snows of Yorkshire*.'

The End